Frederic Harrison

William the Silent

Frederic Harrison

William the Silent

ISBN/EAN: 9783337423605

Printed in Europe, USA, Canada, Australia, Japan

Cover: Foto ©Andreas Hilbeck / pixelio.de

More available books at **www.hansebooks.com**

WILLIAM THE SILENT

BY

FREDERIC HARRISON

"The Prince is a rare man, of great authoritie, universally beloved,
verie wyse in resolution in all things, and voyd of pretences, and that
which is worthie of speciall prayse in hym, he is not dismayed with any
losse or adversitie."

Dr. WILSON to Lord BURLEIGH, 3rd *December* 1576.

London
MACMILLAN AND CO., LIMITED
NEW YORK: THE MACMILLAN COMPANY
1897

To Emma Queen-Regent

OF

HOLLAND

IS INSCRIBED THIS LIFE

OF HER GREAT ANCESTOR

FOUNDER OF THE

NATION'S INDEPENDENCE

CONTENTS

CHAPTER VII

CHAPTER VIII

CHAPTER IX

CHAPTER X

CHAPTER XI

CHAPTER XII

CHAPTER XIII

CHAPTER I

ﾉﾞWHEN we study the foundation of the United
Provinces," says a great French writer, "we learn how
a State, from an origin almost unnoticed, rapidly rose
into greatness, was formed without design, and in the
end belied all human forecast. Those large and wealthy
provinces of the mainland which began the revolution
—Brabant, Flanders, and Hainault—failed to achieve
their freedom. In the meantime, a small corner of
Europe, which had been won from the sea by infinite
labour, and had maintained itself by its herring-fishery,
rose suddenly to be a formidable power, held its own
against Philip II., despoiled his successors of almost all
their possessions in the East Indies, and ended by taking
under its protection the monarchy of Spain " (Voltaire,
Essai sur les Mœurs, cap. 164).

The man who inspired, founded, and made possible
this marvellous development was William, Count of
Nassau, titular Prince of Orange, surnamed the Silent.

B

The eloquent epigram of Voltaire records the result of his achievement. His career, like his nature and his circumstances, was made up of anomalies and filled with complex elements. The man who organised the national rebellion of Holland, by birth a German count, became by inheritance a Flemish magnate and a sovereign prince. A Lutheran by family, he was brought up a Catholic, and died a Calvinist. His early years were passed as a soldier and minister of the Empire, as ambassador and lieutenant of the King of Spain, and as a grandee of boundless magnificence. Himself the mainspring of a national and religious insurrection, his best energies were spent in moderating the political and religious passions which were at once the cause and the result of the struggle. Personally a devout man, he professed in succession all the three great forms of Christian belief, whilst steadily opposing all that was extreme and all that was violent in each. His memory is still passionately cherished in his adopted fatherland : first as the founder of an illustrious Commonwealth, then as the father of a long line of able statesmen and ruling princes, and finally as a martyr to the cause of national independence and liberty of conscience.

William, the eldest son of William, Count of Nassau, and of Juliana of Stolberg, was born in the hereditary castle of Dillenburg, in Nassau, on the 25th of April 1533, the eldest of five sons and seven daughters. By birth he was, through many generations, of pure German race, the heir of one of the smaller ruling houses of the Empire, a House which had produced many chiefs illustrious in war and in council, and which by a series of splendid alliances had amassed titles, offices, and vast

possessions in Germany, in the Netherlands, and in
France. By a singular fortune the boy William, then
aged eleven, was named by the will of his cousin René,
dying on the field young and childless, as heir to the
immense fiefs of the Nassau race in the Netherlands,
together with the puny State of Orange on the Rhone,
and the barren title of sovereign Prince of Orange. From
his twelfth year William of Nassau bore the style of the
petty princedom which he never visited, and he transmitted the titular sovereignty to his descendants down
to our own times. At the age of twenty-six, William
became, by the death of his father, head of the House
of Nassau-Dillenburg, the possession and revenues of
which he transferred to his brother John. Thus, whilst
his birth was as noble as any in Europe, fortune concentrated on him a singular array of honours and of
estates. By his four marriages with princely and royal
houses, Flemish, German, or French, he left a family of
twelve children, whose descendants filled an even larger
part in the annals of Europe than did the ancestors of
William himself. The singular complications of this
family history must be reserved for a separate appendix
(see Appendix A); but it may be well to note the
prominent figures of his House who preceded William as
men famous in policy and war.

The courtly historian of the House of Nassau does
not pretend to find in the local legends anything trustworthy before the eleventh century; but we need not
trouble ourselves about the fierce and ambitious
chieftains who held the beautiful, wooded hill country
along the Lahn, on the eastern side of the Rhine, one of
whom was the Emperor Adolphus in the thirteenth

century. Otto I., about the close of that century, is
taken as the stem of the House of Nassau-Dillenburg;
and William himself in his famous *Apology* opens the
history of his House with Otto II., 1311. "It is known
to all men," he replies proudly to Philip, "that I am no
foreigner in the Netherlands. Count Otto, from whom
I descend in the seventh degree, married the heiress of
Vianden; his grandson, Engelbert I., married the heiress
of Leck and Breda; and my ancestors have for centuries
held baronies and lordships in Brabant, Flanders,
Holland, and Luxemburg."

Engelbert I. (1404), marrying Joanna, only child of
the Lord of Polanen and Leck, brought into the House
estates in Brabant; and made Breda the home of this
branch of the family. He became a leading noble in
the court of Burgundy. His grandson, Engelbert II.,
in the second half of the fifteenth century, played a still
larger part, both as soldier and diplomatist, in the
service of the Dukes of Burgundy and the Empire. He
decided the victory of Guinegates, 1479, and was
Governor of Flanders. By a family arrangement,
maintained for centuries, one branch of the House held
the estates in the Netherlands, and the other branch
held those in the Empire, with cross successions on
failure of sons,—when a fresh settlement was made.

On the death of Engelbert II., without sons, and of
his brother John, who had married a daughter of the
Landgrave of Hesse, the vast Netherlands' possessions
of the Nassaus passed (in 1516) to John's elder son
Henry; whilst the Nassau estates in Germany passed to
a younger son, William. This William, by Juliana of
Stolberg, was the father of William the Silent.

Henry, nephew, adopted son and heir of Engelbert
II., surpassed both his uncle and his great grandfather in
magnificence and power.   "It was he," says the *Apology*,
"who placed the Imperial crown on the head of Charles
V."—a service that the Emperor never forgot, which
he rewarded by loading Henry with offices, honours,
and great charges of State.   And, by the favour of
Francis I. of France, Henry obtained the hand of
Claudia, sister of Philibert, Prince of Orange-Châlons.
Philibert, dying without children, left his principality
to René, the son of Claudia and Henry.   Thus for the
first time, in 1530, a Count of Nassau became Prince of
Orange, a petty sovereignty now included in the French
department of Vaucluse.

Orange, a territory of less than 40,000 acres, measur-
ing eight leagues by four, with a population of 12,000,
engulfed in the papal dominion of Avignon, had given
the title to a nominal county or princedom, as is pretended, from the time of Charles the Great; but, in
fact, it was in later years alternately occupied by the
Emperor or a King of France.   In the meantime the
titular Prince of Orange, who only enjoyed his dominions
at brief intervals, claimed to be a free sovereign, not a
feudatory either of the Empire or the French kingdom.
The barren honour was in later times contested in the
Nassau family for centuries, and the puny state was
finally ceded to Louis XIV. in 1713—the title of Prince
continuing to be held by descendants of the Nassaus.

René of Nassau, inheriting the princedom of Orange-
Châlons, followed the Emperor in arms and at court, as
his father Henry and his uncle Philibert had done.
He was a special favourite of Charles V., who made him

stadtholder in Holland ; and, in 1544, gave him high command in the attack on France. In this war, at St. Dizier, René was killed, to the intense grief of the Emperor, who received his last breath. By special permission of the Emperor, René had been empowered to name his heir, and he gave all his possessions and his princedom to young William, his first cousin, then a boy of eleven.

It was thus that, from boyhood, this scion of the princely House of Nassau became entitled to a rank and to estates far greater than those of his own father or his immediate ancestors. He united in himself the inheritance and the titles of the long line of Nassau-Dillenburg, his direct forefathers. His father, who was still alive, acquiesced in his succession, at the age of eleven, to the vast and varied possessions of the House of Nassau-Breda that had belonged to his uncles and his cousins. And, by the testament of his cousin René he also obtained the titular rank and shadowy rights of a Prince of Orange. Thus it came to pass that fortune, by a singular conjunction of circumstances, showered upon the lad an accumulation of traditions, titles, and possessions derived from a long line of warriors, statesmen, and diplomatists, who had absorbed a constant succession of offices, wealthy alliances, and ancestral honours granted by Dukes of Burgundy, Emperors, and Kings of France. The man who founded the Republic of Holland, in the teeth of such powerful kings and princes, was by birth, by tradition, and even in barren honour, their equal and their mate.

William, the father of the Prince of Orange, lived entirely as a German count, administering his Nassau dominions for forty-three years during the stormy period of the Reformation and the religious wars under Charles V. His position was one of great difficulty; pressed alternately by his more powerful neighbours of Hesse and of Saxony, between Lutheran reformers and Catholic reaction, between the Emperor and the rebel League, with a large family of fourteen children by two wives, with an inheritance burdened by counter-claims, lawsuits, and family settlements. He is called "the Rich"; but he was usually quite poor, and was seldom out of difficult situations. On the whole, he steered between the rocks with great prudence, moderation, justice, and good sense. He avoided war, and never shone as a soldier; but his civil rule was fair, generous, and popular. Slowly, very gradually, he adopted the Reformation; and about the time of young William's birth, he formally accepted for Nassau the Lutheran communion. But he did not make it a means of personal aggrandisement, as did other princes, and he never permitted it to pass into persecution. He may be counted a pale, dull, local type and forerunner of his illustrious son.

It was from his mother that William, like Cromwell and so many great men, inherited some of his noblest gifts. Juliana of Stolberg had been married at fifteen to Count Philip of Hainault, the ward of this elder William of Nassau. On the premature death of Philip, William, her guardian, who had been left a widower by the death of a daughter of Count John of Egmont, married Juliana, and took charge of all his ward's children. By her he had twelve children, of whom William the Silent was the eldest, all born in the castle of Dillenburg. She was a woman of strong character, of devout spirit, and affectionate nature, a Protestant of deep sincerity, but temperate judgment, an exemplary wife, mother, and mistress. Her castle was the training home of the noble youths of Nassau, and she bore a long life of calamity and bereavement with heroic serenity and courage. She died at the age of seventy-seven, having had, by her two husbands, no less than seventeen children, and leaving, says Meursius, more than one hundred and sixty descendants. She died only four years before the assassination of her eldest born of the Nassaus. Of her five Nassau sons, four fell victims in the great struggle, the three younger sons dying in battle in her own lifetime.

The castle of Dillenburg, said to have been built about 1240, was a vast and lofty pile rising on a rocky bend of the river Dill, a tributary of the Lahn. A contemporary print of the sixteenth century shows it as a princely fortress of the first rank, with frowning battlements, towers, barbicans, gateways, and outworks, and vast ranges of halls, stores, offices, and barracks, capable of holding at least a thousand persons. It constantly had to receive visitors of rank claiming its hospitality, with a retinue of many hundreds of horses, guards, and attendants. Here for some fifty years lived Juliana of Stolberg, renowned as a capable *châtelaine*. Here all her children were born. After undergoing a series of vicissitudes and attacks, the castle was burnt down in the last century, and remained a ruin until, in 1872, the *Wilhelmsthurm*, a memorial tower, was built on the foundations of the keep, rising from the historic rock to a height of about 130 feet.

The first eleven years of young William's life were passed with his father and mother at Dillenburg. In

1544, upon the death of René of Orange, Count William took his young son to Brussels, where he was formally admitted to his great inheritances, the father ceding any rights to the Netherlands' honours and estates that he might have claimed under the family compact. He also consented, avowed Protestant as he then was, that his son should be educated at the Brussels court of the Emperor, presided over by Mary, Queen of Hungary, sister of Charles V., and his Regent of the Netherlands. Here for nine years, he himself tells us, young William was carefully brought up as a Catholic prince, being trained for high office, as a peculiar favourite of Charles V., who took the strongest interest in him, and gave him as tutor Jerome Perrenot, a brother of the famous Cardinal Granvelle, destined to be the Prince's bitter enemy. Under this tuition William acquired a very wide education; he wrote and spoke with equal ease, French, German, Flemish, Spanish, and Latin. Charles made him first his page, then gentleman of his chamber, kept him near his person, and suffered him to be present at audiences and councils about affairs of State. The earliest fragment of William's that we possess is a letter to the Bishop Granvelle. It is in French, dated from Breda, 30th September 1550, when the writer was seventeen, and shows the young Prince as already full of public business, dutiful and affectionate towards the wily prelate with whom he was to wage so deadly a combat, and full of devout expressions. It is an autograph, but curiously enough unsigned. Perhaps what we have is the rough draft of this judicious missive.

William was just eighteen when Charles gave him as a wife Anne of Egmont, only daughter and heiress of

Maximilian, Count of Buren, one of the magnates of the Netherlands and a trusted general of the Emperor. Anne was of his own age and of as noble birth ; their union lasted little more than six years, much of which` was spent by the Prince in the field or on public service. The forty-eight of his letters to Anne which remain, all written in French, are simple, kindly, and confidential, mainly filled with details of his military life, his anxieties for his troops, his desire to return to his home, his plans, and his hopes.   The union, which on both sides had been an affair of policy and ambition, seems to have been happy on the whole ; but the records of it are slight, and it had no remarkable character.

In the same month as his marriage, July 1551, the Prince was appointed captain of two hundred horse, raised in the following December to two hundred and fifty, and in April 1552 (*ætat.* 19) he was named colonel of ten companies of foot.   In that year the League against the Emperor was formed between the German princes, headed by Maurice of Saxony, and Henry II. of France.   Henry invaded Luxemburg and took many strong places.   The Prince was sent with his command to defend the frontier.   And from this year he was occupied during the summer and autumn months in campaigns against the French king, which continued in a desultory warfare, and with alternate success until the peace of Cateau-Cambrésis in 1559.

The young soldier of nineteen was first employed, under the orders of the Queen-Regent, in raising a force in his ancestral Holland provinces, and in May 1552 we find him organising a force at Thorn on the Lower Meuse in Limburg.   The numerous letters and despatches that pass between himself and the Queen, and his letters to his wife at home, exhibit him hard at work, and in continual movement on the Upper Meuse and the Sambre, but not engaged in any important action. King Henry's campaign was at first a brilliant success ; he burst into Lorraine, and took Metz, Toul, Verdun, which remained part of France. The Imperial army may have sufficed to protect Luxemburg ; but Henry passed southwards into Alsace. William was not permitted to lead his troops to join the Emperor in his disastrous siege of Metz, but was ordered to invade Artois, and after taking part in that successful campaign, his force was disbanded (November 1552), after he had received from the Queen-Regent a letter of warm acknowledgment of his services and his zeal. In spite of his natural anxiety to see his wife at home, William did not return, but went on to join the Emperor at Thionville, as he was about to raise the disastrous siege of Metz, the Prince apparently being bent on affairs of his own rather than those of the Empire.

In the following year (1553) Charles, rousing himself from the prostration caused by his diseases and his collapse before Metz, and putting his troops under Emmanuel Philibert of Savoy, made a successful and savage attack on the French in Artois. The Prince of Orange was invested with an important command, but we do not know what part he had in the cruel storm and destruction of Thérouanne and Hesdin and the wasting of the country around. He there saw war in its most pitiless form, and he was continually receiving, at the hands of the Regent and the Emperor, new and superior commands.

All through the winter the Prince was engaged in organising fresh levies in his own fiefs. In May 1554 he was appointed first Commissioner at Antwerp, and was summoned to Brussels to consult with the Regent; and in June he received a commission as commander of four squadrons of cavalry beside his own troop. The campaign of 1554 was short, sharp, and somewhat indecisive. The Prince took part in the campaign of Renti and Béthune, which resulted in some successes to the Emperor, under the command of Emmanuel Philibert, now Duke of Savoy.

The winter and spring of 1555 were, as usual, spent in organising fresh levies, and in July of that year the Prince received the signal honour of being named by the Emperor Commander-in-Chief of the army round Givet, numbering 20,000 men. If we can trust the rhetorical and somewhat eulogistic *Apology*, the Prince had held such command more than a year before, in the temporary absence of the Duke of Savoy. In 1555 he was but little over twenty-two years of age, and he was preferred to the command at a critical moment of the Emperor's career, over the heads of veteran soldiers much senior to himself.

The French had captured Mariemburg on the border of Namur, and were threatening Namur and Brussels. The task of the Prince was to protect Brabant, and to recover Mariemburg. He did not succeed in the latter, but he effected the former object by founding the new fort of Philippeville, on a site selected by him and named after the Emperor's son. In the *Apology* we are told how the youthful captain was pitted against such veterans as Nevers and Coligny, yet he succeeded in building

Philippeville and Charlemont under their very eyes (*à leur barbe*). The campaign was rendered very arduous by heavy rains and by the ravages of the plague, by the difficulty of obtaining supplies, by shortness of money, and the ill-humour and mutinous temper of his mercenaries. The archives record an immense amount of discussion by letter as to the wants of the army, as to the site of the new forts, and retaliatory raids upon the enemy in France. Though continually urged to undertake a forward movement, the Prince referred the matter to a council of war, with the proverbial result. He held chief command of the army round Philippeville for six months from 22nd July 1555 to 27th January 1556, during which time he had constructed and garrisoned the new fort of Philippeville, of which the site and armament was left to his sole discretion. He prevented any further invasion into Hainault, but otherwise accomplished little worthy of note. The one hundred and fifty letters that during this period passed between himself and the Government at Brussels (at times almost daily), exhibit him as labouring with inexhaustible energy and adroitness to organise and hold together a turbulent army of ill-paid and ill-supplied mercenary troops of different nationalities. The striking note of his command is *prudence;* he exhibits much more the wariness and patience of a diplomatist in a negotiation than the dash and enthusiasm of a warrior in a campaign. His letters are those of Secretary of State rather than of a Commander-in-Chief. At times he is absorbed in questions of finance. He is at twenty-two already more the statesman than the soldier.

In the October of 1555 the Prince was summoned

from his camp to be present at the formal abdication by
the Emperor of his hereditary dominions in favour of
his son Philip II. This magnificent and elaborate cere-
monial fills many a brilliant page in the histories of that
age. In the great hall of the palace of Brussels,
crowded with Knights of the Golden Fleece, nobles,
prelates, courtiers, and delegates from the States, the
Emperor appeared, leaning for support on the shoulder
of the youthful Prince of Orange—Charles being, at the
age of fifty-five, an old man broken by disease and toil.
The paternal interest that the Emperor had shown to
the Prince, and the confidence he had placed in him now
for eleven years, thus found a striking expression. And
when Charles finally resolved to surrender the Imperial
crown, he charged the Prince with the mission to
Germany. These marks of favour are duly recounted
in the *Apology*, wherein the Emperor is uniformly
mentioned in terms of profound respect. It would seem
that Charles looked forward to his pupil and favourite
being the mainstay of his son Philip on his new thrones.
How many things would have gone otherwise had this
expectation been fulfilled! For a time, Philip seemed
willing to bestow on the Prince the confidence that had
been given by his father. Within a few weeks he was
named by Philip one of his councillors of State, and in the
following January, at the first chapter of the Order of the
Fleece held by Philip at Antwerp, William was admitted
a Knight, a distinction which his father, the Count of
Nassau, had refused on the ground of his Protestant
faith.

The Prince returned to his command the day after
the abdication, and the despatches which he sent to

Philip contain appeals for money, supplies, and muni-
tions, even more urgent than those which he had sent to
the Emperor and the Regent; and, if possible, they met
with an even scantier attention. On the 29th December
he writes to his wife: "Our camp is in a state of heart-
rending destitution; we have not a denier left, and the
soldiers are dying of hunger and cold, but they give no
more heed to us at court than if we were all dead.
You can imagine what a stock of patience I need to
have." Nothing was done on either side during that
indecisive campaign, except that the Prince had
effectually prevented Coligny, his future father-in-law,
from advancing into the Netherlands, and by his new
forts had guaranteed the defence of Brabant.   In
January the armies on both sides were disbanded, and
in February 1556 a hollow and almost nominal truce
for five years was signed at Vaucelles.

   With the departure of Charles V. to Spain, and the
installation of Philip II. as king, the career of the
Prince enters on a new phase. He had hitherto been
the pupil and the favourite of one of the greatest
soldiers and most astute statesmen of that astute and
warlike age. He was in full possession of vast estates,
and had the right to be addressed by sovereigns as
"My cousin." He kept a regal state in the splendid
Nassau palace at Brussels, and had palaces at Breda
and elsewhere. He was attended by nobles and pages
of gentle birth, who lived at his expense. Besides that,
he kept open house, and gave magnificent entertainment
to envoys and foreigners of rank. His civil and military
offices involved him in enormous charges. As General-
in-Chief, his nominal allowance had been 500 florins a

month, whilst he had to spend (he tells his wife) 2500 florins per month. In his *Apology* he declares that his missions and military services had cost him more than 1,500,000 florins, that he had never received as pay more than 300 florins a month, " which was not enough to pay the wages of the servants of his tents." This royal munificence, both public and private, had seriously encumbered even his enormous revenues — a matter which he took with a light heart, for he writes to his brother Louis : "As in the beginning, so now, and it will be for ever after, we come of a race who are very bad managers in youth, though we improve as we get older. I have cut down the cost of my falconers to 1200 florins, and I hope soon to be out of debt." Everything was on the same scale. The twenty-four nobles and the eighteen pages who formed his suite, the tables loaded day and night with choice dishes and wines, required an army of cooks and servants. As a measure of economy he in one day discharged twenty-eight cooks, who bore a high reputation as having served in his palace; and, later on, Philip wrote from Spain begging the Prince to let him have a certain eminent *cordon bleu* from the household at Breda.

The Prince himself was devoted to the chase, to falconry and tournaments, to dancing, masquerades, and courtly entertainments. His costume and retinue was on the scale befitting that age and his own youth and rank. His personal graciousness and courtesy were on a par with his lavish hospitality. Even his bitter enemies celebrated his winning manners and gentle dignity. His character is thus drawn by Pontus Payen, a sincere Catholic and opponent :—

Never did arrogant or indiscreet word issue from his mouth, under the impulse of anger or other passion ; if any of his servants committed a fault, he was satisfied to admonish them gently without resorting to menace or to abusive language. He was master of a sweet and winning power of persuasion, by means of which he gave form to the great ideas within him, and thus he succeeded in bending to his will the other lords about the court as he chose ; beloved and in high favour above all men with the people, by reason of a gracious manner that he had of saluting, and addressing in a fascinating and familiar way all whom he met.

The same writer goes on to accuse the Prince of want of courage in the field. William of Orange proved his real courage in a thousand ways, and is beyond the sneering depreciation of a catholic scribe. But his indomitable spirit of caution and his genius for political finesse unfitted him for supreme command in presence of an enemy whose forces he recognised to be greatly superior to his own. His caution naturally seemed timorous beside the dashing chivalry of Egmont and the wild recklessness of Louis of Nassau. The same charge of cowardice used to be made against Alva ; and it is continually brought by the *sabreurs* against the strategists. It is, however, plain that William of Orange never was, and with his growing habits of intense caution never could have made, a great soldier. His successes were won on the field of indomitable constancy, sagacity, faith, and enthusiasm—not on the field of battle. Our own Cromwell is one of the very rare examples in history of fiery courage in war, combined with inexhaustible caution in policy.

William, in his youth, as we see him in the fine picture of the Museum of Cassel, was a man somewhat above the medium height, spare, well-proportioned, and fairly strong. His complexion was rather brown, his

C

auburn hair rose from his brow in thick curls, his brown eyes were large, bright, and penetrating. His head is well set upon his shoulders, the forehead open and domed; the nose was long, powerfully formed, and wide at the base. The chin is fine, round, and massive, and in early youth shaded with a light down of auburn hair. The mouth is full, closely set, and rather severe and melancholy. The general aspect of the man, even at the age of twenty-five, was that of power, self-control, intensity, and profound thoughtfulness. Such was the young hero who was destined to measure his genius against the master of the Old and New Spain.

CHAPTER II

GENERAL AND MINISTER—SECOND MARRIAGE—IN
LOYAL OPPOSITION

1556–1564

THE three years of war which Philip II. waged with
Henry II. of France, and which closed with such
splendid success, opened with small promise, and ex-
hibited some of the worst features of bad military
organisation. The confusion of mercenaries of different
race and language, enlisted in small bodies by soldiers
of fortune, on special terms for limited periods, and
allowed to pillage in lieu of pay, was combined with the
minute and jealous interference of a pedantic tyrant.
He, like some feeble Byzantine Emperor, would keep the
conduct of the campaign in his own hands, whilst seeking to foment rather than to remove the sources of separation in the heterogeneous elements of his own armies.
The ultimate success of Philip was due to the magnificent
qualities of his Spanish veterans, and the military genius
of one or two amongst his generals. To the Prince of
Orange fell the thankless task of allaying discontents,
consulting the King on details of the campaign, and
importuning him for the needed money and supplies.

No more dreary record of mismanagement can be read than the letters that passed between William and Philip whilst the Prince was in command of the forces round Philippeville. "Sire," writes the Prince (5th January 1556), "have pity on the Spanish infantry, which, for lack of pay and out of sheer starvation, is scouring the low country round, plundering the peasantry in mere need of food. These disorders I cannot repress, much less can I punish them, for necessity has no law." The exasperation (7th January 1556) is such that the country people are talking of taking up arms at the sound of their tocsins to defend their homes, such tumultuous assemblies being likely to prove most dangerous. The whole story reads like a page from the secret history of the Sublime Porte and its starved regiments.

During the year 1556, following upon the hollow truce of Vaucelles, the Prince was employed in negotiations partly to induce the Estates to grant supplies, partly to raise new mercenary forces, partly on missions to the German princes. It was a strange task to be imposed on a young soldier of twenty-three, but the Prince was from boyhood more politician than warrior, and for two years he exerted the whole force of his tact and adroitness in obtaining grants for the King, and in bringing the German *Rittmeisters* to accept his niggardly offers. In the brilliant campaign of 1557, the Prince seems to have had only a subordinate part. Philip took the field in May with a splendid army of Spanish, German, Netherland, and English troops, under Emmanuel Philibert, Duke of Savoy. It was Count Egmont whose impetuous valour decided the great

victory of St. Quentin (10th August), followed within
the month by the storming of the fortress, the capture
of the Constable Montmorency, the Admiral Coligny, and
a crowd of French nobles.   It is clear from three letters
of the Prince to his wife that he took part in the siege
of St. Quentin, and the other forts on the Oise,—a campaign which carried the arms of Philip in triumph to
within sixty miles of Paris. But there is no evidence whatever of the particular services that William rendered ;
and accident or the jealousy of the King may have de-
prived him of filling any conspicuous place in the campaign.

   Nor had the Prince any leading part in the brilliant
campaign of 1558, which destroyed the military power
of France.   He is ordered on service to Namur, to meet
the assaults of the Duke of Guise in the Luxemburg,
but we have no record of his operations ; whilst, again,
the fiery valour of Egmont won the splendid victory of
Gravelines, near Calais, and left Henry of France
prostrate and disarmed.   The moment had arrived for
negotiations, which had already been begun by the crafty
Bishop of Arras on the one side, and the intriguing
Cardinal of Lorraine on the other.   Within a month
of the victory of Gravelines, Philip had ordered the
Prince to open informal *pourparlers* with Marshal St.
André and the Constable Montmorency, both prisoners
of St. Quentin, the Marshal having been lodged on
parole at the Prince's palace of Breda.   These overtures
led to a formal negotiation between the two French
chiefs on the part of Henry,—the Prince, Ruy Gomez
de Silva, and the Bishop of Arras on the part of Philip.
The treaty of Cateau-Cambrésis was eventually concluded (3rd April 1559).

There is little doubt that the chief hand in this masterly negotiation, and in composing the despatches which still remain, was that of the astute Bishop. But the Prince, though yet but twenty-five, had no small part in the work, and we need not treat as exaggerated the claim he makes in his *Apology*.

"As to this Treaty, which was as disastrous to France as it was honourable and profitable to Spain, if I may be allowed to speak of my own part, the King could not deny (had he a trace of grati- tude left) that I was one of the principal instruments and agents to secure him so advantageous a peace ; for it was at the instance of the King himself that I opened the first secret negotiations with the Constable and Marshal St. André. The King assured me that the greatest service in the world that I could render him would be to conclude this treaty of peace, which he desired to obtain at all cost, in order that he might return to Spain." And this is borne out by several authorities and by the admission of his Catholic enemy, Pontus Payen who says that the Prince "held the first rank amongst the envoys of the King, and won high esteem on both sides in this affair."

The Prince was selected as one of the State hostages to reside with Henry, in order to guarantee the execu- tion of the Treaty, the other hostages being Egmont, the Duke of Alva, and the Duke of Aerschot ; and, accord- ingly, William went to Paris in June 1559, and it was there that took place the famous incident which won him the name of *The Silent*. The story has been ad- mirably told by the Catholic, Pontus Payen, and it is precisely confirmed by the *Apology* itself, and other authorities. Pontus thus relates :—

One day, during a stag-hunt in the Bois de Vincennes, Henry, finding himself alone with the Prince, began to speak of the great number of Protestant sectaries who, during the late war, had in- creased so much in his kingdom to his great sorrow. His conscience, said the King, would not be easy nor his realm secure until he could see it purged of the "accursed vermin," who would one day overthrow his government, under pretence of religion, if they were allowed to get the upper hand. This was the more to be feared since some of the chief men in the kingdom, and even some princes of the blood, were on their side. But he hoped by the grace of God and the good understanding that he had with his new son, the King of Spain, that he would soon master them. The King talked on thus to Orange in the full conviction that he was cognisant of the secret agreement recently made with the Duke of Alva for the extirpation of heresy. But the Prince, subtle and adroit as he was, answered the good King in such a way as to leave him still under the impression that he, the Prince, was in full possession of the scheme propounded by Alva ; and under this belief the King revealed all the details of the plan arranged between the King of Spain and himself for the rooting out and rigorous punishment of the heretics, from the lowest to the highest rank, and in this service the Spanish troops were to be mainly employed.

All this the Prince heard without a word and without moving a muscle.

This incident not only gave the eloquent Prince his paradoxical name, but it proved a great epoch in his life,—it is hardly too much to say an epoch in the history of his age. Writing more than twenty years afterwards in his *Apology*, he says :—

I confess that I was deeply moved with pity for all the worthy people who were thus devoted to slaughter, and for the country, to which I owed so much, wherein they designed to introduce an Inquisition worse and more cruel than that of Spain. I saw, as it were, nets spread to entrap the lords of the land as well as the people, so that those whom the Spaniards and their creatures could not supplant in any other way, might by this device fall into their hands. It was enough for a man to look askance at an image to be condemned to the stake. Seeing all this (he continues in his impetuous way) I confess that from that hour I resolved with my whole soul to do my best to drive this Spanish vermin from the land ; and of this resolve I have never repented, but believe that I, my comrades, and all who have stood with us, have done a worthy deed, fit to be held in perpetual honour.

It is possible that the desperate struggle of twenty years may have somewhat coloured the Prince's memory, and that his conversion from being a magnificent prince and a trusty servant of the King of Spain into an ardent champion of liberty of conscience and national independence, may not have been quite so sudden as he had come to think it. And, as we shall see, the *Apology* was not at all throughout the work of his own pen. But, again, Pontus Payen tells the story almost exactly as does Orange himself.

The Prince, having thus wrung his secret from the King, maintained his composure for two or three days, and then obtained leave to make a journey to the Netherlands on private business of importance. No sooner had he reached Brussels than he explained to his intimate friends what he had heard in the Bois de Vincennes, giving a sinister meaning to the excellent purposes of the two Kings, who (he said) designed to exterminate the great chiefs so as to fill their own treasuries by confiscations, and ultimately to set up an absolute tyranny under pretence of extirpating heresy. And when he left the city, he counselled them to make the withdrawal of the Spanish troops a formal demand in the States-General about to be held at Ghent.

This is the point at which the whole life of the Prince receives a great change. He was now twenty-six, when he enters on a resolute, but very guarded, career of resistance to the projects of Philip. His first combination (and one, as we shall see, which completely failed) was to form a party of constitutional opposition headed by the great nobles of the country, and resting on the historic rights of the provinces and the States - General. His ideas at this period are fairly stated in the *Apology*. Not only was he shocked by the cruelties inflicted on "the poor people who allowed themselves to be burned," but he saw such signs of insurrection even amongst the higher nobility as pre-saged a Civil War like that from which France had so cruelly suffered. He was too much exposed to the arm of Philip to defy him openly ; and the King knew him to be so able and so powerful a magnate that he did not care to drive him into rebellion. In a Chapter of the Order of the Golden Fleece the Prince secured the election of Hoogstraeten and Montigny, powerful Nether-land nobles, against the known wishes of Philip. He urged on the States to press for the withdrawal of the Spanish troops, and he specially advised them to make this withdrawal a condition of voting supplies. Thus, he told them, they would gain a hundred times more than by humble supplications. Here we have the policy of our own Long Parliament eighty years later.

Philip, who was now resolved on his departure for Spain, was obliged to temporise. He gave evasive replies; appointed Orange and Egmont nominal com-manders of the Spanish contingent, their real leader being Julian Romero. Orange was commissioned as Governor of Holland, Zeeland, and Utrecht, with a donation of 40,000 crowns (also purely nominal). When Philip set forth in great state for Spain (from whence he never returned) he was attended by the nobles, whom he solemnly embraced. Then turning to Orange, he upbraided the Prince for the refusal of the States to vote supplies. This, said the Prince, was the act of the States. " *No los estados ma vos, vos, vos,*" cried the King, a memoir-writer declares, shaking the Prince's wrist. For once Philip spoke in his wrath more truthfully than was his habit in affairs of State.

When Philip withdrew to Spain, where his purpose

was to secure the absolute ascendency of himself and of
Catholic orthodoxy, he left the Netherlands in a most
uneasy condition. The great nobles had impoverished
themselves in peace and in war with ruinous excesses;
the burghers resented the arbitrary suppression of their
historic privileges, the constant exactions of the Government, and the maintenance in their midst of 3000
Spanish soldiers; whilst the Reformation was constantly
making way both in the Dutch and the Belgian provinces. After long deliberation, Philip had appointed
as his Regent his half-sister, Margaret, Duchess of
Parma, a ·natural daughter of the Emperor Charles V.
Margaret was a woman of masculine nature, devoted to
Philip and to the Church, of much capacity for affairs,
energetic, provident, and laborious. A complex system
of three councils was instituted to assist, control, and
counterbalance each other — the principal Council of
State consisting of Perronet, Bishop of Arras, Berlaymont, and Viglius, devoted agents of Philip, with
Egmont and Orange as titular members. It was soon
found that Egmont and Orange were not admitted to
the inner *camarilla*. Business was practically carried on
by the Bishop, a minister of consummate industry, craft,
and perseverance, who, with his two creatures, was the
trusted confidant of the Regent. Orange and Egmont
were only used by them to give some character to the
Council of State, to induce the States to vote supplies,
and to figure as the nominal commanders of the Spanish
forces. Orange, on his side, whilst remaining loyal to
the Regent, used his position to check the advance of
absolutism and persecution. In the formal instructions
given to him on his appointment as Governor of the

three Provinces, and in the secret memorandum accompanying it, he was ordered, he tells us, to put to death "some worthy people suspected of religion. This his conscience would not allow him to do. And he sent them private warning of their danger, holding it right to obey God rather than man."

By the death of his father, William, Count of Nassau (6th October 1559), the Prince, as the eldest son, now became chief of the House of Nassau-Dillenburg. In a fine letter to his younger brother, Louis, he expresses his grief for the loss of so excellent a father, urges them all to follow in his footsteps for the honour of the House, "and this will be easy, if they all dwell together in love and mutual support. He will do his part to help them, to console their mother to whom they owe so much, and to be a father to the sisters who have lost their own." By the family compact, possession of the German estates passed to John, the next brother, and the only one of his brothers who survived the Prince; but Orange still remained Count of Nassau, with a titular interest in the Nassau honours and estates.

The Prince had now been a widower for a year and a half, and he was contemplating a second marriage. Anne of Egmont died in March 1558. Orange had been at Frankfort on a mission to surrender the Imperial crown, and incidentally to attach the German princes to the service of Philip. On his return he found his young wife at the point of death, was himself prostrated with fever and nervous spasms, and writes to the Bishop to pour out his poignant grief. There is every reason to believe in the sincerity of his affection and of his sorrow, though it must be remembered that for the

greater part of their six years of married life, the Prince
had spent most of his time on service away from home.
From camp he had been wont to write to her:—"All in
the world I have is yours"; "Next to God, you are the
one I love best, and if I did not know that your love for
me is the same, I could not be so happy as I am";
"May God give us both the grace to live always in this
affection without any guile." The marriage gave birth
to two children, Philip-William, Count of Buren, afterwards Prince of Orange, the degenerate, Spaniardised,
son of his father, and Mary, ultimately Countess of
Hohenlohe.[1]

It would have been contrary to all the ideas and
habits of the age for a young man of princely
rank to remain long single. Orange himself was of
an amorous temperament, keenly alive to the future
of his great name and House; and already, as he
admits and almost boasts, burdened with an expendi-
ture of a million and a half of florins in peace or
war. He regarded a great alliance to be a natural
duty of his rank and position. As he told Philip, his
friends and relations were importunate for him to
marry, considering his youth, and the interests of his
House. On the failure of two previous proposals, the
Prince flung himself with extraordinary vehemence and

---

[1] As widower, Orange formed a connection with Eva Eliver,
and by her he had a natural son, Justin of Nassau, born September 1559, who became a famous seaman and bravely seconded
his brother Maurice and Barneveldt in the long struggle. Though
only twenty-five at his father's death, Justin was made Admiral
of Holland and Zeeland ; he took part in many desperate enter-
prises ; had an important share in the Dutch support of England
against the Armada ; was joined with Barneveldt in his mission
to Henry IV. and to Elizabeth ; and was pronounced by Lord H.
Seymour to be "a man very wise, subtle, and cunning."

obstinacy to secure an alliance even more brilliant and promising, which brought him a great position, much shame, long anxiety, and his own valiant and astute successor, Maurice of Nassau, ultimately Prince of Orange.

The bride whom the Prince resolved to win was Anne, daughter and heiress of that Maurice, Duke of Saxony, who had so rudely shaken the very throne of Charles V., and granddaughter of Philip, Landgrave of Hesse, one of the most ardent chiefs of the Reformation. Anne, now in her seventeenth year, not ill-looking, but ill-made, somewhat lame, of a violent nature which ended in madness, had been brought up at Dresden by her uncle, Augustus, Elector of Saxony, as a Protestant. She would have a considerable fortune, was entitled to a great inheritance, and her rank and connections offered the most splendid alliance in Germany. The Prince had never seen her; she had no pretensions to charm; the obstacles to such a match were formidable. But the very difficulties seemed to spur him to action, whilst his politic spirit foresaw the advantages of an alliance with the great and almost independent magnates of Central Germany.

Orange was a Catholic, the subject, counsellor, and minister of the most Catholic King, having all his domains within the power of Philip, who held his whole life and fortunes, as it were, in pledge for his loyalty and his orthodoxy. Anne was a Protestant, the daughter of the old Emperor's most dangerous enemy, niece and granddaughter of two devoted chiefs of the Lutheran movement. The negotiations for this adventurous marriage, which were carried on for nearly two

years, form a strange tripartite battle between the Prince
and his family, the German Protestant chiefs, and Philip
with his agents, Margaret and Granvelle. The old
Landgrave was furious that his granddaughter should
marry a Papist, Philip and his Council were shocked
that his subject should dream of marrying a heretic, the
daughter of malignant Lutherans and enemies of his
House. The Prince was forced to compromise, and he
needed all his consummate powers of diplomacy:—
to satisfy Philip that he would remain Catholic, and
that his wife should live "like a Catholic"; to satisfy
the Elector that he was no enemy of the Lutherans
and that he would not force Anne's conscience; and
withal to avoid giving the Elector, the Landgrave,
Philip, or the Duchess any formal or written pledge
whatever.

The bride's relations wrote long despatches in praise
of the Confession of Augsburg; the Prince replied gaily
that a young wife had better read romances than
theology. He wrote to the old Landgrave with almost
evangelical unction; he wrote to the King protestations
of orthodoxy and loyalty. William made several
journeys into Germany, where he won over the Duke of
Saxony, many of the great chiefs, and presently Anne
herself. The long, subtle, and astute despatches which
passed between Brussels, Spain, and Dresden, in French,
German, and Spanish, fill hundreds of pages of the
printed archives. A volume would hardly exhaust the
ingenious and characteristic turns of the long negotiation.
The Bishop is subtle, far-sighted, politic; Philip is suspicious, hostile, but timid; the Elector is blunt, practical,
and secretly anxious to get his niece off his hands and

out of the Empire; the Landgrave is bigoted, obstinate, and angry; the Prince is diplomatic, astute, eloquent, and resolute. He makes profuse promises, but none that he cannot keep without dishonour. He protests that he is a Catholic and means to remain a Catholic. He protests that he can respect the Lutheranism of his wife and of her relations. In all this he spoke substantial truth, and he fairly fulfilled his pledges. "I will say no more," he haughtily replied at the wedding ceremony, "than that I will act as I shall answer hereafter to God and to man."

Another volume might be filled with the story of the wedding, which took place at Leipsic in August 1561. It was splendid even for that age — adorned with royalties, serene highnesses, dukes and prelates, in abundance. All Germany rang with the story of the gathering and its pomp. William, who was now twenty-eight, and had been a widower more than three years, took with him a retinue almost royal. It is said that more than five thousand persons were invited and eleven hundred horses were required. He had desired to have the nobles of the Netherlands of his party; but the Duchess refused this, and permitted only Baron Montigny to go as representing the King. Philip, "willing to wound and yet afraid to strike," dared not show his wrath in public; he sent his formal compliments and 3000 crowns to present a ring to the bride. The ceremony was performed with strict Lutheran rites; festivities were continued for days; and the young bride went to her new home at Breda, passionately fond of her courtly spouse—"as happy as a queen" she wrote to her grandfather.

The Prince had indeed won a victory and a bride which were to cost him dear. A marriage of policy was at that time a matter of course to a man of the highest rank aspiring to a great career. And at this period of life William, as he confesses, was a man of the world, a man of his age. The alliance with the great chiefs of Lutheran Germany offered him a source of permanent strength. He had no kind of purpose at this time himself to become Lutheran, or any other type of Protestant. He intended to conform to the Catholic rites, and he did so conform for years afterwards. He respected the Lutherans and even the Calvinists; but they did not satisfy him. He abhorred persecution, but he loathed fanaticism, anarchy, and violence. He had no intention of fomenting rebellion in the Netherlands, nor of converting it to Protestantism. But he did contemplate a combination between the nobles of the Netherlands and of Germany to stem the autocracy of Philip and to drive back the threatened Inquisition. As an English agent wrote, the marriage had made the Prince a power. He had no dogmatic conviction as to any one of the competing creeds; and in marrying a Protestant princess, he meant to retain a Catholic household, to conform to the Catholic Church, and yet to secure the alliance of Protestant chiefs. Throughout he acted as politician, not as theologian. He was a diplomatist, not a reformer ; a statesman, not a preacher ; a man of the world, not a saint. As he passed into middle life and the terrific struggle which absorbed and killed him, he grew to a deeper conscience and a more spiritual temper. But, at twenty-eight, he was entirely and solely a politic Prince seeking to found a party of honest patriots.

For a time, and until Philip resorted to the terrible
weapon of an overwhelming Spanish army, the constitutional opposition to persecution and absolutism that
Orange organised had a very real success. On his
accession the King, by the advice of Granvelle, had
reissued the edicts of 1550 published by Charles V. for
the suppression of heresy,—"to stamp out this plague
by the roots," said the preamble of the Emperor's
decree. This atrocious code of persecution had not
been regularly enforced, and every attempt to enforce
it added to the public irritation. Next, a complete
reorganisation of the ecclesiastical dioceses of the Netherlands was effected by the Popes, Paul IV. and Pius IV.,
in 1559-60; by this three new Archbishoprics were
created, and the fifteen bishoprics were divided amongst
them. By this system a new form of inquisition into
heresy was practically created. Granvelle was made
Archbishop of the principal see, that of Mechlin, and
was shortly honoured with the Red Hat, so that he is
henceforth known as the Cardinal. To all this scheme
of reaction Orange offered a resolute opposition. He
protested in Council, remonstrated with the Regent,
Granvelle, and the King against the persecution of
heretics, and incessantly, in public and in private, pressed
on the withdrawal of the Spanish troops, on whom hung
the whole force of the Spanish tyranny.

In these efforts Orange was supported by Egmont
and most of the great nobles. He and Egmont resigned
their nominal command of the Spanish troops, and
formally demanded in council their withdrawal from
the country. The Regent, the Bishop, and at last the
most devoted servants of the King saw that government

could not be carried on without this concession. Philip
yielded to necessity, and at last the Spaniards were dis-
missed home. The Cardinal now felt all the difficulties
of his position. Egmont treated him with defiance and
open contempt; and the old intimacy between Orange
and Granvelle was at an end. The Prince and Egmont
wrote formally to Philip to insist on their resignation
of the Council, unless they were admitted to its real
deliberations. Recriminations between Orange and the
Cardinal were constantly despatched to Madrid. A
secret diplomatic duel was waged between them. The
Cardinal inveighs against "the League" formed amongst
the nobles to oppose their King, and against their leader
and chief, who, he astutely suggests, might be sent
away and made governor of Sicily. At last, the wily
Prelate recognised the full power of the grown man,
whom he had known and loved as a boy and then as his
own apt pupil and colleague.

The Prince is a dangerous man (he wrote to Philip), subtle,
politic, professing to stand by the people, and to champion their
interests, even against your edicts, but seeking only the favour of
the mob, giving himself out sometimes as a Catholic, sometimes as
a Calvinist or Lutheran. He is a man to undertake any enterprise
in secret which his own vast ambition and inordinate suspicion
may suggest. Better not leave such a man in Flanders. Give
him a magnificent embassy or a viceroyalty, or *perhaps call him to
your own court.* As to Egmont, he has been led away by Orange ;
but he is honest, a good Catholic, and can easily be brought
round, by appealing to his vanity and his jealousy of the Prince.

These invectives of the Cardinal were not without
justification. From this point certainly Orange was
incessantly working to form some alliance that might
enable the Netherlands to baffle the Spanish tyrant.
He turned, now to the Lutheran princes of Germany

now to the Huguenots of France, now to the Queen of England. He rallied the Flemish nobles in conference, sent Montigny to Spain to remonstrate with the King; when Philip peremptorily orders a force to be raised to help the King of France against the Huguenots, the Prince in Council succeeded in resisting the attempt. A scheme is even formed to obtain the annexation of Brabant to the Empire. Defying the royal opposition, the Prince goes to the coronation of the Emperor Maximilian at Frankfort. There and elsewhere he carries on negotiations with German chiefs. Margaret and Philip are warned that he has some great design on hand. Whatever it was, no solid alliance was effected. At the same time, he is in relations with Elizabeth's agents, Throckmorton and Gresham. But neither Elizabeth nor the German princes were willing to engage in an open defiance of Spain.

The hostility to the Cardinal waxed fiercer day by day. Egmont and other nobles treated him with haughty contempt. The people filled the streets with pasquinades and burlesques. Orange and Egmont worked incessantly against him. As early as 1561, they had formally urged his recall. Montigny's mission had the same object. Throughout the year 1563 a series of despatches were addressed to Philip signed by Orange, Egmont, and Horn, formally demanding the withdrawal of the Cardinal, and refusing to serve with him in Council. The Regent herself began to weary of her imperious *factotum*. Philip remained obstinate, perplexed, and irresolute. At his side rivals of the Cardinal insinuated doubts and suspicions. The savage Duke of Alva, who now appears upon the scene, stoutly

supported Granvelle. "My blood boils, and I am like
a madman," he wrote, "when I read the letters of these
Flemings. Let them be chastised. But, as that is not
possible yet, divide them, and draw off Egmont. *As to
those whose heads are to be cut off*, it is necessary to dissemble." Philip did dissemble. His creatures wrote
from Spain to the Cardinal advising him to withdraw.
At last, in a secret letter, recently discovered, the King
counselled his Minister "to ask for leave of absence in
order to visit his mother." The Cardinal took the hint,
and early in 1564 he finally quitted Brussels, having been
for nearly five years the real ruler of the Netherlands.

The country breathed more freely. The Spanish
troops, the secret *Consulta*, the Cardinal, were all gone;
and Orange-and his League had won in their first great
bout. The nobles were intoxicated with delight; the
people exulted; even the Regent seemed glad to be rid
of her master. The Prince lost no time in consolidating
his victory. It was quite true that he had formed a
real "League," but it was not at all confined to the
nobles, nor indeed to the nobles of the Netherlands.
Through his own family and his new Saxon alliances he
was incessantly organising the active co-operation of
German Protestant princes. But his ideas were also to
bring the people into the struggle. He placed before
himself, we are told, three main objects :—

1. To obtain regular meetings of the States-General.

2. To organise a real, single, and efficient Council of
State that should be the supreme source of government.

3. To obtain a relaxation of the persecution of heresy.

His aim was very much that of our own Long Parliament
eighty years later, and so far it had been an entire success.

CHAPTER III

WE now enter on the crucial struggle, with religion at its centre, which absorbed the last twenty years of the Prince's life, and in the end closed it by the assassin's bullet. Philip, the Spanish troops, *the Consulta*, the Cardinal, had all in turn withdrawn in face of the growing force of the Reformation, and the widespread indignation they each aroused. They had withdrawn— but only to gain time, and for a far more deadly spring. Silently, in the recesses of Spain, Philip was organising a more crushing persecution, a far stronger alien army, and martial law under the ruthless Alva.

It must be remembered that in 1564 Protestantism itself was only in its first generation, everywhere in a state of flux and of rudiment. All persons well past middle life had been baptized and bred up as Catholics. The Council of Trent had only just formulated its final doctrines; the Church of England was still in the making; in the Netherlands, in England, in most parts of Germany, the Protestants were still in a-minority, and themselves divided into hostile sects. In France,

Protestantism had become to a great extent a struggle between political parties. And, almost everywhere in Europe, those who were charged with the duty of government (except the Spanish and Papal fanatics) regarded the various types of Protestantism from the political, not from the spiritual, aspect. This was pre-eminently true of William of Orange, who—even more than Elizabeth of England, and quite as much as Henry of Navarre—placed peace, order, and religious compromise above any question of Bible, doctrine, or worship.

Pontus Payen, a sincere Catholic, loyalist, and admirer of the Cardinal, has thus painted the religion of the Prince, with a pen hostile, indeed, but not purely partisan. He writes in his *Memoirs* about this time :—

As to religion, he behaved with such discretion that the most close observers could not decide which way he inclined. The Catholics thought him a Catholic; the Lutherans, a Lutheran. He heard mass daily, whilst his wife and his daughter made public profession of the Lutheran heresy, even in his presence, without any objection from him. He condemned the rigidness of our theologians in maintaining the constitutions of the Church without making a single concession to the Reformers. He blamed the Calvinists as provoking sedition and strife, yet he spoke with horror of the edict of the Emperor that sentenced them to death ; for he held it to be cruelty to kill any man simply for maintaining an erroneous opinion. He used to say that in all matters of religion, punishment should be reserved to God alone, much as the rude German who said to the Emperor, "Sire, your concern is with the bodies of your people, not with their souls." In short, the Prince would have liked to see established a fancy kind of religion of his own, half-Catholic half-Lutheran, which would satisfy both sides. Indeed, if you look at his inconsistency on religious questions, as shown in his speeches and despatches, you will see that he put the State as something above the Christian religion, which in his eyes was a political invention to keep the people steady to their duty by the fear of God, so that orthodoxy was to him neither more nor less than the ceremonies, divinations, and superstitions that Numa Pompilius introduced in old Rome to tame the fierce and too warlike temper of his Romans.

The practical dilemmas that beset the task of government in such an age were early brought home to the Prince in his own principality of Orange. The new views had long been introduced there from the Calvinist centres in Dauphiny; and the "Orange nursery" had been used as a seat of propaganda. Violent contests had arisen between the two factions. The situation was one of extraordinary difficulty. The State of Orange was engulfed in the papal territory of Avignon, and was close to the dominions of the French King; from either of them it could be overwhelmed or absorbed. The Prince was there a petty Catholic sovereign, dreading religious disturbances above everything. From 1551 to 1559 he had been dispossessed of his dominion. On his restoration he felt himself obliged to forbid public preaching; for, as early as 1560, he had received remonstrances from the Pope and from the Regent in Brussels calling on him to restrain the disorders. He replies to the Duchess that he has ordered his officers to permit nothing contrary to "our true and ancient faith." He writes also to Granvelle to assure him that he will firmly put down the disorders "so injurious to entire Christendom; if he must use force, he would rather resort to the Pope than to the French King." The orders of the Prince (as he probably foresaw or desired) remained a dead letter; and the reform went on. In 1561, he sends fresh remonstrances; but his principal official in Orange himself joins the Protestants. The Pope renewed his complaints, whereupon after three months' deliberation came a stately and diplomatic letter in Latin from Orange to the Pope, in which he renews his own purpose to maintain "the orthodox and catholic doctrine we have received from our fathers, and to punish with prison and confiscation those who openly or secretly teach the contrary." The sonorous missive may have been drafted by an ecclesiastic; it was never intended to be seriously enforced.

Nothing came of these protestations and edicts, and the town of Orange became a hotbed of the new sect under Montbrun, a Protestant chief from Dauphiny. The Prince took no serious steps to suppress the reform. In December 1563, we have a fresh rescript from the Pope in solemn and affectionate warning to his "dilecte fili!" about the horrors still permitted in his princedom —"attende quam indignum sit dominari in urbe illâ tuâ tam manifestum hereticum." If these abominations cannot be purged out, the Pope himself must intervene and throw the whole responsibility of what happens on the Prince. If the language of William is tortuous, his acts are fair, and probably generous. He was still a Catholic, and a determined enemy of disorder; but nothing would induce him to be a party to persecution for belief. Had he boldly announced this to the Pope and the Ministers of Philip, his little principality would have been overrun in a week, and the reformers exterminated in blood. As usual,. he temporises, compromises, promises, prevaricates—and saves for the time a small people from the tormentors.[1]

[1] The history of the petty princedom of Orange in all these years as narrated by La Pise, Arnaud, and others, is a tale of cruel

So soon as the Cardinal had finally withdrawn, Orange, with Egmont and Horn, returned to the Council, where they worked with energy and decision. The Prince obtained a paramount influence, devoting all his skill as a courtier to the Duchess, and toiling from morning till night. Friendly letters pass between Philip and the Prince. A party of "Cardinalists" still struggled to carry out the edicts against heresy, which the Prince set himself to checkmate. Philip, not yet ready with his great scheme, continued to insist doggedly on the execution of the edicts; the Duchess, under the influence of the Prince, replying that it was impracticable, owing to the numbers of the new sects. Orange was now working to form a league between the Flemish and Holland Provinces. It was decided to send Egmont in person to represent to Philip the state of affairs. William exerted all his eloquence. "Tell the King," said he, "that whole cities are in open revolt against the prosecutions, and that it is impossible to enforce the decrees here. As for myself, I shall continue to hold by the Catholic faith; but I will never give any colour to the tyrannical claim of kings to dictate to the consciences of

vicissitudes. It was alternately overrun by forces of the Pope, the French King, and the Huguenot partisans. It was only at intervals even in the nominal control of the Prince, and he rarely had any effective authority there. The Protestants more than once dispossessed the Catholics and desecrated their churches; and the Catholics retaliated with torture and massacre. A horrible sack of the town and carnage took place in 1562, and a second massacre in 1571. The aim of the Prince clearly was to effect a pacification and to establish a compromise, giving liberty of worship and churches to each party. But he was at the mercy of his mighty neighbours; and he can hardly be held responsible for whatever was done. It is one long story, says the Protestant historian, "of martyrdoms, wars, massacres, arson, pillage, treacheries, usurpations, invasions, dragonnades"—a miniature copy of Alva's reign of terror.

their people, and to prescribe the form of religion that they choose to impose. Call the King's attention to the corruption that has crept into the administration of justice. Let the Government be reformed, the Privy Council and the Council of Finance, and increase the authority of the Council of State."

Egmont went to Spain (1565), and was received by Philip with ostentatious honour, evasive words, and mendacious promises. "The end will show the whole truth," wrote Orange to his brother. He felt sure that Egmont had been duped, and made him feel this. It was so. The King redoubled his secret orders to the Duchess. He would lose a hundred thousand lives rather than surrender on the point of religion. Let the edicts be executed. The correspondence that passed from Spain to Brussels in the three years between the withdrawal of the Cardinal and the arrival of Alva forms a monument of bigotry, duplicity, thirst for blood, and incurable bad faith. Every scrap of these endless despatches in Spanish, French, or Italian that pass between Philip, the Regent, the Cardinal, and their agents, between Madrid, Rome, Besançon, and Brussels, still remain to disclose to us their infernal secrets. "Maintain religion, chastise all who act against it; nothing gives me a greater pleasure," writes Philip (29th September 1561). "He is grieved to learn that the people should anger at the burning of a heretic" (25th November 1564). "He urges the Inquisitors to fresh activity; he will spare neither money nor life to maintain the faith" (4th October 1565).

Philip at last was ready, and he spoke out in a fierce rescript from Segovia (17th October 1565) :—

As to the Inquisition, my will is that it be enforced by the Inquisitors, as of old and as is required by all law, human and divine. This lies very near my heart, and I require you to carry out my orders. Let all prisoners be put to death, and suffer them no longer to escape through the neglect, weakness, and bad faith of the judges. If any are too timid to execute the edicts, I will replace them by men who have more heart and zeal.

This rescript was written in French, no doubt as being formal instructions to be shown to the authorities in the Netherlands. At the same time he sent other long despatches to the Duchess in Spanish, insisting on the Inquisition as a *sine qua non* of government, and that all judges and officers should assist the Inquisitors. The Duchess remonstrates, declares that it is impossible to execute his orders. The Inquisition is hateful to the people. The governors of provinces declare that they will not burn 50,000 or 60,000 persons ; they prefer to resign. Orange, Egmont, de Berghes are amongst the most resolute opponents ; they insist on retiring. Every day the irritation grows deeper. In letter after letter the bewildered Regent pours out her alarms, implores her brother to moderate his orders. She begs leave to resign her office. The indomitable bigot simply reiterates his order to execute the edicts.

He writes, in May 1566, that the two things she recommended him to yield—to moderate the edicts and to suffer the States-General to be summoned, the two points mainly insisted on by Orange—were the last things he could grant. He was now making the final arrangements for the Spanish expedition into the Netherlands ; but to gain some more time he writes to the Duchess, in July 1566, that he will approve of some mitigation of the persecution, since "*he abhors nothing so*

much as rigour." Twelve days later he writes to his
ambassador at Rome to assure the Pope that he will not
suffer the least relaxation of the punishment.

As to the pardons publicly announced in my name, whisper in
the ear of his Holiness *that I do not pretend to pardon in matters
religious.* Assure his Holiness that rather than suffer the least
thing in prejudice of religion, I will lose my States and a hundred
lives, for I will not live to be a king of heretics. And if I must
use force, I will carry out my intentions myself, and neither my
own peril nor the ruin of these provinces, or even of all my
dominions, shall stop me from fulfilling my duty as a Christian
prince to maintain the Catholic faith and the Holy See now filled
by a Pope whom I love and revere.

From the time when Philip's fierce letter from Segovia
had been received (the end of 1565) the Prince abandoned
the hope of ever bending the King's purpose by argument.
By his secret correspondents, he knew all that passed in
the royal Council, and he saw that resistance alone could
be relied on. He is said in the Council of State to have
dissuaded any further attempt to influence the King.
He called for the immediate publication of the King's
missives, saying, "We shall soon see the curtain rise on a
memorable tragedy (*egregiae tragoediae*)." It is ridiculous
to imagine that he uttered such words (as an enemy
relates) "with glee" [*quasi laetus gloriabundusque*], if he
uttered them at all. It would be in flagrant contradic-
tion to every word of the weighty letter that he wrote
to the Regent with his own hand to resign his offices.

Madam (he writes, 24th January 1566), as to the decrees of the
Council of Trent, I do not see that they will cause much difficulty,
and all matters of ecclesiastical order I will leave to those whose
charge it is ; they are not in my vocation. As to the Inquisition,
the subjects of these Provinces have been repeatedly assured that
it shall not be introduced here, and this confidence of theirs has

greatly added to the peace and prosperity of the country. As to
the execution of the edicts against heresy, it seems to me very
hard to insist on them in all their details, and I cannot see what
His Majesty can gain from them but to throw the country into
disorder and lose the love of his people. If His Majesty and your
Highness insist on carrying out these edicts, which I see may lead
to the utter ruin of the country, I ask leave to resign my offices
and avoid the stain of failure on me and mine.

He protests his loyalty and patriotism, and declares
himself "a good Christian,"—he no longer says "a good
Catholic."

The decision of the Spanish King to maintain the
Inquisition in all its severity had aroused far wilder
indignation among the more ardent Protestants and the
younger nobles. The chief of these was Louis of Nassau,
the brave, reckless, noble-hearted brother of the Prince,
who was associated with Count Brederode, a wild
debauché, Nicolas de Hames, a violent man, herald of
the Golden Fleece, and several of the active preachers.
Louis, like the rest of his family, was anti-Catholic; the
Flemish Hotspurs were all anti-Spanish. They held
continual meetings, in which the Prince had no part, and
devised schemes of which he could not wholly approve.
There was a meeting at Spa and another at Brussels,
where Louis and his Leaguers drew up and signed the
"Compromise of the Nobles." This was a vehement
protest against the Inquisition and a pledge of mutual
defence. Its language was violent; it denounced "the
gang of foreigners," "their inhuman barbarity," their
"false hypocrisy." It was signed by Louis, Brederode,
and ultimately by some two thousand of the minor nobles
and burghers. The Prince, who did not sign this document, endeavoured to form a league on less violent lines,

beginning with the greater nobles of the land, and looking to assistance from the German chiefs. After a prolonged gathering in his own castle of Breda, they adjourned to Hoogstraeten, where the Prince endeavoured to unite the Knights of the Fleece. Egmont, always vacillating, was unwilling to act, and the combination failed. Orange then seems to have given a qualified support to the League of Louis; and he advised the Regent to admit the "Request" of the Leaguers if it were presented to her without armed force and in respectful terms.

The position of the Prince at this time was one of inextricable dilemma; and his acts and his language are continually varying. He was not yet frankly anti-Catholic; he could see no prospect of throwing off the Spanish yoke; he was not prepared for rebellion; and he could foresee nothing but ruin in a premature appeal to force. He could not approve of the new League; he had no liking for the propagandist preaching; he strongly condemned all outrage and the fanaticism and iconoclasm of the Calvinists. In a confidential letter to his brother he describes his situation. His efforts to prevent the ruin of the country and the shedding of so much innocent blood are treated in the Council as rebellious; on one side is a certain catastrophe, if he does not speak out: on the other side, if he speaks, he is charged with treason. He is now between the devil and the deep sea. He seeks to restrain the violence of his brother and the Leaguers; he seeks to checkmate the Inquisition; he will not be a persecutor. He will not be an inconoclast; he will not instigate rebellion; and he will not abet oppression. Thus the Spanish rulers regarded

him as their enemy ; the Hot-Gospellers regarded him as
a recreant to the truth; the young Leaguers spoke of
him as a lukewarm friend. His familiar letters at this
date breathe despondency, perplexity, foreboding, and
withal an indomitable activity in searching for allies
from side to side.

The "Request," presented to the Regent in April
(1566), was in form a very different document from the
"Compromise of the Nobles." It was a loyal and most
respectful petition to the royal government to counter-
mand the Inquisition and to suspend the edicts on
religion. This petition was drawn by Louis of Nassau
with the sanction of the Prince, as he formally declares ;
and the confederation that obtained the signatures to it
was, through Louis, practically his own organisation.
He supported it warmly in Council, protesting that the
public burnings of heretics roused the people to fury,
and did harm, and not service, to religion. And when
it was proposed in Council to cut the petitioners in
pieces, he indignantly denounced. such a savage act
as degrading to a Christian king. The Regent, who
wished to fly to a fortress, was induced to remain and
receive the petition. Three hundred gentlemen, in a
mock costume of gray frieze, marched in procession to
the palace, where Brederode read the petition to the
Duchess. Surrounded by the Prince, Egmont, and other
councillors, she received it with manifest alarm, and
copious tears—tears shed not from personal fear, but
from dread of the consequences to the King and the
Church. She spoke with dignity, and gave them a
written reply that she must consult the King, and in
the meantime she would give orders to *moderate* the

edicts. The confederates dispersed through Brussels, not without acts and words at variance with their humble petition, and well aware that they had impressed—if not overawed—the Regency.

In the Council held by the perplexed Duchess the Prince had exerted all his eloquence to show that the only way to avoid a dreadful civil war was to act on the prayer of the petition, suppress the edicts, and dissolve the Inquisition. He pointed out that the petitioners were men of honour and influence, and had manifest support in the nation. Egmont shrugged his shoulders, and said that he should go off to "take his cure" at the baths; Berlaymont broke out with the memorable phrase, "Madam, is your Highness to be terrorised by these beggars? By the living God, they should be driven out with sticks!" Aremberg and Meghem agreed with this advice. But in face of the splendid array of this cavalcade of nobles and gentlemen in the streets of Brussels, where they were welcomed by the citizens as defending the public liberties against Spaniards and Cardinalists, more prudent counsels prevailed. Orange remained for the moment master of the situation. The Regent, as usual, temporised, gave vague assurances, promised to refer to the King, and to use her influence in favour of the request.

This temporary success intoxicated the young petitioners. They were beardless youths of rank, some chivalrous, some debauched, partly Catholics filled with patriotic aspirations, or in quest of adventure; partly inclined to Calvinism, but far from being agreed either in matters of religion or of policy. They adjourned to celebrate their victory in a wild supper given by

Brederode in the house of Count Culemburg, a vehement reformer. When all were heated with wine, Brederode rose, and, repeating the phrase of Berlaymont in Council, he drank a health to "The Beggars." He put on a wallet and a wooden bowl, such as vagrants wore. The idea seized the company; all shouted—"Long live the Beggars!" And a mock ceremony of initiation was invented, each brother Beggar swearing to stand true "by salt, by bread, and the wallet, too!" In the midst of the revelry, Orange, Egmont, and Horn appeared. They came to moderate the young Leaguers, and to bring off Hoogstraeten to the Council. They were forced to listen to the new toast — the origin of a party name which for two generations rang through the world; and the revellers broke up without further indiscretions.

The success of the Request and the news of the concessions promised by the Regent, which the confederated "Beggars" spread about and exaggerated, gave a great stimulus to the cause of reformation. Montigny and de Berghes were despatched to Spain (from which prison-house they were never to return) on a mission to explain affairs and to influence the King to moderation. Egmont refused to go again; and Orange told the Regent he well knew that Philip designed his death and confiscation of his estates. The King and his sister now plied the Prince with soft words and gracious messages, and he was more and more in the ascendant in the council of the Regent. As late as the 1st of August 1566, Philip wrote to the Prince with his own hand a letter of fulsome protestations of his affection and confidence, that the Prince was indispensable to his

E

service, and that he would listen to no expressions against him.   A few days after this, the King executed a formal declaration before a notary, in presence of the Duke of Alva, that as his concessions had been made under force, and not freely, he reserved to himself full right to punish the guilty, *and especially those who were the authors and supporters of the seditions.*   To the appeals made to him from the Netherlands, Philip made no answer, except by secret injunctions to maintain the persecution, which, in spite of promises and some show of moderation, was still carried on in places and at seasons.

The great city of Antwerp was now become the chief seat of the Reform movement, which, owing to its connection with Geneva and with the French Huguenots, took a definitely Calvinist form.   Brederode, Louis of Nassau, Culemburg, and other nobles, in active alliance with several Protestant divines, stimulated the preaching of the New Gospel, which was now openly carried on by vast popular gatherings.   "There are more heretics in Antwerp than in Geneva," wrote Cardinal Granvelle in his indignation ; and in that city sat the synod which organised the Protestant consistories.   To the disgust of all Catholics, the medals, badges, toy bowls and wallets of the Beggars were publicly on sale.   Lutherans, Calvinists, and Anabaptists held open meetings in the fields ; their ministers carried on an active propaganda ; and the preaching assemblies were guarded by armed men.   The same gatherings, at times of ten or twenty thousand persons, were continued in all the principal towns.   The Regent and her officials fulminated orders against them, but the local magistracy was quite unable

to suppress them, and the Government had no adequate
military force. "Everything is in frightful confusion,"
wrote the bewildered Duchess to the King; "neither
law, nor faith, nor king have any longer the least hold
on the people." She appealed to the irresolute tyrant,
she appealed to the divided Council, she appealed to
Orange. The Prince told her that he had no power to
suppress the movement, and again talked of withdrawing. "The Prince has changed his religion," wrote the
secretary Armenteros (July 1566). "No one has ever
said this yet so plainly," wrote Philip on the margin.

This is, no doubt, the period at which Orange ceased
to pretend any sympathy for the Catholic Church, yet
he was far from joining any sect. For Anabaptists he
had an active aversion, and at this time he regarded
them as anarchists outside the Christian pale. He had
no sympathy with the Calvinists, and was earnestly
opposed to their revolutionary tactics. He had more
hope from the Lutherans, where all his German alliances
lay. But his inner mind was still for a compromise
between the Churches, mutual toleration, and, if a common worship was impossible, a treaty of peace between
the creeds. He told a confidential agent whom the
Regent sent to talk him over "that the hearts and wills
of men were things not to be forced by any outward
power whatever. He well knew that assassins were
commissioned to kill him, that his life was not safe for
an hour." At last he accepted, reluctantly enough, the
mission pressed on him by the Regent to go to Antwerp,
of which he was hereditary governor, in order to moderate
the excitement. There he was received with wild
enthusiasm, a tumultuous procession, and cries of "Long

life to the Beggars." For some weeks he laboured to effect a peaceable settlement. At length he drew up a scheme by which the reformed worship should be excluded from the city, but should be tolerated in the suburbs, and an armed force was to be maintained at hand to keep order. Whilst the Prince was at Antwerp he succeeded in calming the agitation, and in maintaining some form of peace. But he must have been well aware of the violent passions which were so soon to break forth in devastating fury; and he urgently warned the Regent of the storm which would arise if the preachings were suppressed by force, or if he himself were withdrawn.

The Duchess insisted on the Prince coming to her at Brussels, which, under strong protest, he did immediately after the annual Festival. The 18th August was the day when the city celebrated the public procession of the Virgin. So soon as the Prince was gone, the storm burst. The Holy Image was received in the streets with derision and insult. Insult led to outrage; a mob of ruffians attacked the Cathedral, and, gathering force with numbers and audacity from impunity, they sacked the magnificent church, destroying the images and statues, wrecking the monuments, and shattering the painted glass. It was the work of but a few, not more, we are told, than a hundred; but these, as Strada gravely relates, were assisted by devils from hell. For some days this havoc raged throughout all Antwerp and the neighbouring villages, and from Antwerp it spread through the Netherlands. In scores of towns and through hundreds of churches the scenes of devastation were renewed. For a week at least the outbreak raged unabated. But churches, images, and works of art only were destroyed. There was no loss of life. The Regent in a paroxysm of rage and fear was about to fly to the fortress of Mons. But the Prince and the rest of the Council prevented her flight, and thus the capital was spared the disorders and scandal of iconoclasm. It was soon found to be the work of a miserable rabble, discountenanced by the true Reformers, and most fatal to the cause of the "Beggars."

The storm of the image-breaking, in which many hundreds of churches were desecrated, had a momentary effect in overawing the distracted Regent. Orange firmly refused to take part in a violent repression, whilst he as firmly insisted on her standing to her post. Wild as she was with rage and fear, she still in public called him "her good cousin," and relied on his help, whilst she told the King that he was a traitor. Within a few days of the image-breaking outrages Margaret was convinced that she must bend to the storm. On 25th August she signed articles of arrangement which declared the Inquisition in abeyance, and gave the Reformers liberty of worship in such places as it had been hitherto practised. Louis of Nassau and the Confederates engaged to maintain the royal authority, and not to act in concert against it. The Reformers thought that their cause was gained. The towns broke out into rejoicing. The Prince returned to Antwerp, where he formally restored the Catholic worship in the Cathedral and other churches; some churches he assigned to the Lutherans, some to the Calvinists. He gave no concession to the Anabaptists, whom he regarded as anarchists. He executed three of the recent rioters and banished three others.

The language which the Regent held publicly and in

letters to the Prince was very different from what she
wrote in secret to the King.   She had a formal protest
drawn up and entered on the register of Government
that her act was null and void as the result of force.   In
the cypher despatches she denounces Orange, Egmont,
and the other nobles, declares that she had only yielded
to force, and that every concession was subject to His
Majesty's approval.   This approval she very well knew
would never come.   The news of the outrages had thrown
Philip into a paroxysm of fury.   "I swear by the soul
of my father," he cried, "it shall cost them dear!"   He
tore his beard, he fretted himself into a violent fever,
and even after his recovery he shut himself up in seclusion.   He wrote to his confidants furious letters, calling
the culprits enemies of God, king, and country.   They
were outlaws and public enemies, worthy of death at
any man's hand.   Those who had not opposed their
misdeeds were liable to confiscation, and their lives were
at the King's mercy.   The rage of this sinister bigot was
more deeply stirred by the destruction of ornaments and
figures than by the sacrifice of ten thousand lives.   And
now he, his councillors and ministers, and the whole
Catholic party of Spain, roused themselves up to exact a
terrible revenge.

CHAPTER IV

SEDITION—REBELLION—WAR

1566–1567

IT was now clear to the Prince that they were involved in a struggle for existence, and that he was regarded as the arch enemy of the King. Long and vehement letters pass between the Duchess and Orange, in which, under the form of the conventional courtesies, she reproaches him with all the concessions he had made, protests against all that he proposes to do, and insists on his carrying out the repressive orders of the Government. He, on his side, remonstrates against these cruel and impracticable commands, declares that he is no longer trusted, and asks for the appointment of a successor in his office.

Well aware that, without foreign help, the Netherlands must be crushed by Spain, he sought for allies with indefatigable energy first from one side, then from another. He turned to the French Huguenots, to the German Lutherans, to the Protestant Queen of England. His restless and enthusiastic brother, Louis, made constant journeys to France and to Germany to negotiate for help, and to enlist men-at-arms. His brother John,

at Dillenburg, was the medium of his appeals to the
Lutheran princes.   In a circular letter to the Dukes of
Brunswick, Hesse, and Cleves, the Prince warned them
in guarded language of the critical nature of the struggle.
He turned to the English Queen, inviting to a banquet
Sir Thomas Gresham, Elizabeth's Envoy at Antwerp,
whom he plied with all the resources of his art.   He
solemnly drank the health of the Queen, extolling her
wise and tolerant government.   He told Gresham that
he "had now agreed with the Protestants," and he sent
over a copy of his "Accord," or settlement.   He pressed
the agent to say whether the Queen would give aid to
their cause as she had done to the Huguenots in France
"for the sake of religion."   And he reiterated "that
nothing they could do would content the King of Spain,"
that a heavy reckoning must result, if Philip became
master.

The breach between the Duchess and Orange was
now complete.   In letter after letter to the King she
accused the Prince of settled hostility to herself, to his
sovereign, and to the Catholic religion; she reported
the efforts that the Prince was making to form a party,
to collect armed men, and to resist the royal commands.
On his side, the Prince did not hesitate to assert, even
to members of the Council, that he knew the purpose of
the King was to crush their resistance, to cut off the
heads of himself and the other leaders, and that he was
perfectly informed by his agents at the Spanish court of
what passed in Council, and the purport of the despatches.
There is good reason to think that both had ample
ground for their suspicions.   It was on both sides a
contest of subtlety, ingenuity, and desperate manœuvres

to penetrate the secret policy of each other. The truth was, in the main, perfectly known to both; and both knew that it was known to the other. Orange was now wholly resolved to stake his all in resisting the tyranny of Spain; and the King and his secret counsellors were well aware that the Prince had staked his all, and would leave no stone unturned to win.

By tradition, by temperament, by conviction, the Prince was averse to any democratic methods. He felt the urgent need of an organised party amongst the chief of the native nobility; and of these Count Egmont was the first. He now made a last effort to bring the count into a definite alliance. For this purpose he sent a trusted envoy to Egmont with a carefully worded memorandum of instructions. It urged the vast preparations of Philip in Germany and elsewhere to crush the Netherlands, with which, under pretext of stamping out heresy, the King menaced all, whether Catholic or Protestant; thus he would "reduce the country, them, and their children, to the most miserable slavery ever known." The Prince himself was resolved to withdraw, and would never stay to witness such a catastrophe. Yet, if only Egmont and Horn would combine with him, he would throw himself and all that was his into the cause, and they could ultimately enlist in the struggle the Estates-General of the land. In the meantime, they three should act without a moment's delay. The Duchess, he added, had already commissioned Duke Eric of Brunswick with a foreign force to invade Holland, although this was the official government of the Prince himself. In conclusion, the envoy was to press for a personal interview.

To this Egmont, ever vacillating, consented with an ill-grace, and the momentous interview took place at Termonde on 3rd October. There were present Orange, Egmont, Louis of Nassau, Horn, Hoogstraeten, and some others. Louis complained that Margaret demanded his dismissal from the country; the nobles urged their grievances against the Regent's acts, and they insisted on the designs of the King, who was to come with a foreign army and crush them. A letter from the Spanish Ambassador in Paris to the Regent was produced and read; it was said to have been intercepted on its way to Brussels. In it the King is represented as determined to take vengeance on the authors of sedition, and in particular to put to death Orange, Egmont, and Horn—"the three from whom comes all the mischief." But in the meantime they were to be lulled into security by gracious language until the time came to strike.

The letter was ultimately published as an appendix to the *Apology*, but it is treated by all the best authorities as spurious, and in the form we now see it, it must be unauthentic. It is quite possible that, where both sides were buying secret documents and information, they were not seldom misled by garbled transcripts or deceived by forgeries. The Regent, when Egmont reported this letter to her, indignantly denounced it as fictitious, although her repudiation of an intercepted letter addressed to herself is perhaps not conclusive. Nothing really turns on the letter being genuine or forged. The information it professed to give was entirely true; and it contained nothing that was not fully known to the Nassaus. Philip did mean to kill Orange, Egmont, and Horn—and he did kill them. He did mean to send a

magnificent army to crush the movement of the Provinces—and he did *send* it, though he did not *lead* it,
nor ever meant to lead it. He did advise that the leaders
should be beguiled for a time, and he did seek himself
to beguile them, for he had lately sent letters in his own
hand to Orange and to Egmont full of expressions of
confidence and affection. Whatever the documénts produced and whatever their origin, Orange and his brother
exactly understood and expounded to Egmont the policy
of Philip. It was the policy detailed in voluminous
letters of the King to the Regent, to Granvelle, to the
Ambassador at Rome. It was the policy dictated by
Alva three years before in the letter already cited—
"Raise an army,—chastise all the culprits,—detach
Egmont—and, in the meantime, dissemble."

The impetuous Louis was the chief spokesman at the
conference, whilst Orange supported him and watched
the effect upon the rest. If the King comes with an
army to crush us, said Louis, the nobles would have the
right to resist him in arms; and if he brought in Spanish
troops, they must enlist a force of Germans. It was impossible to trust the King of Spain any more; and they
might even negotiate to transfer the sovereignty of the
Netherlands altogether to the Emperor Maximilian,
still maintaining the monarchic rule and the House of
Austria. Various projects were debated—whether to
resist Philip in arms, to trust to making terms with
him, or to leave the country altogether.

No agreement resulted on any point. The two
Nassaus failed to rouse either Egmont or Horn. The
loyal and chivalrous spirit of Egmont turned from the
idea of defying his King at the head of an army; his

easy simplicity trusted in fraudulent promises and futile hopes; and his vacillation prevented him from taking any serious resolve. He broke off the conference; reported the result of it to Count Mansfeldt, who reported it to the Duchess. Egmont positively and finally refused to act with the Prince. Horn was in despair, sullen and sore; he could see no way that promised to succeed, but he would not take arms. The attempt of combination fell through, mainly by the weakness or loyalty of Egmont, without whom nothing could be done.

Thus ended this critical interview, the details of which we know mainly from the Royalist and Catholic reports. It is one of the singular characters of this struggle that some of the most important negotiations, schemes, and intrigues of both parties are known to us by the secret information supplied to the other side. And, generally speaking, the King and his advisers, and Orange and his confidants, were accurately and immediately informed of the private counsels of the other. The refusal of Egmont was a cruel disappointment and a disastrous blow to the Prince. He never spoke harshly of his unstable and ill-starred comrade. In his *Justification* of 1568, whilst Egmont was in Alva's clutches, he seeks to clear Egmont of any treasonable attempt. And fourteen years later, in his *Apology*, he said with stately and poignant regret : " If my brothers and comrades of the Order of the Fleece and the Council of State had consented to unite their aims with mine, rather than sacrifice their lives so cheaply, we would have staked life and fortune in the effort to keep the Duke of Alva and his Spaniards from setting foot in this land."

The best chance of keeping the Spanish army off was to preserve some kind of order, and to secure a *modus vivendi* between the various religions. The Catholics were still in most towns a considerable majority; they were in lawful possession; they had behind them the whole weight of the Government and the tremendous reserves that the King could command. The Protestants were now emboldened by success; they were ready to stake all on their creed; but they were divided into groups, and utterly without organisation or union. The Prince of Orange was the one man living who, by his character and impartiality, could maintain any sort of order; he was still officially a Catholic, and he was still forced to hold his great offices under the Crown. Reluctantly, despondently, and as a last resource, he continued his efforts to stave off the reign of anarchy and war. In view of the scenes of tumult and outrage which had ensued in Holland, the Regent insisted that the Prince, who was there the Stadtholder, should betake himself to his Government. She sent a trusty counsellor to William to induce him to act and to disarm his suspicions; and in the end, after making a frank admission of all that he knew and all that he feared from Spain, the Prince, on condition of having an adequate armed force, betook himself to Holland on his thankless mission—to moderate the Hot-Gospellers and Icono-clasts, to pacify the indignant Catholics, and to satisfy a remorseless bigot.

He left Antwerp for Holland on 12th October. At Gorkum, near Dort, he found the Reformers on the eve of a fresh outbreak of outrage and iconoclasm, which he succeeded in quelling by an arrangement that the

Catholics should be left in peaceable possession of their churches, and that places outside the town should be reserved for the New Faith. At Utrecht, where he found the foreign levies of Brunswick already proceeding, he made the same arrangement between the two religions; and in spite of the objection of the Duchess, he obtained her assent. "If by exhortation, warnings, or any other means," she wrote, "you can put down these preachings of the Gospel, you will confer a service, not only to God, to the Catholic Faith, and the country, but a service peculiarly grateful to the King." The business, however, of William was exactly the reverse,— it was to secure the preachings in peace and quietness; and he compelled the Regent to endure them.

Thence he went to Amsterdam, where the populace had sacked the convent of the Cordeliers and other churches. The Government at Brussels insisted on their restoration to the Catholics, and that the preachings should be suppressed, or not permitted within the walls. The churches were restored. The preachings could not be suppressed. "Madam," he wrote, "there are so vast a number in Amsterdam, most of them non-citizens from the seaboard, mariners and ignorant men, rude and unable to reason, that it is impossible to suppress the preachings they are accustomed to hold; and, in this winter time, outside the walls, there is nothing but water."—"We cannot change the ancient religion of our State for these sectaries," wrote the Duchess; "let them go to preaching in boats outside the city."—"Preaching in boats is a preposterous invention—who could put that in your Highness's head?" replies William, forgetful perhaps of a famous sermon on the lake from a boat. "They *must* hold their conventicles inside the town." And the Regent is forced to submit. Having established something like order and toleration in Holland, the Prince returned to Antwerp.

From Utrecht William addressed to the States a memoir or manifesto on the religious questions at issue, which is worthy of minute study, as presenting a summary of his views thereon, or rather, as embodying the policy which at this epoch seemed to him statesmanlike. It will be borne in mind that he was himself neither Lutheran nor Calvinist, was actually serving Philip and Margaret as their official governor, and that his aim was to find a peaceful solution of a revolutionary imbroglio. Like his other manifestoes, and indeed like the State papers of that age, it is exceedingly diffuse, allusive, and often obscure or indefinite. Some three hundred words will follow in one involved sentence without a pause. The language is somewhat rhetorical and redundant, the ideas are guarded with provisoes, and there is a manifest desire to conciliate opposite views, to avoid irritating expressions and dogmatic propositions. In essentials it is like a modern State paper in the forms of an age before prose writing had been cast into an art, and with much of the conventional compliments and verbiage of the old official and ecclesiastical style. The substance of it is as follows :—

I have often in mind the deplorable condition of this country, which must end in its utter ruin, owing to the great diversity of opinions, both as to religion and as to its government ; and I grieve to see how few people really take it to heart with a view to find a remedy : some from indifference, some from selfishness, some from cowardice. Now, without presuming too much on my own age and experience, I hold it the duty of every citizen, young or

old, to give to his country what help is in his power in such a
crisis, and not to withhold anything that in his conscience he
believes to be vital to the welfare of the land and the good name of
its Master.

There is no reason to be amazed, much less to fly to arms, because a large part of the inhabitants of this country embrace and
profess opinions contrary to those of their rulers; for history shows
us that this has arisen in all kingdoms, and especially in such as
combine many monarchies, different countries and states under
one sovereign, as are those of His Majesty. These Netherland
States are so surrounded by others which have changed their
religion, that, even if they had never till now heard of any but the
Catholic, they could not be long without change, seeing how much
frequented by foreigners is this land. To forbid aliens access is
impossible, for they make the prosperity of the country; and, together with wars, camps, garrisons, and public preachings, to say
nothing of the actual doings of churchmen, there is nothing sur-
prising in the spread of the new views. But we ought to reflect on
the warnings given us, when we look round on other countries that
have changed their religion and endured religious wars, how they
have suffered extreme desolation, and have passed through all kinds
of calamities and horrors, to the ruin of the land and the loss of
authority to the Prince.

The first thing to be done is to induce the King to confirm
the concessions made by the Regent to the Confederates. They
have served to allay the agitation, and have caused the people to
lay down their arms; and the result would have been greater, but
for the fear that the King intends to revoke these concessions, and
is levying horse and foot, here and abroad, to enable him to undo
all that has been gained. It is useless to patch up the peace of
one district whilst disturbances break out in another. We must
have a general and final settlement. Our country cannot form a
world of its own, isolated from its neighbours. There is no land
in Christendom more completely dependent on a friendly understanding with the nations around us. Our interests point to connection with the Empire, rather than with any other state, and we
should assimilate our institutions to those of the Empire, saving
the rights and privileges of His Majesty in Spain. If the Emperor
Maximilian were to mediate between the two religions, and were
to obtain a general amnesty for the past, a complete pacification
might result. *And this might become the basis of a perpetual League
for guaranteeing the neutralisation of this country*, the common

resort of foreigners for purposes of trade and commerce, the first condition of which is a state of secure peace.

There are seven possible courses that might be taken :—

"1. Suppress by force of arms all preaching and practice of the New Faith.

"2. Banish all who reject the Catholic Faith and confiscate their goods.

"3. Permit all who so elect to follow their own conscience at home within their own boundaries, and to retain the income of their property.

"4. Permit the free practice of any religion, and assign to each certain quarters in each province.

"5. Allow a 'local option' to each town, or to each Seigneur having local jurisdiction, to permit or forbid the practice of the New Faith within their areas.

"6. To permit the Lutheran Confession alone, the Catholic Church and rites remaining untouched.

"7. To permit, along with the Catholic, both Lutheran and Calvinist communions, as is actually done, so long as they shall continue to insist on their differences."

These seven courses the Prince proceeds to discuss. The first three, all of which are persecution in one form or other, he rejects with indignation and horror, as involving the ruin of the country, as well as manifest injustice. The sixth he passes by as unfair and illusory, and that in spite of his own Lutheran birth, wife, brothers, and alliances. The seventh he seems to feel would never be listened to for a moment by Philip or the ruling powers. The fourth or the fifth he seems to regard as the most practicable schemes. Indeed the fourth course—the free exercise of any Christian faith to be assigned to defined quarters and spots—was the plan on which he had been acting with success during the whole struggle since the outrages of August. His conception of the *neutralisation* of the Netherlands in the general interest of Europe, and also his expectation of the dying down of theological dogmatism in the course of centuries are astonishing examples of his political genius, and stamp him as the one statesman very far in advance of his age. Intellectually, he could dream of a fusion of the best elements of the Catholic and Protestant faiths. As a statesman, he thought they might agree to differ by local separation.

He continues (as if foreseeing the long struggle and the Thirty-Years War):—

The resort to force must be both short-lived and ruinous to the country, for it involves the use of foreign mercenaries with all the cruelty, rapacity, and wanton oppression they always bring in their train. We have seen the horrors and outrages they inflict on man and woman, and the ruin to the welfare of our land. As to the banishment of a vast body of Reformers, even if it could be carried out without resorting to force, it would strip the country of its best workers and chief traders—our country which is "the market of Christendom." It might seem more reasonable to allow the private freedom of conscience without public worship, but this would end in atheism and irreligion altogether, like the brute beasts. As to permitting unlimited toleration, we know that the King, his Council, and all Spain would rather see half this land destroyed before they will consent to it. The conclusion is that there must be a compromise whereby the safety of person and property, churches and institutions, be guaranteed to the Catholics; and that there should be secured to the New Faith an exercise of their worship under conditions and limits of place. Thus only can we avoid great effusion of blood and ruin to the country, together with the possible destruction of the Catholic Faith. There is no real obstacle to tolerating a religion other than our own, if we only trust that error must ultimately disappear. The Arian heresy was not suppressed by bloodshed; but after centuries of active life, it was ultimately overcome by the diligence, learning, and devotion to duty of the Catholic teachers themselves. A very large part of our people have embraced the new views, and rather than forsake them they will give up their lives and homes. To crush them into orthodoxy by force is impossible or intolerable. *If their opinions are false, if the Catholic Faith be based on eternal truth, their*

doctrines will melt away in good time, like the snow before the
sun.

Of possible help from without, Orange at this time
had most hope from the German chiefs.   Nothing
effective came from the Huguenots in France ; even less
came from Elizabeth.   This is the epoch at which long
and earnest despatches pass between Orange and the
Elector of Saxony, the Landgrave of Hesse, the Counts
of Nassau, Wittgenstein, and other leading nobles of
the Empire.   William, Louis, and, to a · great extent,
John of Nassau, press for a league of the German
princes to save the existence of the Reform in the
Netherlands.   One after another the princes urge
acceptance of the Lutheran Confession of Augsburg.
They do not put it quite sharply; but their terms
amount to this—that the Netherlanders must abandon
Calvinism and accept Lutheranism as a condition pre-
cedent to receiving aid.   William is now inclined to
adopt the Lutheranism of his House and of his only
powerful friends ; but he saw that Lutheranism had no
real hold on the masses of his own land, and that it was
useless to attempt any further pressure to modify their
Calvinistic fervour.   He pleads their cause earnestly,
piteously, and skilfully.   He says that he is thinking
of declaring himself to be a Lutheran, but that Philip
regards Lutherans as just as bad as Calvinists.   " Surely
the German Protestants will not see these innocent,
helpless Christians crushed without an effort."   But he
pleads in vain.

    " I am no Calvinist," wrote the Prince to the Land-
grave of Hesse, " but it seems to me neither right nor
worthy of a Christian to seek, for the sake of differences

between the doctrine of Calvin and the Confession of
Augsburg, to have this land swarming with troops and
inundated with blood." Neither William nor Louis
could at this time understand how such speculative
differences could keep men apart in such imminent peril.
They tried conferences; they brought Lutheran divines
from Germany to convince the Dutch Calvinists of their
errors; they appealed to the Lutherans not to stand out
for their Confession in a matter of life and death. But
no impression could be made either on Lutheran or on
Calvinist. "Would not the German princes at least
intercede with Philip?" "Would they hinder the
passage of the royal mercenaries from Germany?"
writes William to the Elector of Saxony. Saxony,
Hesse, Wurtemburg, and the rest offer excellent advice,
"to beware of Philip, not to drive him to extremity, to
avoid outrages"; they are full of Christian brotherhood
towards the Netherlanders, but how can these men
persist in their Calvinistic errors? The letters of these
high, mighty, and serene potentates read like theological
essays, polemical phrases abound, the Confession of
Augsburg is a *sine qua non*. In December the Prince
sent a mission, with his brother John and other chiefs,
to make a last appeal to the great magnates. They
were to plead earnestly for the Reformers, to defend
their civic loyalty provided their consciences were not
forced, to detail the enormities committed by the
Spaniards, and the dangers of a new invasion. Some
ineffectual conferences were held. None of the Lutheran
princes would act; even Count Nuenar, William's
brother-in-law, was sorry he could not join; he is not
important, he begs to have himself excused.

The Prince left Holland in January 1567, having brought things to a certain degree of order by a settlement, most ungrateful to the Regent, but so far approved by the States of Holland that they voted him a gift of 50,000 florins—a present which he proudly declined. At Breda he called together a conference of nobles, who made a new effort to induce Egmont to join in resisting the Spanish army. To this Egmont gave an indignant refusal, answering that he would treat as his enemy any who failed in their allegiance to their lord. In February the Prince returned to Antwerp, which was in a state of acute agitation. There were 40,000 Protestants in the city, reported the English agent, all ready to die for their belief. The Regent was now insisting on the withdrawal of all concessions, the dismissal of the preachers, and the restoration everywhere of the Catholic worship, together with exaction from all officials of the new oath " to serve the King in all or any commands." The rumour of this retrograde step drew an angry crowd of 2000 persons round the abode of the Prince, who could only pacify them with difficulty. Efforts were made by Egmont and the loyalist nobles to induce Orange to accept this new oath and to impose it on all under him. But he stoutly refused to have anything to do with it, or even to discuss it with the Royalist partisans.

And now broke forth the long-gathering, expected, inevitable crash of arms, which the Prince had been striving to avert, yet for which he was practically more or less responsible. For more than a year he had been straining every nerve to form an armed confederation to oppose the King; Louis had been flying about to engage troops, both horse and foot; Brederode was fortifying his castle with the Prince's cannon, and he and others were raising armed bands under the Prince's eyes ; Lutherans, Calvinists, and patriots were constantly receiving from his confidants promises of sympathy and aid.   Orange, as a statesman and general who had taken part in great wars and combinations, naturally intended to resist only when he had a powerful organised force and the certainty of further help from abroad.   The impatience of the sectaries plunged them into a series of wild outbreaks which uniformly ended in bloody defeat. Many of these desperate attempts were certainly carried out by intimate allies and agents of the Prince ; several were prepared under his eyes ; he made no serious effort to arrest them.   And yet there is no evidence that he either instigated or approved them.   The truth is, that his twofold position as Minister of the Crown, and yet virtual head of an armed resistance, was a position of hopeless ambiguity and inextricable duplicity.

One of the boldest and most vehement of the Calvinist champions was Jean de Marnix, Lord of Tholouse and brother of Ste. Aldegonde.   He got together a troop of raw, half-armed enthusiasts and made an attack on the Isle of Walcheren.   This failing, he led them to Ostrawell, just north of Antwerp, and there the insurgents posted themselves to the number of 3000.   A Royalist force, under Philippe de Beauvoir, took them by surprise, cut them to pieces, and killed de Marnix under the walls of Antwerp.   Within the city a wild mob of citizens, snatching up any weapon or even tool, clamoured to be led forth to succour their friends.   This useless sacrifice was prevented by the Prince, who, hastily calling together an armed force,

went forward to meet the excited crowd. He was
greeted with execrations and cries of "Vile traitor,"—
"Soldier of the Pope,"—"Minister of Antichrist !" He
had the gates closed, and forced the mob back into the
centre of the town. Here a vast concourse of Calvinists
were gathered; they seized some cannon, opened the
prisons, and prepared for a new sack of the churches
and Catholic houses. The Prince himself was threatened
by a man who levelled an arquebus at his breast, crying
out, "Faithless traitor, it is thou who art the cause of
this massacre of our brothers!"

The next day some 13,000 or 15,000 men on the
Calvinist side were gathered in the Place de Meir, and
formed barricades mounted with cannon. The Prince
acted with extraordinary energy and no less consummate
moderation. He marshalled all the regular forces of
the city; he enrolled some three or four thousand
Lutherans, united them with the armed Catholics in
defence of order, and called for support from the foreign
mercantile guilds. He himself sat day and night in the
council chamber to frame some treaty of compromise.
At imminent peril he again went down to the furious
insurgents in the Meir, calling on them to send deputations to discuss terms of peace and settlement.

On the third day the condition of Antwerp was fear-
ful. There were now three armed bodies posted within
the city, in numbers altogether that were computed at
thirty or forty thousand. "The Calvinists," says the
contemporary Catholic, Pontus Payen, "hated the
Lutherans as much as the Catholics, or worse. They
called them semi-Papists, worse than Papists; nor had
they a good word for the Anabaptists, who were as

much children of the devil as they were themselves. And they would have succeeded in their detestable ends, if the Prince had not stopped them by his wisdom and energy. He, detesting the bloodthirsty temper of the Calvinists, found means to stem their bold attempts with a strong hand." He formed a solid armed force consisting of Catholics, Lutherans, foreign merchants, and the leading burghers of all creeds; the tocsin was rung, and the rioters surrounded. Then, at the head of a deputation from the Council, attended by a hundred men-at-arms, he rode up to the barricades in the Meir. There he had the terms of settlement read aloud, and he proved to them that they were all they could obtain, being free right of worship and exclusion of a foreign garrison. He warned the insurgents that they were outnumbered by two to one, and that further resistance could only end in a new massacre such as they had lately witnessed at Ostrawell. He adjured them passionately to accept the terms. They were overawed, if not convinced. Their preachers accepted the terms. As the settlement was read out, the Prince cried—"God save the King." And, as a sign of submission to his authority, the same cry at last broke forth from the fierce gathering of men who had kept the city in awe for three days and nights. "Thus was the tumult quelled," says old Pontus, "without any spilling of blood, which every one expected to see."

This was one of the most masterly, as well as one of the most hazardous, exploits of the time, crowded as that time was with heroic and brilliant deeds. And it has won the praise of all historians on both sides. The garrulous Pontus, who never would believe in the

Prince's soldierly courage, declares that. Orange then saved the city from pillage and massacre; and, though men chiefly applauded him for protecting the Catholics by bringing the Lutherans and foreigners to their aid, the old Catholic writer believes that it was the Calvinists who have most cause to thank him for saving them, the weaker party, from the condign chastisement they were about to receive. Fortunately we have an excellent eye-witness in our own Sir Thomas Gresham, who wrote thus to Cecil: "The Prince very nobly hath travailed, both night and day, to keep this town from manslaughter and from despoil, which doubtless had taken place, if he had not been,—to the loss of 20,000 men; for that I never saw men so desperate willing to fight." The Prince himself, in a letter to a German friend recounting these terrible days, says that order was preserved only by great effort and labour, and common risk of life and limb; that their escape from death was so marvellous that they feel as if the grace of God had vouchsafed ˙ them a second life. It will earn us little thanks at Court, he knows; but they must look for reward to God, their consciences, and honest people. "I know not how we can find a way out of this strait," he adds, "and we can only commend ourselves to God and the prayers of our friends."

Everywhere the ill-starred outbreaks of the Pro-testants in arms were savagely crushed. Egmont re-duced Flanders. Noircarmes, having subdued Tournay, marched against Valenciennes. He cut to pieces a miserable rabble of half-armed insurgents at Lannoy and Watrelots, slaying and burning some thousands, and laid siege to Valenciennes, which, with the aid of Egmont,

by the end of .March, he had captured. A bloody vengeance was taken, and hundreds of citizens and ministers
were strangled or beheaded. The victorious general
pursued his successes throughout the country, and these
series of defeats struck panic into the whole Protestant
cause. "The capture of Valenciennes," wrote Noircarmes, "has wrought a miracle ; the other cities
submit with a rope round their necks." The victory at
Lannoy, we are told, "had made these hypocrites of
Catholics toss their heads, like so many dromedaries, in
their stiff-necked insolence." The first blood had indeed
resulted in a cruel disaster everywhere to the Reformers.
It is difficult to clear William, if not of complicity with
these miserable struggles, at least of responsibility for
their failure. His agents had given them encouragement and hope. He was himself powerless to control
them, and was still an official of the Government which
crushed them. He was no doubt willing to see them
as formidable and as stubborn as they could be made.
He underrated the discipline and energy of the Royalist
forces, but he never intended half-armed peasants led
by ignorant preachers to take the field.

No thanks, indeed, were ever wasted on the Prince by
the Regent and the Government of the King. Margaret
declared that the terms of settlement at Antwerp were
" strange and preposterous," that it was a surrender to
sedition ; and shortly afterwards she annulled the agreement and forced the magistrates to dismiss the preachers.
But the intolerably false position of William was now
about to end ; and the stubborn, diplomatic contest between this adroit pair had almost reached its close. For
at least fourteen months, ever since William's famous

letter of 24th January 1566, resigning his offices and
refusing to enforce the edicts of persecution, the official
letters of the Regent had contained nothing but com-
plaint, suspicion, reprimand, and refusal to accept his
advice or to confirm his acts.   On his side, his elaborate
replies were able, determined, unanswerable arguments
to convict her of impracticable orders and unfounded
fears.   The forms of politeness are retained.   She
always addresses him as "Her good cousin," and he is
always "the very humble servant of Her Highness,
whose hand he kisses and whom may God preserve."
She, all the while, is writing daily to Philip that the
Prince is betraying him; and the Prince at last declines
to see the Regent, or even to come within her reach.
Yet the diplomatic war goes on incessantly between
Margaret and her great Minister.   In her precarious
position without Spanish troops, she rightly felt that
Orange was indispensable, if the whole country was not
to be plunged into a state of bloody turmoil.   He, on
his side, was labouring to gain time, and to disarm
tyranny by an organised resistance.   She regarded him
as a temporary instrument of order, though potentially
a leader of rebellion.   He regarded her as the official
instrument of a power which he hoped to baffle, and
trusted that he could outwit.

The final breach came over the new oath, which the
bigotry of Philip had invented as a notable trap.   From
the beginning of the year 1567, the Regent had been
urging the Prince to obtain from the troops and officers
under his orders a new form of oath that had been
ordered from Spain.   William put off her demands with
excuses that were not quite serious and hardly civil.   At

last she sends him (8th March 1567) a solemn and per-
emptory demand to sign by way of oath a formal undertaking "*to serve His Majesty, and to act towards and against
all and every, as shall be ordered me on his behalf, without
limitation or restriction.*" Thus directly challenged, the
Prince replies by a positive refusal to sign such an oath
as being both "unprecedented and general," as involving
acts that might be "against his conscience, and to the
injury of the King and the country, and contrary to his
allegiance as feudal lord, and subject of this land." And
he thereupon begs leave to resign all his offices, and to
withdraw from service.

The Regent could not spare such a man, and she
dared not yet defy him : it was just before the outbreak
at Antwerp. She sent an agent to the Prince to induce
him to retain office ; but he was unmoved. He said the
new oath might compel him to act against the Provinces
of which he was hereditary chief, against the Emperor,
or even to kill his own wife. He was pressed to meet
Egmont and Mansfeldt, which he consented to do. The
last interview took place at Willebroek, 2nd April 1567,
in presence of the Regent's agent, who took notes. The
Jesuit historian, who had access to these, relates that
nothing was concluded, as neither Orange nor Egmont
could shake the other. The Prince took Egmont aside
and implored him not to await the tempest of blood
which Spain was about to discharge upon the Netherlands. Egmont was confident that if the country was
quiet, the King would be merciful. "This mercy will
be your ruin ; you will be the bridge across which the
Spaniards will enter this land," said Orange. Sure that
he would never see his old comrade again, he grasped

Egmont in his arms; and so, "both weeping, they took a last farewell."

Thereupon the Prince wrote a series of letters to the King, the Regent, to de Berghes in Spain, to Egmont, and to Horn, in all of which he announced his resolve to withdraw from all offices, and to betake himself to Germany. He seems still to have cherished a forlorn hope that by fair words he might yet avert from himself and from his outlawry and confiscation. He wrote a stately official farewell to the Regent, rehearsing his services and sacrifices, and declaring his loyalty and good faith. He withdrew his daughter, Marie, who had been in the Court of the Duchess for the last three years. To the King he wrote a long justification of his acts as governor, and formally renounced his offices, on the ground that he could not accept the general and unlimited terms of the novel oath demanded, whilst he purposed to remain a loyal subject. To Egmont and to Horn he sent epistles, in the Latin tongue, evidently prepared by some learned scribe, and for the use perhaps of clerical readers, full of sonorous compliments, stately protestations, and official asseverations of loyalty and patriotism. To de Berghes, in Madrid, he wrote, that he could no longer stay to see the ruin of the country, which he was unable to avert. Having satisfied all the conventions, he withdrew to Breda, which he reached safely on the 11th April. The last letter of the Regent overflows with protestations of confidence and affection; she begs him to remain ever true and faithful to his King; she will ever cherish him as her own son; and hopes soon to have again under her roof his dear daughter, whom she loves as her own. She prays the Creator to give him

happiness and a prosperous journey into Germany. The
Prince, it seems, had steadily refused to come within the
grasp of the Regent's bodyguard ; and, indeed, hearing
of the approach of a Royalist force, he hastily set forth
from Breda in what his enemies called a flight. The
official letters, full of affection, trust, friendship, and
loyalty, which he wrote and received, were simply the
custom of the age. He received them, but he did not
trust them. A secret message from the very Cabinet of
Philip revealed to him "that Alva was first and foremost to seize the Prince, bring him to execution
within twenty - four hours." The first clause of the
secret instructions from the King required Alva to
*arrest and bring to condign punishment the chief persons
of the country who had shown themselves guilty during the
late troubles.*

CHAPTER V

In those very days of April 1567, when William of
Orange was withdrawing from the Netherlands in despair, Ferdinand de Toledo, Duke of Alva, was leaving
Spain in triumph, to take command of the punitive
force, and ultimately of the government of the Low
Countries. He marshalled his troops at Genoa; and
thence he led them northwards across the Alps, through
Lombardy, Burgundy, and Luxemburg to Brussels.
This splendid army was one of the most perfect engines
of war ever seen in that age. The total force consisted
of some 24,000 men with 6000 horses. The fighting
men comprised about 9000 foot, Spanish veterans mainly
drawn from the garrisons of Lombardy and Naples.
The cavalry were some 1200 troopers from Italy. These
were joined by a force of German mercenaries, both
horse and foot. They had a due complement of artillery
and engineers; and together they formed a small but
efficient corps of the best soldiers in Europe. A portion
of the infantry were equipped with muskets,—an arm
not previously used by troops in the field,—they were

attended by their squires and bearers; on the march
they were mounted; their armour was gilt and chased,
and each private soldier was arrayed like an officer of
rank.   Two thousand courtezans, we are told, were
enrolled in this force, "four hundred of them in garb as
fine as princesses, and riding their horses." The martial
array of the Spanish soldiery filled all beholders with
admiration, wonder, and alarm.

The organisation of this veteran army was perfect.
Their commander was acknowledged to be one of the
greatest masters of war of his age.   And under him
served the most able captains of horse and foot that
Europe had seen.   In discipline, in commissariat, in all
tactical provisions, this model army was equal to anything in modern war.   The Pope had wished it to
be diverted "to destroy the town of Geneva."   But
without a check, and without a halt, constantly
watched by jealous forces of Swiss, Germans, and
French, the Spanish army in three months achieved
its long and difficult march from the Mediterranean to
Brabant.

Their chief was a consummate and experienced
soldier, now in his sixtieth year.   Charles V. had pronounced him to be one of the three great commanders
of his time.   From the age of sixteen he had lived in
the field or the camp.   The Duke of Alva is well known
to us by the grand portrait of Titian.   Tall, spare,
upright, with a stern but regular countenance, a long
dark visage, gleaming black eyes, close black hair, a
waving beard flowing over his magnificent armour, and
wearing the collar of the Fleece, he looks the ideal of
the resolute, profound, self-centred grandee, bronzed in

war and worn with unremitting cares. Proud of his
imperial descent, he was arrogant even for a Spanish
duke, consumed with ambition, thirsting for wealth,
jealous, implacable, and abnormally prone to cruelty
and deceit. Though neither saint nor devotee, he was
not brutal, not intemperate, not shameless; but tena-
cious enough of his own strange point of honour. He
was a sincere bigot; inexorably convinced that no law,
human or divine, stood between his duty to the Catholic
Church and the Catholic King—that nothing which he
vehemently desired could be otherwise than right. He
had a conscience of his own, and even had, or once had,.
some inner recess of a heart. But fanaticism, pride, and
self-worship made him what for centuries he has remained in the history of Europe—the type of all that
is bloody, pitiless, and false.

Alva had received his original commission from
Philip as early as December 1566, and in the same
month this was communicated to the Regent. It had
caused consternation in her Council, and bitter disappointment to herself. She remonstrated with her
brother; told him that "the very name of Alva
already made the Spanish nation hateful in the Netherlands." With obstinate mendacity Philip had reiterated
that he was coming in person; he tried to pass the
fraud upon his sister, the Council, even upon the Pope.
The Regent urged Alva to limit and restrain the army,
the approach of which was causing such terror. She
prayed Philip to inform her what were the General's
powers. All this the King and his new Viceroy treated
with silent contempt, keeping their own counsel, and
concealing the truth. "I have tamed men of iron,"

G

said Alva ; " shall I not deal with these men of butter ? " Alva, as a Knight of the Golden Fleece, had some qualms about dealing with his brother knights contrary to the rules of this ancient Order of Chivalry. But Philip, by a notarial act in Latin (15th April 1567), authorised the Duke "to proceed to punish all authors of the late troubles, without regard to the Constitution of the Order, *even in the case of Knights of the Fleece.*"

The Duke entered Belgium in August, and was waited upon by the Royalist grandees, including Egmont, who came with a fine retinue and a present of horses. Alva received the count with diabolical good - humour and sarcasm, passed his arm round his neck, and then rode side by side in ostentatious friendliness. Count Horn was also welcomed with cordiality and affection. The young Count of Buren, eldest son of the Prince of Orange, then thirteen, was studying at the University of Louvain. The Duke received the lad most graciously, promised his good offices to him and to his father, and accepted from the Prince a present for his own son. It is even said that the Prince wrote to the Duke a formal letter of compliments. Alva entered Brussels in state on the 22nd August, to the wrath of the Duchess whom he was to supplant, and at once became practically master of the land. He was hardly firm in his seat when the new Reign of Terror began.

The Council of Troubles—henceforth known as the Council of Blood—was instituted ; and it soon became a sort of court-martial, with the Duke as perpetual president, and a few creatures of his own as assessors. Egmont and Horn, lulled into a sense of security, were treacherously arrested. With them, a crowd of men of mark were seized. But as the wily Cardinal Granvelle remarked, "to have seized the Prince would have been more important than all the rest"; and the Duke wrote to Philip that the Prince was "the head of all." Alva did what he could do, in the absence of Orange. In January 1568 a solemn proclamation of outlawry was made against the Prince, "as chief author, supporter, and accomplice of the rebels and disturbers of the peace." And shortly afterwards, the Count of Buren, his eldest son and heir, was treacherously seized in the University, befooled, and carried off to Spain, where he was destined to pass the next twenty-eight years of his life as Philip's prisoner, pupil, and hostage.

This was the signal for the wholesale execution of thousands of men and women—heretics, rebels, suspects, or plainly innocent. "No matter," said the monster Vargas, the Duke's right-hand man, "if the condemned man be innocent; it will be easier for him when he is tried in the next world!" "The heretics sacked the churches, the rest looked on, so all are guilty alike." This is not the place to rehearse the infamous trial and execution of Egmont and Horn, the horrors of Alva's Reign of Terror, and the brutal achievements of the Spanish Inquisition. It has been recounted with pardonable warmth of language by the American historian in a well-known passage, which it is convenient again to quote:—

The whole country became a charnel-house ; the death-bell tolled hourly in every village ; not a family but was called to mourn for its dearest relatives, while the survivors stalked listlessly about, the ghosts of their former selves, among the wrecks of their former homes. The spirit of the nation, within a few months after the arrival of Alva, seemed hopelessly broken. The blood of its best and bravest had already stained the scaffold ; the men to whom it had been accustomed to look for guidance and protection were dead, in prison, or in exile. Submission had ceased to be of any avail, flight was impossible, and the spirit of vengeance had alighted at every fireside. The mourners went daily about the street, for there was hardly a house that had not been made desolate. The scaffolds, the gallows, the funeral piles, which had been sufficient in ordinary times, furnished now an entirely inadequate machinery for the incessant executions. Columns and stakes in every street, the door-posts of private houses, the fences in the fields, were laden with human carcases, strangled, burned, beheaded. The orchards in the country bore on many a tree the hideous fruit of human bodies. Thus the Netherlands were crushed, and but for the stringency of the tyranny which had now closed their gates, would have been depopulated. The grass began to grow in the streets of those cities which had recently nourished so many artizans. In all those great manufacturing and industrial marts, where the tide of human life had throbbed so vigorously, there now reigned the silence and the darkness of midnight.

Such is indeed the language of indignant partisans on the Reformers' side, and it is doubtless over-coloured. But no substantial disproof of the persecution has been ever made by Catholic apologists. And Alva is said to have boasted on his resignation that he had put to death 18,600 persons, not counting all who perished in fight, storm, siege, and massacre.

The elaborate and historic documents in which the Prince had announced to the King, the Regent, and his colleagues his intention to withdraw, contained the substantial truth and the true reasons for his act, wrapped up in the verbiage of diplomatic euphemism. He knew for certain that Alva was approaching with an overpowering army, not only to crush rebellion and opposition, but to punish without mercy, to restore Catholic orthodoxy, and to kill the Prince, his friends, and followers. No man knew so well how helpless was the

country by itself to resist, and how savage a vengeance
Philip had prepared. The recent massacres by the
Regent's troops had effected a calm of terror and despair,
and the royal authority was no longer challenged nor
threatened. The Prince seems to have nursed a fond
hope that such abject submission might disarm even
Philip's revenge ; and that, as he himself was formally
neither Protestant nor rebel, diplomatic assurances might
yet be of use. Outside the reach of Philip's troopers, he
possessed nothing—neither home nor house, income nor
estates—nothing but his barren titles of honour, and the
kind words and good advice abundantly offered by his
German cousins. He now committed the capital error
—one of the few imprudences of his life—in leaving his
son and heir in the University of Louvain. He seems
to have hoped thus to avert or mitigate the confiscation
of his estates, take from himself the imputation of being
a refugee, or enable the Spaniards to accept the boy as
his successor. It was a grievous fault, and grievously
did Orange answer for his fault.

It was on the 22nd of April 1567 that the Prince
hurriedly left his palace of Breda, on the approach of
Noircarmes' troops, and by easy stages withdrew to his
brother John, in the ancestral castle of Dillenburg.
He was followed by his household and his vicious and
crazy wife, Anne of Saxony, who assailed him incessantly
with reproaches and insults. He remained some months
amongst his family, brooding over events, and awaiting
the issue. He declined the offer of the King of Denmark
to give him a safe asylum. And now he seriously be-
thought him of entering the Lutheran Communion. He
writes to the Landgrave of Hesse that he wished to

devote his leisure to studying the Scripture and to pious meditations, and he begs for a learned divine to assist his conversion. The Landgrave is only too happy to see such a disposition, sends off his favourite preacher, and an invaluable work of Melancthon, the *Corpus Christianae doctrinae.* The letters show us the Prince now rapidly advancing in Evangelical orthodoxy. He loses a beloved sister, the Countess of Nuenar; he bears the ill-humours and violent demands of his unworthy wife like a Christian and a gentleman. She clamours to return to Breda, finding Dillenburg unbearable. The Prince remonstrates, insists on her remaining with him in her present condition; and in September 1567, Maurice is born—destined to be for forty years the heroic upholder of his father's work, at last also Prince of Orange, and head of the Dutch Republic. This son was duly christened as Lutheran, the first of the Prince's children to receive the Protestant rite.

The treacherous arrest of Egmont and Horn in the same month, the wholesale seizure of prominent reformers, the institution of the Council of Blood, roused the Prince into active measures, and showed that all his forebodings fell short of the reality. In December he writes to the Duke of Saxony that armed resistance was not only justifiable, but inevitable, and he points out the danger that threatened Germany as well as the Netherlands. In January 1568 the Prince was solemnly summoned as rebel and traitor, and formally outlawed by ban. A few weeks later, by special order from Philip, and at the suggestion of Cardinal Granvelle, the boy-student, Count of Buren was seized and sent off to Spain, and never again saw his father's face.

The Prince replied to the summons and outlawry by a long and somewhat oratorical piece, in which he shows that it was null and void, as against all law and custom. He says the very suspicion of heresy is now treated as wiping out all services, and as proving all charges. The monstrous acts of the new Council of Blood, the seizure of Egmont and Horn, the abduction of his own son, and the abrogation of contracts, laws, rights, and customs, prove that the Duke of Alva is setting up, not the just authority of the King, but a lawless, personal tyranny. He throws back the summons in his face, and claims his right as a magnate of the Empire to be judged by the Emperor, the electors, and other chiefs. Thus, in the sight of all men, did the Prince throw down the gage of battle to the death (3rd March 1568).

In the following month was issued his *Justification*, an elaborate document in nearly fifty pages, written, we are told, by himself, which is not true of the *Apology* of 1581 and many other manifestoes bearing his name. He had the assistance of the celebrated Protestant divine, Languet, who probably supplied the theological commonplaces and the mottoes from the Psalms :—

The wicked watcheth the righteous, and seeketh to slay him. But the Lord will not leave him in his hand, nor condemn him when he is judged (Ps. xxxvii.)

Thou shalt destroy them that speak leasing : the Lord will abhor the bloody and deceitful man. Lead me, O Lord, in thy righteousness because of mine enemies (Ps. v.)

They gather themselves together against the soul of the righteous, and condemn the innocent blood. But the Lord is my defence ; and my God is the rock of my refuge (Ps. xciv.)

The *Justification* opens with a historic review of the Nether-lands, from the first introduction of the Edicts against the New

Faith. The Prince is scrupulous to speak with respect of the late Emperor, and even as to Philip, he throws all blame upon the royal ministers and agents. He speaks with pride of the services of his countrymen in the long war with France, and of the forty millions of florins that they contributed to the service of the Crown. For the descent of the country from the height of prosperity and loyalty to its present state of calamity and disturbance, he throws the whole responsibility on evil counsellors, especially on Cardinal Granvelle. The Prince himself had consistently resisted all attempts to persecute and to introduce the Inquisition, by speech in Council, by remonstrance with the Regent, by his offers of resignation, by repeated letters to the King. If he had remained in any official position, it was solely by the refusal of Regent and King to relieve him ; for the Cardinal, like Dionysius, tyrant of Sicily, desired to keep some popular noble in the ministry, well knowing how deeply he was hated. After the departure of the Cardinal, he (the Prince) was retained in office at the urgent entreaties of the Regent, little as he coveted such duties himself. He then inveighs against the Cardinal, who upheld the Edicts and Inquisition by which more than 50,000 persons had been cruelly put to death and driven into exile, so that the whole country was thrown into transports of rage and horror.

He then gives a history of the conversion of the bishoprics which involved the revival of persecution, the mission to Spain of Montigny, and other deputations to protest against the Inquisition, the subsequent mission of Egmont, and the decision of the King to maintain the Catholic orthodoxy with all the rigour of the Spanish Inquisition. This, and this alone, was the sole cause of the agitation, and not "the ambition or the machinations of the Prince." It was against this new form of religious persecution that the Federation of the Nobles was directed—a movement that did not originate with him, but the certain result of which the Prince had pressed on the Council. And the same of the Petition of the Nobles, which was a loyal remonstrance to the King to respect the ancient constitutions of the land. To throw the responsibility of the Confederation of Nobles on the Prince, who was not a member of it, to make him answerable for the acts of men, to whom he never gave assistance, is to substitute *pro summo iure, summam injuriam.* No place, town, fortress, or government where the Prince was in actual command has ever broken out in insurrection, or into outrage to churches and ecclesiastics.

The interview at Termonde was a friendly gathering, where the letters of the Spanish Ambassador to the Regent were discussed, but no resolution was taken to resort to arms. He defends himself from many minor charges : from any complicity with Brederode, with the attack on Zeeland, with the insurgents of Ostrawell. As to his work in pacifying the disturbed provinces and towns, the Prince speaks of it with pride as a just and wise measure of tolera- tion, it being impossible to secure public peace, except by per- mitting the exercise of the new faith, even to the extent of their possessing temples of their own. *How can a temple offend any man more than the building of a secular house? And is it not more conducive to public peace and order that a congregation should meet quietly in a temple of their own, rather than by public processions and open meetings.* "Such are the false and frivolous pretences whereon they now seek to ruin me, in spite of all my services and sacrifices and that of my warlike ancestors. They set at naught rights, law, custom, and rob me of my honour and my child, dearer to me than life. And all this is done not to my despite but that of the King, whose contracts and oaths they would trample under foot. May God grant His Majesty, by the light of His divine grace, to see and understand the purposes of his true and loyal servants, now so sorely calumniated, persecuted, and afflicted ! "

This document was circulated in German, Latin, Dutch, English, and Spanish, as well as in the original French. Though it uses Evangelical forms, it is not the work of a theologian. It is the work essentially of a politician, of a diplomatist, and in substance is like a modern State paper at the opening of a war. William was one of the first politicians in modern Europe to understand the importance of political manifestoes addressed to the public opinion of Europe. The paper is in parts rhetorical in form, but essentially based on powerful arguments. In substance, its statements are true as well as convincing, though we cannot literally accept the truth of all his assertions as to his freedom from complicity with the acts of his friends.

This defiance was followed by energetic action all along the line. The time indeed was ripe. Alva was revelling in slaughter by fire and by sword—his Lenten offering to his master and his God "will exceed 800 heads." But, meanwhile, Orange had been using his year of exile in organising a general war. According to the confession of one of his captains, when a prisoner awaiting execution, it had been judged necessary to raise 200,000 florins, half of this to be found by Antwerp, the towns of Holland, and the rich refugees in England. The Prince found 50,000 florins, Louis 10,000; John of Nassau pledged his lands; the Prince pledged his plate and jewels; help was expected from Germany; and envoys were sent to implore it from Elizabeth. An attempt to seize Alva by a *coup de main* failed. The plan of campaign was, that three independent expeditions should invade the Low Countries, from the south-west, from the east, and from the north. French Huguenots and Flemish refugees were to invade Flanders from Artois; a second corps was to invade Limburg from the Rhine and the Meuse; a third was to descend upon Friesland from the Ems. The Prince was to hold reserves on the Lower Rhine between the two Eastern armies, and watch events.

All of these expeditions were doomed to fail; the two former in immediate and bloody collapse. The first, an undisciplined rabble of some 2000 men, in Artois, were instantly driven out, cut to pieces, and the prisoners hanged. The second of nearly 3000 men, who invaded Limburg, were almost as suddenly routed and slaughtered by a picked body of Spaniards, whom the Duke had detached to meet them. The third, under

Louis of Nassau, had a momentary success, which it could not maintain or use. The fiery Louis had collected in Groningen, in North Holland, a force of some 3000 horse and foot, against whom Alva sent two veteran corps of 4000 men, with strict orders to act in concert, and not separately. One of these Louis, with great skill and courage, succeeded in entrapping in the dykes and morasses of the left bank of the Ems, cut them to pieces at Heiligerlee, killing their commander, Aremberg, but losing his own younger brother, Adolph. It was a gallant exploit, which proved that Spanish veterans were not invincible—at least in the dykes of Holland; but it led to no result, and was saddened by the first victim offered up by the family of Nassau. In the words of the *Wilhelmuslied*,—

> Sijn siel in eeuwich leven
> Verwacht den jongsten dach.
> (His soul in life eternal awaits the Last Day.)

Alva was roused to fury by this reverse. He issued a fierce sentence of banishment against Orange, Louis, Hoogstraeten, and others, with confiscation of all their property—the revenues of the Prince being valued at 152,000 florins. Batches of eminent men were executed day by day, first Villars, the commander of the second expedition in Limburg, and then Count Egmont and Count Horn. Within a month, the Duke had reached North Holland at the head of a splendid army of 15,000 men. He found Louis near Groningen with a far inferior force that did not exceed 10,000 all told, ill-equipped, disorganised, and mutinous mercenaries. The battle that ensued at Jemmingen was a horrible butchery, which exterminated the entire command of Louis. He was caught in a trap, out-manœuvred, deserted by his own men; and after doing all that wild valour could effect on the field, just saved his own life at last by swimming across the Ems.

The strategy and tactics of Alva were faultless; his Spanish veterans fought like heroes; all his combinations were exactly carried out; and, almost without loss, he wiped out the principal force of the invaders in one bloody ruin. The Duke, still unsated, resolved to teach the country a memorable lesson in terror. With fire and sword, rape, plunder, and outrage, his army poured over the country, covering it with blood, ashes, and corpses. He was rewarded with a message from the Pope that his Holiness was much gratified to learn all that the Duke had done in the Netherlands. He marched in triumph through Amsterdam to Utrecht, where he held a review of his army, now consisting, we are told, of 30,000 infantry and 7000 cavalry.

Thus ended in utter ruin the first collective effort of war that the Prince had organised. It is impossible to doubt that the scheme was singularly weak, that the Prince had overvalued his own forces, and no less fatally underrated those of the Duke. The three invading expeditions were separated, each from the other, by no less than 150 miles, so that they could not act in concert, or give or receive mutual help. The Duke, with disciplined forces outnumbering the invaders two or three times over, and in military qualities surpassing them as ten to one, was in the inner circle, with ample resources, equipment, stores, and material. It was the old story of a great master of war, at the head of a disciplined

soldiery, crushing isolated parties of unorganised and
motley levies.   Louis and many round him fought with
desperate courage, but large bodies of their so-called
troops were unwilling to fight at all.   Well might Alva
say, "He had tamed men of iron; should he not tame
men of butter?"   He had done so.   And this makes
his bloodthirsty vengeance the more wanton and savage.

These crushing disasters did not dismay the Prince
or his brother.   A few days after the defeat, Orange
writes thus to Louis:—

"We must have patience and not lose heart, submitting to the
will of God, and striving incessantly, as I have resolved to do, come
what may.   With God's help, I am determined to push onward,
and by next month I trust to be at our appointed rendezvous.
Watch Alva closely, and contrive to join me as arranged," etc.
And the chivalrous Louis writes to his agent in England:
"Our army is partly dispersed and partly defeated, but our heart
is as good as ever, and we hope soon, by the help of God, to have
a better force than before to save the Church and the cause."
William had sought before the battle to moderate the impetuosity
of Louis, urged him to withdraw before Alva, and to fortify himself
on the German frontier.   After the defeat, William has no word
but of affection, encouragement, and counsel.   The disaster had
struck terror throughout the Netherlands, and turned the German
princes into Job's counsellors.   One after another called on the
Prince to lay down his arms.   "Our friends and allies are all
turned cold," wrote he to Louis.   The Emperor formally summoned
him to withdraw in peace.   In a series of public and private
manifestoes, Orange now appealed to rulers and to the people.

On the execution of Egmont and Horn, the Prince (through his
own agent) had addressed to the Emperor a most powerful and
touching appeal.   The savage terrorism of Alva, he says, cries to
God for vengeance, and covers with dishonour the country and the
King.   Let the Emperor know the particulars of "this inhuman
tragedy," the crowning act of which has been the execution of
Egmont and Horn, and placing their heads on stakes in the public
place.   These acts of the Duke are a violation of the rights and
ordinances of the Empire, as well as of every law, human and divine.

It will be the ruin of the Netherlands, where the establishment of the Spaniards must be a standing menace to the Empire. Again, in a direct appeal to Maximilian, in August 1568, he rehearses the story of "the atrocities committed by Alva and his sanguinary creatures, the inhuman executions and persecutions of thousands and thousands of innocent persons since his ill-omened arrival in this country." And again, with great skill, he presses on the Emperor the risks to the Empire of the planting of a Spanish slavery in the Netherlands. Even now, in diplomatic documents, the Prince avoids a direct attack on Philip, who himself about this time had the curious impudence to assure the Elector of Saxony "that he would be delighted to see the Prince justify himself and recover his estates. He can count on impartial justice, *and it is not possible for him to suspect anything else from the Duke of Alva.*"

From the Emperor, William turned to Elizabeth, to whom he sent an envoy with an urgent appeal for help, "that the pure word of God might not be extirpated by the incredible cruelties of Alva." He was no rebel; he had taken up arms to defend the faith; he himself had always felt a sincere desire to be of service to the Queen. From rulers he turned to the people, and he issued an elaborate manifesto and appeal to all comers, which is a summary of his previous *Justification*, giving a history of recent events and throwing the whole responsibility " on the indescribable wrongs and villainies daily perpetrated by the Duke and his people, so that a man with any self-respect would rather die than see before his eyes such cruelties and tyranny as now are practised." The paper was doubtless the work of a professional writer, and bore for inscription the 94th Psalm : "They gather themselves together against the soul of the righteous, and condemn the innocent blood. But the Lord is my defence ; and my God is the rock of my refuge." It was followed by a formal address to all subjects of the King

in the Netherlands, in which he inveighs against the
introduction of the Inquisition and the attempt to
establish a Spanish tyranny in a country having an
ancient constitution of its own. His Majesty has been
so utterly misled by the false witness and evil counsels
of his Spanish advisers that the Prince and his friends
have raised an army to resist them "for the honour of
God, the propagation of His word, the protection of the
faithful, the service of the King, the preservation of the
country, the saving it from ruin, the maintaining its
liberties and privileges, and to spare it the cruel tyranny
of the Spaniards." And this document bore as legend
the device which Orange now adopted on his banner,—
Pro Lege, Rege, et Grege (*For Law, King, and People*).

Throughout this series of manifestoes, the Prince
labours to show that he is not undertaking a *rebellion ;*
that he does not dispute the King's lawful authority ;
that his aim is conservative, not revolutionary. To the
jealous dignity of the Emperor, of the German dukes,
of Elizabeth, in the eyes of the nobles, and even of the
burghers of the Netherlands, the armed resistance of
Orange was a sheer act of rebellion against a lawful
sovereign. He felt the difficulty and shared the senti-
ment, being himself a sovereign prince ; nor had he yet,
even in thought, conceived the idea of an independent
Republic. These documents were perhaps all of them,
more or less, the work of trained men of letters ; but in
substance they are the thoughts, and, to a great extent,
the actual drafts of William himself. Diplomatic as
they are, encumbered with rhetoric, with subleties and
with euphemisms, it cannot be denied that they all tell
the same tale, and make the same appeal, whether

addressed to Emperor, dukes, Queen, or people; whether they be secret despatches or public manifestoes; whether meant for Germans, for Hollanders, for Flemings, or for Englishmen, for Catholics, or for Protestants. Adroit as is the pleading, violent as is the indignation, and variable as is the religious tone of them, they all coincide in this, that his single aim is to get rid of the horrible persecution and the Spanish tyranny; to save the ancient constitution of the land, not to overturn it; to give freedom to the new religion, not to make it supreme.

Despairing of any help from Germany, or from England, and seeing into what a state of panic Alva had thrown the Flemish towns, the Prince turned to the Huguenots of France; and in August 1568, he was negotiating a formal alliance with Coligny and Condé. They were to bind themselves to mutual succour and support in the Low Countries and in France, in order to resist tyranny and maintain liberty of religion. Early in September the Prince had collected, it is said, 18,000 foot and 7000 cavalry, with fourteen cannon, round Treves—mostly German and Walloon mercenaries, ill-disciplined, and greedy of pay. These numbers are not trustworthy, and such an army would have but a fluctuating roll. Alva was ready for him, with an army about one-third less numerous, but greatly superior in quality. The tactics of the Duke were simply to wear down the Prince without coming to close quarters, till his mutinous and unpaid troops should disperse of themselves. And in this the great Spanish captain was entirely successful.

The Prince led his army with skill and foresight,

and surprised the Duke by crossing the Meuse on to
Flemish soil.   For a month the Prince sought to bring
on an engagement, changing his camp from day to day ;
but the Duke as continually foiled him, and avoided
battle.   On 20th October Alva succeeded in cutting off
William's rear-guard and destroyed a force of 3000 men.
The inevitable want of money, provisions, reinforcements, and material caused violent discontent, which
broke out into incessant mutinies.   Not a man stirred
in the terrorised towns ; the promised contributions did
not arrive.   The consummate strategy of Alva had
triumphed almost without a blow. · The large army of
Orange was melting away, or threatening his life in
their tumults.

Having penetrated into Brabant, where he reached a
point within a few leagues of Brussels, between the
battlefields of Ramillies and Waterloo, the Prince found
that he had effected nothing, nor obtained any sign of
help, and therefore he decided to disband the greater
part of his force, and with the wretched remnant to
throw himself into France.   He was now at the mercy
of his own soldiers, who were without food, supplies,
clothes, or pay, clamouring for arrears, and refusing
even to disband without them.   Of the 300,000 florins
promised from the Netherlands, he had not received
12,000.   To Charles IX. he wrote evasive and humble
letters that he had entered France "as a sincere well-
wisher and servant."   As the dark year 1568 had closed,
the condition of the Prince seemed utterly hopeless.
" Orange is a dead man," wrote the Protestant Languet ;
" his men desert him, and threaten to cut his throat and
sack his ancestral domain "; " he will be caught and

annihilated as was his brother at Jemmingen." However, he managed to make his way to Strassburg; sold his remaining plate, and mortgaged his last domain, to pay his mercenaries. "We may regard the Prince now as a dead man," wrote Alva to Philip; "he has neither influence nor credit." "They are broken, famished, cut to pieces" [*desechos, hambreados, degollada la mayor parte de su gente*].

It was but too true. In a few months his large army, once estimated even by his enemies at 30,000 men, had vanished; 8000 of them had perished miserably without any loss to the Spaniards. His last stiver was gone, his last estate mortgaged, his very person had been pledged to pay his angry mercenaries. But he did not abandon the cause of free religion. The three brothers, William, Louis, and Henry, a lad of eighteen, flung themselves into the Huguenot campaign in France, with a few followers, and served with Condé. Louis and Henry were in the bloody defeat of Jarnac, where Condé fell. William was away and had no part in the fight. They all then joined Coligny, and took part in the disastrous campaign in the heart of France that led to the rout of Montcontour. Here again Louis distinguished himself with heroic energy both in the battle and in the desperate retreat; but the Prince had left the army some days before on a secret mission. His German followers were again mutinous; he himself regarded the Huguenot rising as without aim or hope; he told Brantôme that he saw no hope in this expedition, but that he should appear again. Even now it is not clear how, why, or whither he went. He is said to have made his way in disguise across France into Germany. Some said he was

gone to La Rochelle; others said to England to see
Elizabeth; others declared he was to head a rising in
the Netherlands. None of these are at all likely. He
was no doubt bent on organising from Germany a new
force to resist Philip, and experience taught him how
little was to be expected from the Huguenots of France.
He was now apparently dogged by hired assassins, whom
he sought to escape. It is certain that his mysterious
disappearance in the crisis of a campaign seriously
impaired his reputation with friend and with foe. And
a chorus of exultation and derision rose from the Spanish
side at what they called the flight and degradation of
their arch enemy.

In his own days and in ours the opponents of the
Prince have spoken slightingly of his courage and his
military qualities, especially of his excessive prudence
in the field. As to his personal bravery, it seems
ridiculous to doubt it of a man whose whole life was one
of hairbreadth escapes from furious mobs and relentless
enemies, who chose a career of incessant war and combat
when he might have gone to live quietly with John in
Nassau, who boldly faced raging fanatics at Antwerp
and Amsterdam, and mutinous troopers in a dozen camps,
who lived cheerfully for years surrounded by murderous
conspirators and hired assassins. But it is certain that
he felt none of the joy of battle that throbbed in the
soul of his gallant brother Louis, or his chivalrous rival,
Egmont. He never had loved battle with his peers; he
was always for the tactics of Fabius, and not of Hotspur.
But his resources as a tactician must have been of a
high order, for he had commanded large armies against
Coligny and also against Alva, without ever having

in battle been defeated by either of these great masters of war.

In the higher field of comprehensive strategy he must be judged to be wanting. His grand campaign against Alva, even with superior numbers, was a melancholy failure, doomed to defeat from first to last, with an impracticable plan, that was constantly varied or abandoned. Even the accumulated disasters did not open his eyes to the uselessness of opposing such a general as Alva at the head of such disciplined veterans by a promiscuous levy of German and Walloon hirelings, serving for pay and plunder under a private flag. It is, no doubt, equally true that he could get no others. Had he the genius for war of Cromwell he might have seen, as did Oliver at Edgehill, that nothing could be done "with such fellows"; that he needed "men who had some conscience in their work." Orange had not Oliver's genius for war. As Granvelle wrote sneeringly to Philip, "The Prince has no head for such things; he writes too many manifestoes for a man of action." It is true that he was not a great soldier, but he was a great statesman. And his very want of genius for war throws still more glory on his greater genius as a statesman, as his excessive caution in the field heightens our sense of that indomitable resolution to persevere for the cause which he beheld defeated in a hundred combats.

Seldom has a chief of men withdrawn more utterly ruined, discredited, and abandoned than was William of Orange as he made his lonely way back to Nassau. He was now indeed the "Prince without land" of the legend. He had neither estate, nor resources, nor friends, nor home. He was actually driven out of his ancestral home to wander up and down, as even the vast castle of Dillenburg, with its miscellaneous population, was not considered to be safe as a residence. The German princes all turned from him ; the Lutheran preachers denounced the Calvinists as rebels who ought to be destroyed, and reproached him for having to do with such sacrilegious ruffians. From his retreat at Arnstadt he wrote to his brother John, " Whilst our adversaries are still at work, we seem to be asleep. Unless God work a miracle in our behalf, there will be an end of religion for many a long day. For no man will risk himself in its behalf, when they see how soft and without heart are they who might preserve it " [*la flosseté et peu de corage*]. Rumour had it that the Prince was dead. A Spanish councillor believed it, and wrote, "We need fear no more when the head is gone." But William was not dead, nor was he sleeping. He was still labouring incessantly, nor, whatever others did, did he lose hope and heart.

CHAPTER VI

IN the worst crisis of his fortunes, the forlorn Prince was afflicted with sore trouble at the hands of his unworthy wife. Anne of Saxony, the young bride of seventeen, whom, in 1561, he had brought home to Breda, "happy as a queen," had turned out a thorn in the side of a husband now embarked in a disastrous struggle. Anne, though not wanting in ability or energy, was proud, jealous, sensual, and intensely selfish. Regarding herself as a member of the sovereign caste, she showed violent ill-humour that she was not so treated in the Flemish Court. · After three years of marriage, the Prince told the Regent in confidence that his wife was leading a strangely morbid existence. A year later the extravagance of her conduct and the misery of their home was notorious; and William asked his brother to consult the Elector of Saxony as to what should be done for his niece. Year after year the Prince remonstrated with her and appealed to her relations in vain. She treated him with insolence, "as if he

were a lackey or a negro "—"for a Nassau was more fit
to be her domestic than her husband"—publicly complaining, scolding, and thwarting him, and at last ogling
her favourites in his presence.

The patience with which he bore her insults is treated
by the hostile writers as little to the husband's credit,
and even by his friends it was regarded as weakness.
When he was driven out of the Netherlands in 1567,
she loaded him with reproaches of cowardice.   At
Dillenburg she made herself intolerable to the Nassau
family, who so hospitably received her and her retinue,
shut herself up, and repaid their goodness with contempt.
Her condition, whilst her husband was away, a penniless
outcast fighting for a cause apparently hopeless, was
certainly one to try the nature of a wife of the birth and
nurture of Anne.   She railed, intrigued, and quarrelled ;
and at last, against the wish of her husband and his
family, she eloped to Cologne, where she took up her
abode with a somewhat ample retinue of twenty-two
persons.   Here she abandoned herself to intrigue, ill-
temper, and vice.

Her husband, her uncle, her relations, made constant
efforts to reclaim the wretched woman.   Augustus of
Saxony sent a confidential agent to see her, and then to
report to John of Nassau.   They advised her to submit
to her husband and return to Dillenburg.   This she
obstinately refused, and proceeded again to appeal to
the Elector, to the Landgrave of Hesse, to the Emperor
at Vienna, and even at last to Alva himself.   She told
them that the Prince being civilly dead as an outlaw,
she was a widow and entitled to a widow's estate.   In
1569 William wrote a fine appeal to his wife.

Why had she refused to return to him, as he had so often asked her to do ? Had she not promised before God and the Church to leave all things on earth and cleave to her husband ? He would no more ask her to come back, but he was bound to remind her of her duty and her vows.   When a man is sunk in troubles, there is no consolation so sweet as that which a wife can give,—to see her patiently bearing the cross which the Almighty has given her husband to bear, and all the more when he is suffering to advance the glory of God and purchase the liberty of his country.   There was very much he desired to say to her, which he dared not write, and his friends had warned him against coming to any place where he might be seized.   If she would meet him at Frankfort, he would come.   Would that in his misery he might have the pity of his wife, and not be left to strangers !   She had suggested to him to take refuge in France or in England.   Alas ! the poor Christians in France were like to be in as sore strait as those of the Nether-lands—or even worse.   And as to England, he would not write, but he could show her how hopeless was that thought.   They could no longer choose an asylum.   The question was who would receive them.   Neither sovereign nor free city would take them— neither the Queen of England, nor the King of Denmark, nor the King of Poland, nor the Princes of Germany, now that he is threat-ened with the ban of the Empire.   Of all this he would be glad to speak, if they could meet ; but, to save his life, he is obliged to be continually passing from place to place.   It would relieve him to see her, even for a day or two, in the affliction that he endures. His future is uncertain ; it is in the hands of the Almighty, who has laid this trial on him for his sins.   Would that His Holy Spirit might give both him and her guidance to act so as they shall be able to answer for their actions in the Last Day.

To this and many another such appeal from her husband Anne returned evasive and insolent replies, obstinately refusing to leave Cologne, and growing more and more outrageous in her tone.   At last, in 1570, William, in a pathetic letter to the Landgrave of Hesse, sends him the whole correspondence, declaring that it is more than he can endure, in all the trouble which is racking his brain, to find that instead of comforting him

in his disasters, his wife is pouring a thousand curses on
his head. Let it be seen whose fault it is; for he,
William, will swear on his soul that he desired only to
live with her according to God's ordinance. They seem
to have met once; but the only object of Anne was to
obtain money for her wasteful household.

She had now formed a guilty connection with John
Rubens, a refugee from Antwerp, and father of the
painter. He fully confessed his guilt, and when arrested,
asked only for death by the sword. Her letters exist
proving the amour, of which a child was born, a child
never recognised by the family. The miserable woman
had long been the victim of her passions — she had
taken to drink, to scandalous excesses of all kind. She
had no doubt seduced the unfortunate secretary, as her
family seemed to believe. The Nassaus by their local
law were entitled to put to death her adulterer, if not both.
They imprisoned Rubens for some years, and sent Anne
into seclusion, her children being removed and carefully
brought up by John at Dillenburg. She became more
violent and crazy, a burden and shame to all her relations, attempting the lives of those about her. She was
now obviously insane. The Prince regarded her as
dead; spoke of her as *celle de Saxe, jadis ma femme*,
and handed her over to her own blood relations. She
was taken charge of by her uncle, the head of her
paternal house, the Elector of Saxony. Augustus,
according to the barbarous habits of the age, shut her in
a dungeon, where food was passed through an aperture,
and a preacher attended daily to expound the word
through a grating, and improve her soul. After six
years of confinement, the wretched woman expired in

1577, a confirmed maniac. Such was the end of William's alliance with the great House of Saxony, which sixteen years before had so stirred the official world in Germany and Spain.

In his extremity William of Orange found a brotherly helper in the very worthy John of Nassau, now Chief of the House of Dillenburg. The ancestral castle was always a home to the outlawed Prince; here was received the wayward wife and all her household, and here the family were constantly gathered together. The venerable mother still lived, a beautiful and pathetic figure in this true-hearted and affectionate race. Juliana of Stolberg, the mother of five sons and seven daughters by William of Nassau the elder, was the type of the loving, thoughtful, stalwart, God-fearing matron of the Lutheran age. Her noble letters which remain breathe in every line a mother's tenderness, deep piety, and unshaken fortitude. She consults William—[*mein herzlieber Her und Son*]—about the education of her youngest son, and many other family arrangements—she too is often consulted by him. She writes to the Prince and to Louis letters of intense love and profound devotion. There is a strange pathos in her quaint old German in its uncouth spelling. She took a keen interest in every phase of the great struggle—but with her it was always and essentially a struggle for religion :—

" Put your trust in God alone; He only can save you and yours; they who put their confidence and hope in Him will never more be forsaken [*dan die iren vordrauen und hofnung uf Im setzen, die werden in cwigkeit nit verlossen*]. I pray God to strengthen the good people in Haarlem. My mother's heart is ever with you, dear love. [*Hertzallerliebster Her, mein meutterlich hertz ist allezeit bei, E. L.*]" When the Prince is attempting to negotiate with the French king, the mother implored him not to trust in any help that may be against God (it was after St. Bartholomew). "God can save when all earthly aid is gone. He will never abandon His own." After the fatal defeat of Mookheath, she writes with resignation in her anguish. "Verily I am a wretched woman [*bin worlich eyn betreubtes weib*]; and never can I be delivered out of my wretchedness until the dear God shall take me to Himself out of this valley of tears, which from my heart I pray Him may be soon."

With such resignation to the will of God she saw the death of three sons in battle for the cause. When Don John in 1577 was making overtures for peace to the Prince, the aged mother writes thus to her son (she was then seventy-four): "I sorely fear that the promised pacification may be a source of harm to souls and all, for Satan goeth about like a prowling wolf in a sheepskin, and will bring destruction on many a pious Christian. But our Lord Jesus Christ, to whom all power in heaven and in earth has been committed by His Heavenly Father, is able to deliver out of every strait those who call on Him and trust Him in their hearts. It is better to lose things here on earth than to lose that which is eternal [*Es ist besser das zeitlich dan das ewig zu verlieren*]. I pray my lord and dear love to look to the inner truth of things, and not to be deceived by fair words into being led into a place that may be fraught with peril, for the world is full of deceitfulness [*dan die welt ist listig.*]"

So she continued, counselling and praying for her great son to the last, and died at the age of seventy-seven, in 1580, just before the issue of the *Ban*, leaving an immense number of descendants, and a name of spotless devotion to her duty, her family, and her creed. There exists a fine portrait of her in old age—a thoughtful and stately dame. She was as tender as she was judicious, as indefatigable as she was wise. But her dominant character is an intense personal piety and Gospel religion, which in weal and in woe she ever pressed upon her children. She was the Puritan saint in the martyr family of Nassau.

The sons were worthy of such a mother. John, now the lord of Dillenburg, though three years younger than his brother the Prince, was a fine type of the Lutheran magnate. He resembled his mother in devotion to his family, in sterling good sense, in active self-sacrifice, and in genuine piety. His letters are more full than any others of the brethren of evangelical religion, of practical judgment, and considerate benevolence. He deeply burdened his family estate, and ruined himself in a cause which was not his own, nor that of his own fatherland. He flung himself with ardour into the Prince's undertakings, though he was constantly seeking to restrain the more dangerous adventures, and to counsel prudence. His letters are almost as biblical as those of his mother, and have more worldly wisdom than those of his brother Louis. Whilst William, Louis, Adolph, and Henry are fighting the Spaniard and rousing the people, John was making himself the father of the whole clan, and his castle was their refuge in need. He busies himself with the education of his younger brothers and sisters; and after the disgrace of Anne he carefully and tenderly brought up the children of the Prince. He was invaluable as an envoy and mediator, and laboured with energy and skill to gather the German magnates to the aid of his brother and the cause. He is continually addressing the chiefs around him by missive or in person, and was also employed in negotiating with France. In all this, especially after the death of Louis, John " was the Prince's right arm."

The two elder brothers passed their stormy lives in mutual affection and perfect trust. John regards William as his royal chief; William treats John as his ever-trusty

brother in counsel and in arms. But William is loth to
expose John to the risks which all the other brothers
met by night and day. "How can we venture to lose
the last stay of our house? Is it not indispensable to
have at any rate one left to maintain relations with the
princes of Germany, and the other sovereigns and cities?
No one can do this office better than you, from the
entire love you bear our just cause, and also from your
intimate knowledge of all our negotiations and affairs."
Over and over again the Prince will not suffer John to
run the risks which were the very breath of life to Louis.
He insists on his renouncing a perilous journey. "It
would be the greatest disaster which could befall our
House if any untoward accident befall you, which may
God avert!" "Do not hesitate to open letters addressed
to me. Your love for me and the absolute confidence
between us make me feel that I cannot have any secrets
from you."

Accident removed him from the fatal field of Mook-
heath, so that John did not share the doom of Louis and
Henry. He alone of the five brothers lived out his life,
and died in honour and peace at the age of seventy.
William Frederick, a grandson of John, married Agnes, a
grand-daughter of William, and from them has descended
the royal House of Holland, so often allied to our own
and other royal houses of Europe. John had neither
the genius nor the iron tenacity of William, nor had he
the chivalrous enthusiasm of his younger brothers. But
he was an affectionate, true-hearted, religious man, of
sterling good sense, homely wit, and honourable nature.
A fine portrait in later life records his outer man as that
of a stalwart, honest, solid German chief, somewhat

overwhelmed at times by the tremendous vortex of care
into which his life was plunged.

The next brother was Louis, nearly five years younger
than the Prince, the Bayard of the Nassau race. His
heroism in the field, his fascination of manner, his
chivalrous frankness, made him the idol of all with whom
he served. The Landgrave "adored him as a demi-god";
the Hollanders continually called for him. "*Bref tout le
pays vous attend comme un ange Gabriel,*" wrote William to
his loved brother, his sword, his mouthpiece, his pride.
Louis began campaigning at the age of twenty in the
great victory of St. Quentin, and thenceforth on a
hundred fields he showed romantic courage and unconquerable buoyancy of soul. Smaller and slighter than
William, he had a frank and handsome face, with a
singular resemblance to our own Sir Philip Sidney, who
died in the same cause a few years later almost in the
same field. His bright countenance was never so radiant
as in the thick of a desperate *mêlée*. He had much of
the charm and eloquence of his brother, but little of his
sagacity and nothing of his prudence. He was the life
of incessant combinations, many of which William could
not countenance, and most of which broke down from
causes which a less sanguine temper could foresee.

Louis, like the rest of the Nassaus, was born and
educated a Lutheran. But he came in manhood to full
sympathy with the Calvinists, and had more in common
with the Huguenots of France than with the German
Lutherans. With the French Reformers he was so
completely at home that he was looked on as the prob-
able successor of their great chief, the Admiral Coligny.
Louis was sincerely religious, and saturated with the

biblical ideas of his fellow-Reformers; but this did not prevent him from being the boon companion and idol of such wild spirits as Brederode, or the gay courtier in the palaces and châteaux of France. He carried on incessant negotiations with the German and French princes, and even with Elizabeth and Charles IX. Walsingham wrote home that he was eloquent and insinuating as he was open and loyal. Though he was the soul of a dozen confederacies, he never lost his character for straightforwardness and honour. His noble letter to Charles IX., a solemn warning, says Michelet, addressed by a dying man to a dying man, remains to this day as a monument of his bold and earnest heart. He fascinated all whom he addressed, as he inspired all whom he led to battle. His banners were inscribed — *Nunc aut nunquam : Recuperare aut mori.* Skilful as a captain, he was capable, like his kinsman Prince Rupert, of sublime imprudence as a commander. Indefatigable and ingenious in negotiations, he was continually foiled by events and outwitted by his inferiors. His heroic and brilliant career came to an early end in the fatal swamps of the Mookerheide, where he perished miserably at the age of thirty-six along with his young brother Henry. None knew how or where they fell, or where their bodies lay.

Adolph, the next brother, had died six years before this, in the victory of Heiligerlee, in his twenty-eighth year. He too from his early youth had taken arms in the Protestant cause, and had fought against the Turks. His bearing was gallant, his character noble and modest. At Heiligerlee, says Languet, victory was saddened by the loss of Count Adolph—"*praestantissimum juvenem.*"

" Fighting in the front of battle, he encouraged by his example his men, who were wavering, and did much to give his brothers this victory by his valour and his blood."

Henry, the Benjamin of the Nassau House, was by no less than seventeen years younger than the Prince, who had taken the most lively interest in the education of the lad. The mother felt the deepest anxiety for the youngest of her children, and letters are continually passing from her to William, Louis, and the others as to the best mode of training the last hope of the house. Like all the rest, he had a thoroughly scholar-like education; but at the age of nineteen he joined his brothers William and Louis in the disastrous campaign against Alva and Anjou, which ended at Jarnac and Montcontour. He continued to fight with honour at the side of Louis, and perished with him in an unknown swamp in the cruel rout of Mook. He was but twenty-three. Two months after the battle the aged mother writes a piteous letter that she can learn nothing of the fate of her " *hertzlieben sohn Heynrichen* "; " but God's will be done on earth, and let us pray that in His mercy and loving kindness we may all be gathered to Him in eternity."

CHAPTER VII

THOUGH the Prince had been completely foiled by the
Royalist troops of Spain and of France, though he had
withdrawn from the field into a secret retreat, it was
only that he might more ardently devote himself to his
true task, that of organising a new resistance to the
oppressor. "The spirits of all men are so crushed,"
wrote Languet, "that their only hope is in the clemency
of a most savage tyrant." Orange alone did not despair.
His activity was prodigious, and in less than two years
he threw Alva himself into great embarrassment.

He worked day and night, sending despatches and
emissaries in every quarter—to England, Cleves, Germany, to the Hanse towns, to the Dutch towns, having
secret interviews with his agents there, and issuing
commissions to trusty officers, civil and military, to act
in his name. He sold and pawned, borrowed and
begged, to raise funds. Alva said, "The Prince will
have much ado to escape from his creditors." He had
pledged his own person, William wrote; but if they

I

hold him to a known place of residence, all may be lost. Will not the Duke of Saxony take a certain casket in payment of 6000 florins? As to the debt of 10,000 florins, he can do no more. Cannot John find a sound horse to send him; and where are his trunk hose that went to be mended? His two expeditions of 1568 and 1572 are said to have made him indebted for 2,400,000 florins. He warns John to have his castle of Dillenburg securely guarded night and day, "in these terrible times of villainy"; he cannot come there with safety himself, as his unpaid *Rittmeisters* might seize him, or the Duke of Alva might have him poisoned.

But now, out of the depth of affliction, there arose the first sign of that unnoticed, unexpected force which was ultimately to transform the whole struggle and to decide the issue. It came as a little cloud out of the sea, like a man's hand. This was the first naval success of the "Beggars of the Sea." For some time past the Huguenots had issued letters of marque to privateer ships from the west coast of France. Coligny had seen the great possibilities which this opened to the Protestant cause; the result showed the importance during half a century to come attributed to the port of La Rochelle. Fresh from the bloody field of Jemmingen, Louis of Nassau wrote (July 1568) that "they were resolved to harass the enemy by sea"; and Coligny and Louis seem to have induced the Prince in the following year to issue commissions to various officers by sea. A brother of Brederode, an Egmont and others, served on shipboard; and a de Berghes, Lord of Dolhain, was named as Admiral of the Fleet.

These commissions purported to be issued by the Prince as a sovereign waging lawful war; and, in the double-dealing way characteristic of Elizabeth, they were from time to time recognised or repudiated in English ports. These irregular fleets, with ships procured in England, Holland, or Germany, were manned by mixed crews of refugees and desperadoes, French, Walloon, Dutch, or German, who soon carried on what was little less than miscellaneous piracy. Dolhain, in September 1569, had under his command some 18 ships with 3000 men, and in a few months he had captured 300 vessels, some of them with a treasure of 30,000 thalers. The excesses, atrocities, indiscipline of these wild corsairs were a sore trial to the conservative, prudent, systematic temper of the Prince.

From his retreat at Arnstadt William endeavoured to restrain these excesses and control his sea-rovers. He denounced their "drunkenness and disorder," recalled Dolhain, and appointed de Lumbres his admiral (August 1570). He now seriously reorganised the marine forces, drafted a scheme for their operations, and named as harbours of refuge Rotterdam, the Zuider Zee, or Brill. He orders that they shall attack none but such as serve the Spaniard, and carefully abstain from molesting neutrals, or even Philip's destined wife. A minister was to serve on each ship, who was to preach the Word morning and evening; no foreigner could command a ship; no bad character should be enrolled; and all violence, mutiny, and misconduct was to be strictly punished. It is difficult to see how the Prince could expect to enforce these rules from the fastnesses of Nassau: as a fact, they were a dead letter;

and the excesses of these "Sea Beggars" were the terror of the coast. One of the most desperate was William de Lumey, a count of La Marck, a descendant and imitator of the famous Wild Boar of Ardennes. He wore the Beggars' costume, and had sworn not to cut his beard till he had avenged Count Egmont's death. Crews of refugees and outlaws of various races, led by men like de Lumey, scoured the Netherland coasts and estuaries, pillaging, burning, and slaying all whom they chose to treat as Catholic enemies. Priests and monks they put to death with horrible tortures; magistrates and officials of the Government they held to high ransom. Their audacity, their exactions, their outrages, increased day by day. They attacked the navy from Spain, and seized the treasure. Alva himself, we are told, dared not risk the voyage back to Spain.

Under the organising genius of the Nassaus, these marine expeditions began to assume a far more serious form. They were now acting with the Huguenots of France. Louis, in La Rochelle, was raising a large force to land at Brill, to co-operate with a simultaneous invasion of Hainault by William. Elizabeth, still determined not to bring on a war with Spain, had so far yielded to their entreaties for aid, that she allowed the Sea Beggars to use her ports, and to recruit for Orange in her realm. "They are going too far, I admit to you in private," said Burleigh, "in favouring the corsairs; but you may avow it has no sanction from the Queen." Alva now took vigorous measures, and forced Elizabeth to disclaim these underhand doings, and to issue a proclamation against helping the rovers. Her act had a startling result, unlooked for by herself, by Alva, or by Orange.

A fleet of some twenty-five ships of the Sea Beggars under de Lumey and Treslong, being suddenly driven from the English coast and denied supplies, cruised off the shores of North Holland, in search of provisions and plunder. Contrary winds drove them into the mouth of the Meuse before Brill (1st April 1572). The terrified burghers, who were told that the fleet carried 5000 men, first parleyed and then fled. The Beggars stormed the gates, captured the town, cut the dykes round it, and, though but a few hundred strong, fortified themselves with cannon on the walls, proclaiming the Prince of Orange as lawful Stadtholder. They sacked the churches and monasteries, arrayed themselves in the priests' vestments, drank out of the golden chalices from the altars. They murdered and tortured the monks and priests, and then issued an address to the towns of Zeeland, that they were come not to harm the people, but to destroy priests, monks, papists, and idolatry. Refugees poured in from England and elsewhere; a force sent by Alva was beaten off, but took a cruel vengeance on Rotterdam, which had declared for Orange.

Neither William nor Louis at first approved of this wild raid by a handful of rovers. They were organising a combination on a large scale of Huguenots and Hollanders, with concerted action by sea and land. They were not yet ready; and they were not pleased by a lawless and premature *coup de main*, which they would hardly believe could be followed by any result. But the instinct of the people of Holland flamed up at this daring stroke. Mad as they were with rage and despair, this foothold in the sea-swamps of Voorn seemed to them a plank to seize in the shipwreck. An electric

shock of hope ran through Zeeland and Holland. They
shouted the rhyme, "On April-Fool's Day, Duke Alva's
specs [Bril] were snatched away!" Caricatures were
published showing this in the act, with the Duke
exclaiming, *no es nada* ("it is naught"). This explosion
of popular fury, opening a vast revolution in modern
history, by what was in itself an unpremeditated and
trivial incident, like the storming of the Bastille in
1789, really laid the foundation of the Free Netherlands. On 1st April 1572 the Dutch Republic began
to rise out of the sea.

Neither the Nassaus, nor Alva, wholly unfamiliar as
they all were with maritime war and "the sea-power,"
had for the moment seized the vast importance of this
casual stroke. But they all soon learned that it must
be promptly treated. Louis, then at Blois conferring
with the French princes and king, keen partisan chief
as he was, immediately sent off his secretary to try if
Flushing also could be seized. Treslong and his Beggar
seamen, Alva and his engineers, all understood the
crucial importance of Flushing, which the military
genius of Louis had perceived from the Loire. Flushing,
on the island of Walcheren, commanded the estuary of
the Scheldt; it was the key of all Zeeland, and the
gate of Antwerp, whence the importance of this point
of vantage from that day to ours. The Duke was
well informed of its importance, and had already com-
menced a citadel there on the model of that which
Paciotto, his Italian engineer, was constructing at
Antwerp. But Alva, who at first had treated the
Sea Beggars as *nada*, was too late, and made a fatal
blunder. The citizens rose in revolt, sent for aid to

Brill, from which Treslong dashed down to their help. Beggars and refugees flocked to the standard of Orange; they drove off the Spaniards, and became masters of the whole isle of Walcheren, excepting Middelburg. Paciotto was caught and hung, the Spanish prisoners were slaughtered, and the patriots, or rovers, raided far and wide, sacking convents and churches, and even threatening the mainland round Ghent. Within ten days the Beggars were masters of Delfshaven and Schiedam near Rotterdam, where a movement took place; and before long all the important towns of Holland, Friesland, Guelderland, and Utrecht, joined the Prince.

He now fully understood the vast possibilities that accident and audacity had flung into his arms, and he seized the occasion with passionate energy. Fourteen days after the seizure of Brill, he addressed from Dillenburg a stirring proclamation to all states, magistrates, burghers, and citizens of the Netherlands. He called on them as Stadtholder of His Majesty for Holland, Zeeland, Friesland, and Utrecht, to win freedom and redemption from the slavery they endured at the hands of the cruel, bloodthirsty, foreign oppressors [*slavernye der wreder, utlandigher, bloet - dorstigher verdruckers*]. He rehearsed the horrors of the Inquisition, the monstrous taxation, and the suppression of free conscience and the Word of God. He vowed to help them with might and main, not renouncing their allegiance to the King, but asserting the ancient rights and privileges of these Provinces.

He sent off separate appeals to the burghers and magistrates of Middelburg, Gouda, Enkhuisen, and other

towns to act with spirit. These were stirring incentives
to patriotic effort, to throw off the Spanish yoke, to
save their wives and children from the tyrant by the
help of Almighty God, and not to forget that it is
impossible for him to bring troops to their aid, unless
he is enabled to pay and supply them. He was still in
Germany, concerting with his brothers and the French
Huguenots a combined attack on Alva from the Rhine
and the Meuse. He could not foresee how utterly all
these armies on land were destined to fail. Nor could
he quite foresee all that was destined to be achieved by
the scanty fleets on the sea-board. The islands of
Voorn and Walcheren together commanded the estuaries
of the Rhine, the Waal, the Meuse, and the Scheldt.
"Flushing will become another La Rochelle in the
hands of the rebels," wrote one of his ablest captains
to Alva. In truth, Zeeland became the *pou stô* whence
the Holland mariners were to find sea-captains whom
Alva could not match, and squadrons which his veterans
could not reach, where refugees and comrades could
join them from England and from the coast of France,
whence invincible fleets were to issue to drain the very
life-blood of Spain, and ultimately to snatch from them
their Indian Empire.

When the Prince, after the disasters of 1569, withdrew from France to Germany, Louis of Nassau remained
as the right arm of Coligny, his chivalry, energy, and
personal fascination making him a leading spirit in the
Huguenot cause. Now occurred one of those perpetual
changes of front characteristic of this age of Machiavellian intrigue, balance, and counterpoise. Seeing the
Huguenots prostrate before the Catholics, it occurred to

the wily Catherine and the imbecile Charles IX. that the time had come to rehabilitate the losing side. The indomitable Coligny and the ardent Louis of Nassau seized the opportunity, and for some two years they seemed to control the councils of France. By the peace of St. Germain (August 1570) the Protestants were recognised as capable of all public offices ; four important places were put into their charge ; the two Nassaus were declared the King's "good kinsmen and friends," and the principality of Orange was restored to the Prince, who, said rumour, was now to transfer his allegiance to France. By a secret article Charles agreed to give two millions for arrears of pay to the German auxiliaries. Louis took charge of the rovers from La Rochelle, and held constant interviews with the French king and his advisers.

Coligny and Louis now urged on France the bold and tempting policy of humbling Spain, and driving her from the Netherlands. It was a real danger for Philip ; but here again, in this age of counterpoise, it awoke the jealousy of Elizabeth and the German chiefs. Louis won over Walsingham, if not Burleigh, but the imperturbable wariness of the Queen gave him a final rebuff. Louis found the feckless Charles more amenable, and the French king actually entered into personal engagements to help the Nassaus. The falsehoods, so freely poured forth by Catherine, her sons and her creatures, did not deceive the sagacious envoys of Spain, who knew that, so far as words could go, the crown of France was pledged to the cause of Orange. They had gone so far as to open a map and thereon to reapportion the whole of the Netherlands between the French, the

English, and the Nassaus. There is no evidence that William, any more than Elizabeth, ever seriously committed himself to this policy; the reckless Louis as usual used his brother's name in a dozen different intrigues. But Philip's agents at last reported that a combined set of attacks were to be made on Alva from different quarters: one by Orange, another by Louis, and a third by Coligny, the King of France secretly giving his support. It was a real policy, even a great policy, if honestly treated—the policy indeed of Henri IV. and of Richelieu—but it was premature, and impossible of execution, because in that age every politician distrusted every other politician, with abundant cause; and no politician, except William and Philip, could be trusted to maintain any definite policy for two months together. Confidential letters and envoys now passed constantly between the Prince and the French king; but we know nothing of the details agreed.

The position of Alva had now become almost critical. He had instituted a novel system of taxation, which aroused the fiercest hostility in the Netherlanders, who had the ancient right of taxing themselves. One per cent on all property, fixed or moveable, 5 per cent on every transfer of fixed property, and *10 per cent* on every sale of goods, were new and crushing impositions. The last tax, known as *the Tenth Penny*, drove the good burghers to fury. It was the very delirium of tyranny which could dream of exacting from the richest traders in Europe 10 per cent on every transaction. The opposition was so general and fierce that even Alva was forced to compromise, and at last agreed to accept two millions of florins annually for the two years ending

August 1571.   At that date he again began to insist on
his Tenth Penny.   But now even Philip's creatures
cried out against it.   His ambassador from Paris wrote
that the Duke was ruining the country by *desta negra
decima;* the land was being depopulated; there was
but one cry, *vaya, vaya, vaya,* the Duke must go.   The
cardinal's confidants told him that Brill was lost "owing
to that Tenth Penny."   To smooth his way, Alva published a *pardon,* which was simply laughed at; but he
stuck to his tax; and, as trade had ceased—"the bakers
refused to bake, the brewers to brew, the tapsters to
draw"—the Spanish financier ordered eighteen traders
to be hung at their own shop doors, to encourage the
rest to do business and save his Budget.

But the tyrant felt that he was failing.   He was
racked with gout; he implores Philip to send him a
successor; he would be cut in pieces rather than resign,
if he thought he could still serve the King; but the
obstinate impatience of taxation shown by the Flemings
was such that he is not duly supported—"owing to the
hatred the people bear him, in consequence of the
chastisement he found it necessary to inflict, with all the
moderation in the world [*por el castigo que en ellos ha
sido necesario hacer, aunque con toda la moderacion del
mundo*]."   This letter of 26th April 1572 is a psycho-
logical document.   The Duke honestly relates the loss of
Flushing and the difficulties of the Spaniards, the want
of money, the universal hatred, the paralysis of the
Spanish veterans whom he dared not to move, the need
of a successor less odious than himself,—the Duke still
proudly conscious that he has served his God and his
King with devotion and with clemency.   Philip doggedly

stuck to his Viceroy and his Tenth Penny; refused to let Alva go; but he secretly consented to some moderation, and he sent Medina-Cœli to assist, to watch, and ultimately to supersede the Duke.

And now Louis of Nassau struck his stroke, not less daring than that of Brill, but destined to have no such result. Dashing suddenly out of France into Hainault, with a small army, raised by Charles's money, he seized Valenciennes, took Mons by stratagem, and fortified himself there (23rd May). At the same time the Sea Beggars at Flushing seized a valuable Spanish fleet with an immense treasure on board, and nearly captured Medina-Cœli himself. It was believed that the towns of Brabant and even Brussels were threatened. But neither William nor Coligny were yet ready to support the impetuous Louis, who was not very well received at Mons and was unable to advance. Alva hurried down a strong force to blockade Mons under his natural son, the gallant captain Don Frederic; and, as a still speedier device, he sent in two hired spies to poison the Count in his house. Violent struggles were going on in the councils of France; and, in spite of the power of Coligny, who was now called "the King of Paris," the Court hesitated to make open war on Philip's Viceroy.

But William was now ready. For two years he had been working incessantly to raise an invading army and to organise an internal rising in Holland. The latter prospered far more speedily than the former, which needed funds. He had now something like a complete provisional system of leaders and agents awaiting his signal to rise. Troops could not be had without money. But of late large sums had been rolling in from English

Protestants, from France, and elsewhere. Since the peace of St. Germain, subsidies had secretly arrived from France, and recently a sum of 200,000 crowns had been sent by Charles himself. The sea-rovers had captured treasure ships, and the refugee congregations in England and France had sent contributions in response to the Prince's appeal. The seizure of Brill and Flushing had given the fund a new life ; and large resources were now coming in to the Prince, just as the Duke's Tenth Penny and his gigantic fortresses had drained his exchequer dry. George Certain (William) and Lambert Certain (Louis) were doing a roaring trade, and their cypher correspondence of merchant ventures began to show a promising balance.

At the end of June 1572 the Prince left Dillenburg at the head of 1000 horsemen. The next month he crossed the Rhine north of Dusseldorf with a considerable force. At his summons as Stadtholder, the representatives of eight Dutch towns assembled at Dort, where Philip de Marnix, Ste. Aldegonde, addressed them in a fervid speech in the name of the Prince. The congress responded to this appeal by proclaiming the Prince as their lawful Stadtholder under the King, and they voted supplies for three months. De la Marck was appointed Admiral, and a regular government instituted. By the middle of July, William had an army of 20,000 horse and foot: with them he crossed the Meuse and took Roermond, which his people savagely sacked, murdering the priests. Coligny was promising him to lead in person powerful supports ; and the vanguard of these, 5000 strong, had already advanced towards Mons when they were cut to pieces by the Spaniards. In the meantime nearly all Holland had declared for the Prince. Alva told the King that only two towns there, they having a Spanish garrison, could be trusted. On the 21st of August the Duke writes to Philip a long despatch on the difficulties of his position; his army cannot yet be mustered to take Mons, on which so much hangs: both in Flanders, Brabant, and Holland, the revolt is raging and successful.

The hopes of William rose high. On 11th August he wrote to John—"We may see how miraculously God defends our people, and makes us hope that, in spite of the malice of our enemies, He will bring our cause to a good and happy end, to the advancement of His glory and the deliverance of so many Christians from unjust oppression." He continues to enlarge on his desperate want of more funds; but on the other hand he has just heard from Coligny that he is about to join him with 12,000 arquebusiers and 3000 horse, and the Admiral implores the Prince not to engage the enemy until their forces were united. This letter is still dated from the camp round Roermond, 100 miles from Mons, where Louis is closely beleaguered; and, in spite of the advice of Coligny, of the want of money, of the need of combination, it is difficult to see why the Prince should not have dashed forward to Mons and Louis, instead of occupying himself with despatching ten pages of narrative and brotherly confidences to John at Dillenburg. Both in his own age and in ours his deliberate strategy has been bitterly condemned.

Coligny never came. His mangled corpse was being dragged about the streets of Paris in the massacre of St. Bartholomew, 24th August 1572. That terrific

thunderbolt out of the blue dashed to the ground the
rising fortunes of the Prince and of his fatherland.
The intrigue which cut down the heads of the Huguenots
belongs to the history of France and of Europe; to the
Netherlands it came as a crushing blow which for years
set back their chance of deliverance. For all the
ascendency of Coligny at court and the gallantry of his
followers, France definitely rejected the Calvinist
Reform; the Catholic chiefs were as resolute, as ambitious, as willing to fight it out, as the Huguenot chiefs;
they had a great popular majority to support them, and
were bent on even more desperate ventures. The
struggle had long been a rivalry between the Papal and
the Calvinist aristocrats to get control over the royalty
of France—the Court meanwhile, with a perfidy and
treachery that have never been surpassed, intriguing
with each in turn to keep itself free from the grasp of
either. The ascendency over Charles of Coligny, a man
with an iron will and a great policy, in result only
forced Catherine and Anjou into the arms of the
Catholics, to share the blood feud of the Guises. Where
murderous hatreds and furious ambitions had kept a
warlike nobility for years at fever-heat, a sudden outburst of passion was enough to fire the entire arsenal of
fanaticism and hate. Intrigue followed intrigue; fresh
reprisals followed each murder; then came the Red
Wedding of Henry of Navarre, the mutilation of
Coligny; Huguenot plots—Catholic plots—midnight
murders—a popular frenzy—and torrents of blood
through the streets of Paris and the cities of France.
The Huguenots lost for ever their last real chance of
being masters of France.

The Prince felt all the consequences of this *exécrable meurtre*. In a cypher letter to John he writes : "Quel coup de massue, cela nous ait esté, n'est besoin de vous discourir." "Our one hope of human aid was in France. By all earthly calculations we should have been to-day masters of Alva, and had him at our mercy. It cannot be told how this has ruined and thrown me. back, for I trusted to the 12,000 arquebusiers that the Admiral promised me." He pressed on, urging John to procure him some fresh arquebus men from France. A month after taking Roermond, at the junction of the Meuse and the Roer in Limburg, the Prince advanced towards Antwerp and Brussels, taking many towns on his way, his German troops scouring the country with horrible excesses, pillaging and destroying freely, and advancing within a league of Brussels, which, with Louvain, shut its gates upon his force. Here he received positive news of the massacre of August; and as the French king's messenger reports : "Il s'est merveilleusement trouvé estonné et en extreme fascherie, en sorte que sur ce il commença à entrer en grande crainte et défiance de Vostre part et de n'avoir plus le bon succès en ses affaires qu'il attendait."

Heartbroken he struggled on. He got possession of Malines, half-way between Antwerp and Brussels, of Ter-monde, between Brussels and Ghent, and of Oudenarde, between Ghent and Lille. Both Ghent and Bruges expected an attack. Early in September he was close to Mons, where he had been for three months eagerly expected by Louis and his men, with prayers, entreaties, and even reproaches. He now seemed to be on the top of a wave of success. A girdle of towns round Brussels,

from the Scheldt to the Meuse, was in his hands.   His
army was now larger than any the Spaniards could bring
into the field.   Had he been a great master of war at
the head of disciplined patriots, even now he would have
joined Louis, crushed Alva, and roused all the Netherlands in arms.   But he was not a great master of war,
and he led, not patriots, but a motley host of foreign
mercenaries, greedy, lawless, and ferocious.   They
claimed the right to recoup their arrears by plunder;
they murdered, burnt, and pillaged; and the country
people, scared by their excesses, and panic-struck by
Alva, gave no real support.   William advanced with
caution and by slow stages, hardly master of his own
disorderly army.   The Duke knew that his rival's force
was formidable, "with some 6000 good cavalry."   One
of the acutest observers wrote: "If the Prince acted
with spirit he would crush Alva; if Alva acted with
spirit, he would crush the Prince."   This was true.
Both were masters of Fabian tactics; but the Fabian
tactics which served the Duke were the ruin of the
Prince.   William led a loosely organised crowd of free
lances.   Alva commanded unconquered veterans, led by
consummate soldiers.

The Duke was now at the head of his army at Mons,
having deliberately drained Brussels itself of his Spanish
garrison.   His position, he well knew, was critical; but
he still speaks with proud confidence in his despatches
to Philip.   And well might the commander of such
soldiers feel confident.   On the night of the 11th September Julian de Romero led a night surprise, or *camisada*,
into the camp of the Prince.   Six hundred arquebusiers,
with their white *shirts* over their armour, mounted

K

behind as many troopers, dashed into the enemies' lines,
cut down the sentinels, butchered the men asleep, and
for two hours spread confusion in the camp, which they
fired, and returned with a loss of only sixteen men.
Romero himself made straight for the Prince's head-
quarters, and nearly cut him off. William was asleep;
but, as his habit was, in his clothes, with arms by his
side and his horse saddled. His favourite lap-dog, who
lay on his couch, roused his master and saved his life;
and thus he lies beneath him to this day in bronze on
the Prince's monument and statues in Delft and at the
Hague.

After this serious blow, which disorganised his army
even more than it reduced it, William beat a hasty
retreat.   He was without provisions, his troopers
mutinied and refused to act, he was surrounded, and
with the wreck of his force sought to make his way
back into Holland.   In the retreat he was nearly killed
by his mutinous mercenaries, who talked of surrendering
him to Alva; whilst an assassin, hired by Alva, penetrated to his quarters and dogged his steps.   The incident
of the midnight surprise is not one that deserves to be
commemorated in bronze.   Maledictions and insults
followed the beaten general in his retreat: " *Perde il
credito*," wrote the Venetian envoy; " *Fort desrompu
et triste*," wrote the envoy of Charles.   Again a great
combination, organised after years of negotiation, had
suddenly collapsed, and a powerful army, collected with
incredible labour, had penetrated to the walls of Brussels,
only to disband itself in ignominious rout.

To the ardent soul of Louis of Nassau, shut up in
Mons, the massacre of the Huguenot chiefs struck a

death-chill. "His sorrow was so bitter that he was ill for three months." Within a few days after the retreat of William, Louis was forced to capitulate. He obtained from Alva unexpectedly favourable terms, which, even yet more unexpectedly, Alva punctiliously observed. The French king, whose envoy was ordered "to keep on amicable terms with Orange and with Alva, encouraging both," pressed the Duke to refuse quarter and massacre his prisoners. Alva, who is said to have denounced the St. Bartholomew crime, and who wished for the moment to exhibit his clemency as a contrast, suffered Louis with his German troops to evacuate the fortress with their arms, and gave them an ample escort to join the Prince, treating them with the high-bred courtesy of a Spanish hidalgo. Such was the fantastic point of military honour as understood by the Viceroy of Philip. The man who habitually employed assassins would not be himself an assassin. He stuck at nothing to murder the Prince, but "he would cut off his right hand" rather than butcher Coligny fresh from a friendly embrace. The monster who sent innocent thousands month by month to the rack, the scaffold, and the stake was himself the mirror of chivalry in presence of the noble foeman whom he had beaten in fight.

Louis, prostrate with fever, and fainting by the way, was honourably escorted in a litter to Roermond, where rumour had it he was dead. Thence by slow stages and in many dangers he made his journey home to Dillenburg, and his mother nursed him back into life. His Huguenot followers returned to France, and the French king took care to have them quietly butchered at the frontier. Charles was now quite eager to show Philip and Alva that he was a good Catholic, and had no desire for a war with Spain. He knew that Alva's officers had captured his letters to Louis, wherein the King of France freely promised the Nassaus money and men. To the mind of a Valois it was but natural that, being found out, he should now turn against the men with whom he had intrigued.

The Prince of Orange was utterly crushed, but even now would not give way to despair. His men would neither fight nor obey. They were encumbered with waggon loads of booty; and the panic-stricken towns fell off, one after the other. Again he implores John to make fresh efforts with the German princes in this crisis, "seeing that the massacre of Protestants touches them more closely than they think." Next, as the French Crown had swerved round to the enemy again, he turns to Elizabeth, sends her an envoy to press on her the vast change in affairs that the massacre disclosed. "I am resolved," he writes to John in September, "to go and plant myself in Holland or in Zeeland, and there await the issue which it shall please Him to ordain." And again in October he writes: "I am bent on going to Holland and Zeeland to maintain the cause there, so far as this may be possible—*ayant délibéré de faire illecq ma sépulture.*" His instinct was right. The Southern Provinces, that we now call Belgium, were not to be saved for a Commonwealth and for Calvinism; the Northern, that we call Holland, were destined in the course of time to grow into the rich, artistic, victorious, and aspiring Dutch Republic. Holland and Zeeland, with their sea-board and intricate waterways, in perpetual contact with England and the high seas, were the nucleus out of which the Dutch Republic was finally destined to emerge. And so to this day the ancient Church of St. Ursula in the Groote Markt of Delft enshrines in serene silence the sepulchre of William of Orange.

CHAPTER VIII

1572-1574

FROM henceforth William of Orange was settled in Holland, and he clung to it whilst life remained. After the *débandade* of his mutinous army, amidst constant perils from traitors and assassins, he passed the Rhine, and pressing northwards with a few followers, he tried to strengthen the defences of Zutphen, Kampen, and other places. "Alone and abandoned on every side," he writes to John, he crossed the Zuider Zee; and, having reorganised the Government at Haarlem and at Leyden, he fixed his residence at Delft, which became his permanent home.

Now begins that series of terrific struggles in the Dutch towns and their heroic defence, whereby, in spite of defeat, massacre, and horrible sufferings, they wore down the armies of Spain; and ultimately, by endurance of agony rather than by military success, achieved the independence of the Northern Provinces.

On entering Mons, after the retreat of Count Louis and his soldiers, Alva exacted a bloody vengeance on the citizens, which was prolonged till the time of his successor. He then proceeded to sack Mechlin, which ill-fated town was delivered over to butchery, torture, rape, and indiscriminate plunder, till every article of value, sacred or profane, had been rifled by the infuriated soldiery, thirsting to recoup themselves their arrears of pay. Philip was informed by one of his agents that they had not left *un clou aux murailles*, and had tortured wives, maidens, and boys to force them to reveal concealed money. Alva assured Philip that this chastisement was the manifest purpose of God, but they had not had chastisement enough. He passed on with his valiant son, Don Frederic, to the Northern Provinces. Dripping with blood, and laden with spoil, his soldiers stormed Zutphen, where the same scenes of horror were repeated. The Duke reports to Philip that he had ordered his son "not to leave a man alive, and to set fire to the city in various places." This, he adds, had been done, and promises a most blessed result.

When butchery and rape were exhausted, Don Frederic passed on to Naarden, a little town on the Zuider Zee, near Amsterdam. The massacres at Naarden were even more horrible and more systematic than at Zutphen. The population was exterminated and the city burnt to the ground, which even the Jesuit historian calls "not a punishment, but a crime." Alva duly reported this work to the King, who congratulated the Duke on exacting so well-deserved a vengeance, and Don Frederic as being so truly the son of his father.[1] Alva, it must be remembered, was always straight-

---

[1] This monumental phrase of Alva's in a report to the King (19th December 1572) deserves to be recorded in the original—*Degollaron burgeses y soldados, sin escaparse hombre nascido* ("They slaughtered citizens and soldiers, without leaving a man alive").

forward, frank, and perfectly conscientious in his own
sense of duty to his King and his God. He conceals
nothing, palliates nothing ; he neither denies his
failures nor exaggerates his success; his record of
massacre and tyranny is all signed with his own hand.

The bloody progress of Alva from Hainault to the
Zuider Zee had crushed out all sign of opposition, and
he proudly reports to the King the places which he had
subdued and occupied.   He then fixed himself in
Amsterdam, resolved to stamp out resistance in the only
corner where it remained—the narrow sea-board of
Holland and Zeeland, which lay behind its vast dykes,
half-sunk beneath its salt marshes, from Walcheren to
the Helder.   In this historic strip of swamp, little more
than 100 miles long, and hardly more than 20 in breadth,
were enacted those prodigies of valour, endurance, invention, and martial energy, which ultimately drained
Spain and set up the Dutch Republic.   The heroism
and the ferocity were equal on both sides ; and if the
Spaniards were supreme in every art of war, the Dutch
were supreme in indomitable endurance.   Nearly in the
centre of this narrow strip of dykeland lay Delft, where
the Prince had planted himself for life and death, and
whence northwards and southwards he directed the
desperate defence.

Unused as were the Spaniards to the sea, to ships, to
fens, and to ice, they betook themselves to them all
with marvellous audacity and resource.   The exploit of
Mondragon, who relieved Tergoes by leading 3000
veterans, at low tide in the dead of night, in a march of
ten miles through a swamp where the water reached
their shoulders, was, as Alva reported to Philip, one of

the most astonishing feats in the records of war. Again, when a fleet was frozen up in the Zuider Zee, Don Frederic attacked it on the ice ; and, when the Hollander arquebusiers advanced to the charge on skates, Alva ordered 7000 pairs of skates and taught his men to use them in battle.

Between Amsterdam and the ocean lay the rich and noble city of Haarlem, almost surrounded by shallow lakes, and connected with its neighbours by causeways, which were pierced by an intricate system of sluice-gates. Don Frederic opened the siege with a magnificent army, said to amount to 30,000 men, with whom he at once attempted to storm the city. How he was driven back by a furious rally of the whole population, how assault after assault was defeated, how his mines were met by counter-mines, and the breaches in the wall made by Spanish cannon were countered by new walls raised inside, how every device of the engineer's art was baffled by the ingenuity of the defence, how the valour of the Spanish veterans was kept at bay by the heroism of men, women, and children in the town, how a regular corps of 300 fighting women shared in the hand-to-hand grapple of sortie and assault, how the relieving parties sent by the Prince to succour the city both by sea and land were cut to pieces by the solid investing army, how after seven months of terrific sufferings the city was starved into surrender, how Alva celebrated its capture by a new general massacre,—all this fills some of the most thrilling pages of history, but it cannot be rehearsed at large in this brief record of the Prince's life.

During the seven months of this tremendous siege (10th December 1572 to 12th July 1573) William was

working day and night to save the doomed town. He
sent in small parties and urgent appeals whilst the lines
were still open, and then messages by carrier pigeons
when they were closed. He wrote imploring letters to
his brothers in Germany to come to the rescue with a
force, and he organised such relieving parties from the
north and from the south, by land and by water, as he
was able to collect. He besought aid from England, from
France, from Germany, but all in vain. Three thousand
men whom he sent under de la Marck were cut to
pieces. Another 2000 under Batenburg were destroyed.
Sonoy's party from the North and a flotilla collected on
the Haarlem lake were annihilated; and by the end of
May the last fleet the Dutch could muster was swept
from the sea.

Then a despairing cry arose from the Hollanders to
make a last effort. Soldiers there were none; but 4000
volunteers were enrolled, and the Prince consented to
lead them on this utterly forlorn hope. He protested
publicly and in his private letters that it was a mad
venture to lead a few thousand untrained burghers
against a great Spanish army securely intrenched. The
citizens and troops insisted that his life should not be
sacrificed in what they all felt to be a hopeless effort.
Batenburg, who took the command of this devoted
band, fell into a Spanish ambuscade and was routed and
killed. " It is the will of God," wrote the Prince to
Louis, "and we must submit; but I call my God to
witness that I have done all that in me lay to save the
city, utterly desperate as I knew the attempt to be."
His own officers despaired, and said that unless he had
some secret alliance with a potentate, resistance was

hopeless. "When I took in hand the defence of these oppressed Christians," he said, "I made an alliance with the mightiest of all Potentates—the God of Hosts, who is able to save us, if He choose."

Don Frederic had lost 12,000 men during the long siege, the garrison had been reduced from 4000 to 1800, and he had butchered in cold blood more than 2000 prisoners, but he could still lead 16,000 men, gorged with blood and booty, to finish his work by destroying Alkmaar. By the end of August he had invested this little city, which stands on the northern spit of Holland, some twenty miles north of Haarlem and of Amsterdam, between the ocean and the Zuider Zee. It was defended by some 2000 men, more than half of whom were un- trained burghers. Alva duly reported to his King his intention on taking Alkmaar to leave not a single creature alive (*passar todos a cuchillo*), because his clemency at Haarlem had led to no good result. Again he warns Philip not to give way to tenderness, and to rest assured that every living soul in Alkmaar shall be slaughtered (*en Alckmaer anima nascida que no se pase por el cuchillo*). Don Frederic attempted to carry the town by storm as he had tried at Haarlem; but, after four hours' assault by his choicest troops, he was driven back, leaving a thousand of his men in the trenches. The burghers, whom a Spanish officer declared looked like fishermen, not soldiers, then sent forth instructions to cut the dykes and flood the city. Secret orders were sent by the Prince, inclosed in a rod, to open the sluices and admit the sea. The Spanish army found itself begirt by a rising tide. Before this new enemy even the valour of Don Frederic quailed. He hesitated to sacrifice a fine

army in combat with the ocean; and after a hot siege
of seven weeks, Don Frederic led off his drenched and
diminished forces to join his father in Amsterdam.

This memorable repulse, the first retreat of a great
Spanish army, with the revelation of the new power
that Holland could call to its aid, the exhausting siege
of Haarlem, and the still more exhausting and disastrous
repulse from Leyden, soon to follow,—these mark the
turning-point of the mighty struggle, and begin the long
epic of the expulsion of Spain from the Northern
Provinces. The whole story is told us by Alva himself
in his reports. He was as obstinate as he was merciless;
no less devoted than capable; the frank historian of the
heroism of his enemies and of his own ferocity. When
Don Frederic told him that the men of Haarlem did all
that the best soldiers in the world could do, and asked
for leave to abandon the siege, the Duke told him
fiercely that he should hold him no son of his if he retired
before he was dead or victorious. When Orange began
to cut the dykes round Haarlem, the Duke admits that
he had never in his life been in so great peril, and that
if the causeways were flooded he should be driven himself to surrender. "Never was seen on this earth," he
writes, "such a war as this. Never was a fortress so
well defended by men. They have an excellent engineer,
who has devices that were never yet heard or seen
(*cosas nunca oidas ni vistas*). The defenders are stronger
than the assailants."

Without pay, without food, without supplies, the
Spanish troops plundered far and wide. License led to
mutiny, and desperate plots of treason and revolt. A
royal secretary informed Philip that his soldiers, ever

since their arrival in 1567, had committed murder, rape, robbery, and extortion, so that the land was being left deserted and trade had disappeared. The Catholic prelates joined in an appeal to the King to curb "the furious excesses" of the soldiery. "Never before," wrote Alva, "in all the forty years of his service had he suffered such grief as by these mutinies. He will go to the troops and deliver himself up as a hostage ; and he warns Philip that things are as bad as they can be." A second mutiny breaks out at Haarlem. His admiral, Bossu, is defeated and taken prisoner. The Spanish veterans are insubordinate ! Without more money all is lost. The sailors as well as the soldiers clamour fiercely for their pay. Never in his life-long service has the Duke felt such distress and suffered such pain.

Ever and ever more piteously the Duke implores the King to hasten his successor. He was now, in truth, a man broken in health, in credit, and in self-confidence. "I am a dead man," he wrote, "but, dead as I am, I can feel the ingratitude of the King for all my services." The whole Royalist world threw on him all their dis- asters. "This people," the secretary wrote home, "hate the Spaniards worse than the devil, and foam at the mouth at the very name of Alva." The Jesuit Strada long afterwards sums up the story thus : "*Albani perse- veram invisamque Belgis administrationem fuisse belli occasionem principiumque non abnuerim.*" Up to the very last, the pitiless fanatic maintained his reign of terror. A few days before his resignation he superintended the most revolting burning of a noble prisoner over a slow fire, and he murdered the French Huguenot chief, Genlis, secretly in his dungeon, giving out that he had died of disease. His parting advice to the King and to his successor was " to burn down every place in the country not actually occupied by the royal troops, even if it were to need eight or ten years for the land to recover. It was idle to attack the cities one after another; the only practical plan was one general destruction." In November 1573 the great Assassin resigned office, and was succeeded by the Grand Commander Requesens, having in his six years of power put to death, as we are told by the Dutch historians and by the Prince himself, 18,000 persons, and accumulated round his name a mass of loathing beyond any recorded in modern history.

The retreat and disgrace of Alva mark the point in the long struggle at which endurance and constancy were about to triumph over cruelty and force.

During all this time the web of intrigue and negotiation was being unceasingly woven by some of the subtlest brains and the most indefatigable workers whom history records. The combinations are of infinite variety and rapidity of change, and almost every step in the maze of intrigue is now open to us in the despatches and memoirs that survive. Volumes would be needed to unfold in detail the kaleidoscopic variations which pass from chancery to chancery, from court to court. But although the combinations seem to vary from day to day, like the surprises of a game of hazard, we can see now that the rulers of each country held steadily to a clear and intelligible policy of their own, perpetually striving to reach it by continually shifting means.

Spain, France, and England stand forth as the three dominant powers—Spain, with far the most powerful armies and the highest renown; France, with all her vitality and resource, and the advantage of her central position ; England, far weaker than either by land, but really superior to both on sea.   Round these three great powers are grouped the Netherland Provinces, themselves divided into the rich, conservative, Catholic South, and the hardy, revolutionary, and Calvinist North ; Scotland and Ireland attached to England by physical bonds, which were to a great extent neutralised by historic tendencies ; and Germany, also divided into a Lutheran North and a Catholic South.   All these countries (except Spain proper) were again divided and shaken by the indomitable zeal of the new religion, and by the counter-reformation inspired from Rome and Toledo.   The Catholic power held official command in France, the Reforming power held it in England, with a permanent Catholic conspiracy in England, and a formidable Protestant rebellion in France, with Protestant pretenders to the throne ; whilst even in Catholic Spain there was a party of political moderates, as well as a party of uncompromising fanatics.

The power of Spain seemed (and for the first half of Philip's reign perhaps really was) an ever-present danger to France, as well as to England, weakened as both were by religious divisions.   If Philip, now the absolute master of the Iberian and Italian Peninsulas and also of the Indies, could establish himself as equally absolute in the Netherlands, with their great commerce, wealth, and maritime aptitudes, the position of France, surrounded on three sides by her mighty rival, was one of continual peril.   So, too, were Spain in undisputed command of this huge empire, and so face to face with the Thames and the eastern sea-board of England, it was no less a standing peril to England, all the more that Philip was the sovereign who represented the Catholic reaction, as Elizabeth was the sovereign who represented the Reforming interest, and that, with Catholic Ireland at her side, and her Catholic cousin as her sole heir, the position of Elizabeth was one of extreme danger. Philip, again, could not rest under the fanaticism of his own nature, of his churchmen and people, and the pride and ambition of his consummate warriors; and thus the recovery of his richest Provinces and the extirpation of the Calvinist heresy was to him a matter of life or death. Thus it was that, for a generation or more, the critical struggle swayed backwards and forwards across the revolted Provinces; and European complications revolved round their future settlement.

In this tangle of interests and alternation of perils, each of the great powers naturally, and perhaps inevitably, pursued a policy of counterpoise and doubledealing. The proud motto of our Henry VIII. had been—*Cui adhaereo, praeest.* The new motto was—*Ne quis praesit, caeteris adhaereo* ("If one gains the mastery, I support the others"). It was of vital importance to France and to England that Philip should be occupied by insurrection in the Netherlands. Both France and England were willing to give assistance to sustain the revolt, so far as they could do so, without forcing on a war with Spain, and without imperilling their own position between the Catholic and Protestant interests at home. France and England could not form any serious and lasting league with each other, apart from

all national antipathies, because the Valois could not cease
to be Catholic, nor could Elizabeth cease to be anti-Papal.
Nor could either sovereign form any serious or lasting
understanding with Spain, because to do so would hand
them over to their own fanatical Catholics, and drive
their Protestant subjects into uncontrollable rage.

If France began to obtain control of the Netherlands,
it alarmed England and drove her to resist such a
scheme. If England began to do the same thing, it
alarmed France. Hence it resulted that the diplomatic
history of Europe during the life of William the Silent
was an almost unparalleled maze of unscrupulous intrigue and shifting combinations, wherein the claims of
religion, honour, mercy, and truth were regarded by all
statesmen as mere phrases, so far as foreign countries
were concerned, and wherein subtle and patriotic men
strove *per fas et nefas* to safeguard their own country
and augment its strength. Machiavelli's *Prince* was in
its most brilliant vogue.

In the centre of this desperate game stands William
of Orange, with a policy not less able, and certainly less
tortuous, than any around him. He is as indefatigable
as Philip or Cecil, as subtle as Walsingham or Granvelle,
as ingenious in combinations as ever were Elizabeth
or Catherine. But in all the whirl of intrigue he has
steadily in view one dominant idea—*free life* for the
Netherlands, with liberty of worship, their old charters,
and no Spanish soldiery. From this he never swerves.
To secure it he would accept the suzerainty of France.
He would accept the suzerainty of England. He would
accept incorporation with the Empire. He would accept
partition of the provinces between France, England, and

Germany, subject to the local privileges and freedom of religion. He sought for a royal Podestà from abroad. He would even advise submission to Spain, if adequate guarantees could be devised to secure the cessation of religious persecution and the withdrawal of Spanish troops. With these conditions as an irreducible *mini-mum*, William was continually scheming for some new alliance: to gain some external aid, however slight, precarious, and even sinister might be the hope it held out.

It was an age when motives of self-preservation over-rode in statesmen all questions of moral principle and of personal feeling. With them all, the universal rule was—that your enemy of to-day might be your friend of to-morrow—that to-morrow you might be fighting your friend of to-day—that frank alliances must be made even with those who had murdered your friends or sought to murder you—that you must suppress such words as "never," "impossible," "unendurable,"—must nurse no resentment, yield to no affection, trust no one, shrink from no plot yourself, and suspect all plots in others. The Catholic enthusiasts on one side, the Protestant enthusiasts on the other, were burning to serve God at the cost of blood, destruction, confusion, and crime. The patriots were fired by national glory; the people were moved by inveterate prejudices and affections. But the leading statesmen, and especially the sovereigns, kept their eyes fixed on the main chance —the safety of their own country and throne, without personal prejudices and without passion. Within a few months of the Bartholomew Massacre, Elizabeth ex-changed ostentatious courtesies with the Valois princes

and William the Silent was concluding an alliance with
Charles IX. Philip and Alva sought the friendship of
Elizabeth, whom they had plotted to assassinate. And
Elizabeth alternately sent money and men to the
revolted Provinces, and then tried to force them into
abject surrender, when, abandoned by her, they flung·
themselves on France.

The salient feature of the policy of Orange in this
incessant gyration is the indomitable patience with
which he met continual desertions, and his magnanimous
self-control under cruel disappointment and cutting in-
dignities. Elizabeth might send him men and money,
and as suddenly recall them ; she would encourage,
menace, or desert him, as the safety of England seemed
to her to require—she might even add to the politic
artifices of diplomacy the restless caprices of a spoilt
beauty, but the Prince met all her moods with dignified
composure ; he gave her credit for patriotism, if not for
sincerity. Again and again, undeterred by rebuffs, he
importuned her to give him such help as she thought
fit. He seemed always ready to admit that, to the
Queen of England, the safety of England was paramount
and the welfare of the Netherlands but a move in the
great game. And he quite understood that Elizabeth
herself held in detestation both Calvinism and rebellion,
by which indeed her policy at home was circled and em-
barrassed at every step.

The expeditions of the Sea Beggars, which led to the
seizure of Brill and Flushing, were mainly supplied from
England, with the full knowledge of Elizabeth and her
ministers ; and this continued until Alva's vigorous
action forced her to withdraw her aid. The close union

of the Nassaus with Coligny and the French Crown drove Elizabeth to take up a hostile attitude to the Dutch, but she suffered English soldiers to gain a footing. Immediately after the Bartholomew Massacre, the Prince opened fresh negotiations with Elizabeth. From her he obtained little or nothing; but, under her eyes, he received large sums and bands of volunteers from the Protestant congregations. He sends over agents to England to collect funds and raise troops, and he enters into a formal treaty of mutual help with English merchants. He is said to have received £250,000 from London. But the Queen would give him no open support.

As the siege of Haarlem was drawing to its fatal issue, the Prince made a desperate effort to induce the English Government to help them. He protested his devotion to the Queen and his wishes for her prosperity. He had informed her of his negotiations with foreign powers, and had pressed her to accept the protectorate of Holland and Zeeland. If the Low Countries were crushed, the Spaniards were certain to turn their forces against England. If the Queen would accept these sea provinces (and they would put in her hands as a guarantee Flushing, Brill, Rotterdam, and Enkhuysen) she would immensely strengthen her command of the sea, for the Spaniards in the peninsula had no such havens, shipping, or mariners. He protested indignantly against the imputation that he was a rebel, or was heading a rebellion.

He declared before the Almighty Majesty of God that these wars were not for ambition or gain. He had steadily refused the sovereignty himself, and he could always withdraw (if he pleased) to a quiet life in his own hereditary domain. The war was one solely in defence of religion and the freedom of the people—a cause for which he would refuse no travail or danger till the last drop of his blood were spent. The Estates pressed on the Queen to take full possession of Holland and Zeeland; they were resolved, if she refused, to throw themselves on the French, who would then be masters of the Low Countries. To prevent that, let the Queen put herself at the head of a Protestant League, and, with the aid of the German Protestant chiefs, effect some peaceful settlement of the revolted provinces. *Rather than they should fall into the Spaniards' hands they would not only die with their country, but, before they died, they would entangle the same with such a devil as should root out the name of the Spaniards for ever amongst them.*

In spite of this eloquent appeal, warmly supported now and many times by her own counsellors, Elizabeth steadily rejected the tempting offer. She was at this very time disposed to make some arrangement with Alva and with Philip. She was very willing to see the Netherlands embarrass and exhaust Spain. From time to time, as it suited her moves upon the board, she allowed them to have men, money, and ships. She always took care not to drive them to despair, not to suffer them to be utterly exterminated. She would not accept their protectorate; she would not let any other power accept it. She would give no official countenance either to rebellion or to Calvinism—much as she was willing to profit by both in enabling her to ·hold her ground against France and Spain. She would not risk her very existence by a premature war with Philip; she would not encumber her country with a new Calais and new continental appanages, however tempting they might seem. Nor would she, semi-Catholic head of an Anglican episcopacy, put herself at the head of a motley anti-papal confederacy of Lutheran adventurers, Huguenot rebels, and Calvinist fanatics. In a word, during the whole life of William of Orange, Elizabeth played fast and loose with the cause of the Low Countries, alternately helping and abandoning them, now encouraging, now rebuking, not willing to see them crushed, not daring to protect them. It was not until after the death of William, as the inevitable war with Spain was approaching, that Elizabeth sent an army to the Netherlands ; and even then she prosecuted the war with so poor a heart that it achieved no result. She could not bring herself to act on their side, and when she did act she was too late.

In the same spirit as with Elizabeth did the Prince deal with France. First he sought and obtained aid from the Huguenot rebels, and personally fought against the royal armies. Not long after he seeks and obtains aid from the King, and is in close but secret alliance with Catherine and Charles. Then the massacre of St. Bartholomew was a cruel blow to all his hopes, coming on the top of the horrid murder of his own dearest friends. Yet nine months later he is again negotiating an alliance with Charles, still fresh from the Huguenot slaughter. When Anjou, the principal instigator of the massacre, becomes Henri III., William congratulates him and enters into terms of friendship. When the miserable Alençon seems willing to throw his lot in with the struggling Provinces, Orange gives him a steady support, in spite of the incurable treachery of the man, and the insolent menaces with which in turn Elizabeth assailed him. His one inflexible idea is to save the land of his adoption from the Inquisition and from Spanish tyranny, however false, however blood-stained were the hands which necessity impelled him to grasp, however treacherous and grasping were the powers at whose feet he bent himself to sue.

The restless Louis of Nassau was hardly recovered from his prostration before we find him occupied with new negotiations with the French king, with the German princes, the Emperor, and even Philip. In all this William takes no active part except to gain time and to insist on his unalterable conditions—First, "*The reformed religion according to the Word of God and freedom of worship*"; Secondly, "*The Commonwealth and the whole land restored to its ancient privileges and liberty*"; Thirdly, "*Strangers, and in particular Spaniards, in civil or military employment, to be withdrawn.*" Besides this, the King should pay the soldiers whom the Prince had engaged. He does not think that Philip will accept these terms, nor that the German princes can obtain adequate guarantees for their faithful execution. It need hardly be said that they did not succeed; nor did the King of Spain, who did not pay his own men, pay the troops who had been fighting against him for heretics and rebels.

The Prince had more hope from France, which during his whole career was the quarter to which he most inclined. And in the spring of the year succeeding the St. Bartholomew, he again permitted his brothers to negotiate with Charles. But he warned them that, after the massacre, it was very difficult to induce the Protestants to trust the French Court. His terms were still —freedom of worship for the Reformers, war in the Netherlands on Spain, or money and men to carry on the war for themselves, the French to retain what they could capture, except in Holland and Zeeland, and to have a protectorate of these. These were the terms which he constantly offered to France. It was at the time when, strangely enough, proposals for a settlement in the Netherlands were made simultaneously on behalf of the French king, eager to clear himself of the stain of the massacre and to assist his brother to the Crown of Poland, and also on behalf of the King of Spain, then eager to obtain the Imperial Crown.

The Prince did not personally take part in any of these negotiations. He was willing to try if anything could come of them—always subject to his inflexible conditions. The powerful and outspoken letter of Louis to Charles IX.—one of the most daring appeals ever made by a private person to a sovereign—may have touched the conscience of the dying King. The ardent young hero was loaded with protestations of support from the French Court and received a very large sum of money. With this he raised an army of 6000 foot and 3000 cavalry—all, alas! inexperienced volunteers or disorderly mercenaries.

At the head of this force Count Louis crossed the Rhine in a stormy February of 1574, having at his side his brothers John and Henry, and Duke Christopher, son of the Elector Palatine. Orange raised 6000 men in Holland and tried to join his brother, warning him in vain not to be caught in a trap alone. But the Spanish captains, rushing upon Louis, drove him back staggering down the Meuse, with a lawless and mutinous army, entangled in the swamps of the Meuse and the Waal. At Mookheath, near Nijmegen, what remained of the

little army was outmanœuvred, crushed, and exterminated,—Louis, Henry, and Christopher perishing, as
was supposed, in the bloodstained stream. And thus
the gallant Louis disappears from his brother's side,
where he had fought, schemed, and toiled with such
reckless audacity and such indomitable ardour.

Shortly before this William publicly professed the
Calvinist faith. A minister wrote to London—"Our
godly Stadtholder has come to the communion, and
therein has broken the Lord's bread, and has submitted
to discipline, which is no small event." Born and baptized as a Lutheran, bred a Catholic, the Prince had
again professed the Lutheran faith in middle life ; and
now, at the age of forty, he joined the Calvinist communion. He never pretended that any of these changes
of creed was a matter of conviction. In all his intimate
letters to his family, letters of entire sincerity and
candour, there is no allusion to his change of profession.
The letters breathe an unmistakable spirit of personal
piety, trust in the goodness and mercy of God, and
reverential submission to His will. Beyond that, all
questions of theology and of worship were to him subordinate matters of personal opinion and local ordinance.
From time to time he joined that communion with which
it seemed to him best to work in the supreme cause of
freedom of thought and public liberty.

We are told that as a young man William had had
a secret interview with the eminent jurist, François
Baudouin, who had an Utopian idea of a fusion between
the Catholic and Protestant faith. William's practical
sense rejected this as a working possibility, but throughout his whole career he was willing to respect the good

side of every creed, and stoutly resisted the evils in all.
Why cannot you live together in amity? was his permanent attitude of mind. Against persecution in any
form his whole nature flamed up with indignation—
equally whether the victims were Catholic, Lutheran,
Calvinist, or Anabaptist. As he said in a noble speech
in the Council of the Regent, in 1566 :—

> In all earthly things there must be order, and above all other
> things in religion, to maintain the peace of the country and salva-
> tion of souls. But it must be such an order as can be accepted.
> By the Inquisition religion is sacrificed, for to see men burned for
> holding what they feel to be right, sorely troubles the people
> and raises a case of conscience—whereby judges lose all credit and
> authority.

As a statesman, religions appealed to him in their
social, and not in their doctrinal aspect. Like Elizabeth,
he would have been content to remain Catholic, had it
not been for the papal persecution and exclusive pretensions. Like Henri IV., he frankly changed his
nominal communion from political necessity. But he
was free from the levity of Henri and the intolerance
of Élizabeth. He neither jested nor excused his change.
In all his various professions he was equally tolerant
towards Catholics, Lutherans, and Calvinists. He continually told all Protestants that he could not see what
need divide them, nor why any one sect claimed the
right to dictate to the rest. His one dominant idea in
religion was to get rid of all persecution and to tolerate
different forms of worship side by side. The atrocities
committed by his own partisan chiefs, Count de la Marck,
Sonoy, and the rest gave him deep anxiety. Catholics
had very naturally regarded him as a secret heretic ;

Lutherans. then looked on him as a time-server; and
Calvinists still regarded him as a weak vessel. He
treated all these charges with serene indifference. So
far as he dared, he punished the authors of outrage and
crime. As a matter of statesmanlike policy, he openly
and quietly united himself with that theological communion wherein he saw that he could best serve the
cause of civil and religious liberty. And when he joined
the communion, he held to it with perfect loyalty and
unswerving moderation.

Again and again in his private letters William pours
forth, along with unhesitating trust in Providence, his
sense of isolation and bereavement. "It is not possible
for me to bear alone such labours and the burden of
such weighty cares as press on me from hour to hour,
without one man at my side to help me." "I have not
a soul to aid me in all my anxieties and toils." Ste.
Aldegonde had been captured, and would have been
executed by the Spaniards had not the Prince vowed
to deal the same by Admiral Bossu, whom he had taken
in fight about the same time. The excitable and eloquent secretary languished in prison, and implored the
Prince to surrender and abandon the struggle. In a
noble set of letters, full of feeling for the despondent
prisoner and of stern resolution, William patiently
rebukes the impatience of his friend, and rehearses the
enormities of Philip and of Alva. In public and in
private he poured forth stirring appeals to the struggling
cities and to the world around. The war went on with
varying fortune, horrible sufferings, and heroic deeds.
Here and there a town was won, a commander captured,
a force repulsed. By the beginning of 1574 William

was master of all Holland, except Amsterdam and Haarlem, and of all Zeeland, except South Beveland and Tholen; and Leyden still resisted the utmost efforts of Spain.

. Disaster, defeat, and isolation did not crush the Prince. In a long and exhaustive letter to John, who by a lucky accident had escaped the slaughter of Mook, William pours forth his grief for the loss of his brothers, and his plans for the time to come.

" If they be dead, as I can no longer doubt, we must submit to the will of God and trust in His divine Providence, that He who has given the blood of His only Son to maintain His Church will do nothing but what will redound to the advancement of His glory and the preservation of His Church—however impossible it may appear. And though we all were to die, and all this poor people were massacred and driven out, we still must trust that God will not abandon his own." And then he goes on to detail at great length his schemes and his necessities, hardly knowing, he says, what he is doing, with his head so racked with a multitude of cares and sorrow for the loss (as he fears) of his brothers. Letter after letter to Louis had received no answer, for Louis was lying dead in his unknown place of rest. And this most intimate letter to John was intercepted by Spain, and was recovered and sent to Maurice long years after his father's death.

To understand the nature of William of Orange we cannot do better than study this long letter to John, written at the moment of a great disaster and cruel bereavement. The text fills twelve pages of print, and is full of piety, tenderness, pathos, politic schemes, strategic and diplomatic instructions, and unconquerable determination. He ends thus :—

" If no prince or power will give us help, and for want of it we are all to perish, so be it in God's name ! Yet withal we shall have the honour of having done what no nation ever yet did, of having defended and maintained ourselves, in so petty a land, against the mighty and horrid efforts of such powerful enemies, without any aid from others. And if the poor people of these parts, abandoned by all the world, still resolve to hold out as they have done till now, and as I trust they will continue to do, and if it do not please God to chastise us and utterly destroy us, *it will still cost the Spaniards the half of Spain, in wealth as well as in men, before they will have made an end of us.*" Stirring and prophetic words !

All this time the Prince was dogged by assassins. He had for years been on his guard, and had escaped many attempts. The correspondence of Philip and his officers contains continual references to schemes for this end. Philip on the margin of reports wrote—" They show little pluck not to kill him ; that is the only remedy." Cardinal Granvelle urged the King to have William and Louis both put out of the way " like Turks." Spanish, Italian, German, French, and English assassins were put upon the work ; but either their heart failed them or the Prince caught them. The French as well as the Spanish envoys are constantly reporting the same conspiracies. Philip's agents write—" The King approves of the plan and would be rejoiced to have the world rid of both brothers."

When Requesens succeeded Alva, he was expressly ordered " to despatch (*despachar*) William and Louis of Nassau. He was to find determined men and offer them an adequate reward. But the King was not to be known as the authority for it." Requesens obeyed, and made large offers, but after many months he writes back to Madrid that he has little hope of success, *unless God help him to do it.* (*De hacer matar al principe d'Oranges, si Dios no lo hace, no tengo esperanza.*) Not only, says he in despair, does God show no favour to our assassins, who are mere rogues and swindlers (*chocar-*

reros y sacadineros), but the beggars are trying the same thing against us! So far as the Prince is concerned that charge was false; but he had his secret information, even in the cabinet of Philip, and received notice of all that passed there, it is said, by the agency to no small degree of women. He avoided, arrested, and executed certain of these assassins, and terrified the rest. It was the age of assassination; and no court and no nation was wholly free from the taint. In the Papal, Spanish, Italian, and French governments it was one of the recognised weapons of constituted powers. There is no evidence, direct or indirect, that William at any time gave his sanction to the murder of an opponent. But the last twelve years of his life were passed in constant peril of assassination, to which in the end he fell a victim.[1]

[1] The sixth volume of Gachard's *Correspondance* (pp. i.-clxxiv. and 1-246) is occupied with documents relating to these various conspiracies. It forms an amazing repertory of official assassinations.

CHAPTER IX

THE collapse of the baffled tyrant at the end of the year
1573 marked a real turn in the long struggle. The
successor of Alva was expected to bring a change in the
tactics of Spain. To some extent he did this. And
now, after six years of war, the drain upon her resources,
the chaos in her civil and military administration, the
heroism of the Hollanders, and the indomitable energy
of their leaders, slowly and amidst many disasters were
seen to tell. Spain began to parley; even Philip
listened to a compromise; chronic mutiny and anarchy
among his soldiers turned their victories into defeat;
and exhausting repulses now began to alternate with
their dear-bought triumphs. In the result, thenceforth,
for some four or five years, the cause of the patriots and
of Orange was in the ascendant, down to the advent of
Alexander Farnese, Prince of Parma, whose supreme
genius in war and in craft again restored the mastery of
Spain.

The crushing defeat which the skill of d'Avila and
the gallantry of his troopers had inflicted on Louis at

Mook-heath was neutralised by a mutiny of the Spanish forces. They clamoured for arrears, chose an Eletto, or dictator, pillaged and rode riot far and near; and, forming an independent army of free lances, they defied Requesens and seized on Antwerp until their demands were satisfied at the cost of the city. These mutinies, and the orgies of outrage and extortion to which they led, undid the work of their arms, and drove the Netherlanders of the Southern Provinces into union more effectively than did the heroism of the men of Holland and the fervid appeals of the Prince.

Paralysed by bankruptcy, anarchy, and mutiny, the Grand Commander was driven to hope something from negotiation, which he first intended as a ruse. There now begins a long series of abortive attempts towards a compromise, which revealed the exhaustion of Spain; whilst, owing to the license of the mutinous troops, the union amongst the provinces was consolidated or renewed. And thus, in the end, the overthrow of the young Counts of Nassau and the last army that could be raised from without, was compensated by a closer combination within, and deeper hatred of the Spanish oppressor.

The war was no longer a monotony of massacre for the patriot forces. The repulse of Don Frederic from Alkmaar had been followed up by the defeat of Count Bossu, the Spanish captain in the Zuider Zee. Mondragon was now in desperate straits in Middelburg; and the gallant Boisot, in a furious sea fight under the eyes of the Grand Commander, destroyed the Spanish ships which were sent to his rescue. The capitulation of the fiery Mondragon and the capture of Middelburg marked the epoch when the Spaniard was forced to recognise the

Hollanders as "belligerents," not as rebels, and the Prince as their lawful Stadtholder, and not a proscribed outlaw. The second siege of Leyden opened with as little hopes of any immediate victory for the King as did the first. Altogether, as the struggle gradually but inevitably drifted into a maritime war, the superiority of the Spanish veterans ceased to tell, and the heroism of the Dutch seamen reaped its reward.

It would be an endless and unprofitable task to set forth in detail the subtle and repeated overtures made to the Prince in order to bend his resolution and bring the Provinces to submit. Spain at last recognised that through him alone could any settlement be effected. He was approached by many agents and from various quarters and lands. Throughout the whole of these complicated negotiations we find him holding on to one inflexible set of conditions, which, he saw but too clearly, nothing but dire necessity could ever wring from Philip. Over and over again, he says, our terms are these: 1. Withdrawal from our country of all Spaniards and foreigners. 2. Free exercise of the Word of God according to the Gospel. 3. Restoration of the ancient rights, privileges, and liberties of the land. And for these three concessions there must be given solid guarantees. These were his terms (he tells his brothers, November 1573): "I have already stated them in my letters, and I have nothing else to propose."

The overtures began first with indirect hints and unauthorised suggestions of third parties, which raised vain hopes, and have led hostile writers into absurd misrepresentations; to these succeeded letters and at last interviews by the Prince's personal friends; and finally there were long and complicated conferences between regular envoys. All came to nothing. Neither the Prince nor the Dutch ever yielded a single point of their irreducible *minimum*. And, as William well knew, Philip had no intention whatever of accepting any one of the three terms, which, from first to last, remained antecedent conditions *sine quibus non*.

To put aside the vague suggestions for reconciliation thrown out from time to time from Germany, France, and England, we find Julian Romero, the fierce soldier who led Egmont and Horn to the scaffold, writing most courteously to the Prince and soliciting a personal interview. This however, in a ceremonious answer, William declines, for reasons which he politely omits to state; but he offers to send two confidential agents to meet the General, whilst urging him to lay before the King the terms on which peace might be had. At the same time Ste. Aldegonde, his spirit cowed or perverted by captivity and its terrors, is induced to write imploring the Prince to yield. In firm and noble letters in reply, William insists that he cannot act without the States, that it is impossible to surrender the country to the mercy of Spain, that he is resolutely labouring to prosecute the war, and withal to protect the prisoner and to secure his release. A few months after his own installation as Governor, Requesens obtains Philip's sanction to a new attempt by the agency of Dr. Leoninus, a professor at Louvain. This learned diplomatist deputed a certain Hugo Bonte, formerly Pensionary of Middelburg, to sound the Prince at Bommel. The envoy received the usual answer. The Prince rejected the idea of "Pardon" altogether; if he fell in the struggle, he would have died with a glorious name; and however mighty was the King of Spain, they put their trust in a King still mightier than all kings.

The envoys of Spain persisted; and Bonte was sent on a second mission two months later to Rotterdam, to propose a conference between delegates from the insurgent States and delegates from the Royalist party. Orange raised difficulties as to any safe-conduct or promise given by Spain. When the envoy urged that no change of religion could be tolerated, the Prince replied that the Turks freely permitted various sects in their Empire, and even the Pope tolerated the Jews. If they were driven to extremities they would put their country into some strong hand as protector—for their land "was a beautiful damsel, handsomely attired, for whose hand there were many suitors, a land so strong and well armed that it might resist even the Grand Turk." The comparison was much quoted, for it contained a truth of wide significance.

Other envoys were sent, who received the same reply; and at last Requesens released Ste. Aldegonde on parole and sent him to treat with the Prince at Rotterdam (July 1574). After a long interview on minor points William answered that he had done and would do nothing without the assent of the delegates of the States. As to himself, if they should think it right, he would leave the country, for he sought nothing for himself. Nothing, he said, could be done whilst the foreign troops remained. Let them be withdrawn, and the States would decide on their future lot. The despatch which the envoy carried back to his prison from the

States was not one that held out much promise of a
settlement, either in substance or in form.

At the close of the year 1574, after more than twelve
months of unprofitable negotiations, the Grand Commander sent Dr. Leoninus with Bonte on a further
mission to the Prince. The solemn report of the
learned and verbose civilian is weary reading. William
kept him for months at arm's length ; and at last, in a
long private interview, cut short his subtleties and
formalities, told him that freedom of religion was an
indispensable condition, and that both the States and
himself could put no trust in any promise of Spain,
whose "clemency" was a mockery, and whose phrases
would not deceive them. These futile *pour - parlers*
resulted in nothing but a yet more futile conference at
Breda, which was protracted from the beginning of
March to the middle of July 1575. Ten delegates
from the States met the agents of Philip, with the
Prince's brother-in-law, as representing the Emperor.
The Prince himself took no personal part in the debates,
which he followed and directed from Dort. Philip, now
seriously alarmed, like the Emperor, desired to end the
struggle. Orange and the States desired it no less. But
neither Philip nor Orange would yield a point on the
only material questions at issue.

These various attempts at negotiation, carried on for
some twenty months, had done nothing but convince
both sides that the contest must be fought to the bitter
end. From first to last the Prince had never expected
the smallest definite result, nor had he given any one
reason to imagine that he did. He permitted these
overtures to go on, without hope and without guile.

Plainly and consistently he maintained one uniform policy, which he stated in full—a policy as impossible to reduce as it was beyond hope to obtain. But an indirect end resulted which he may have foreseen, and could not regret. Time, on the whole, favoured the revolt. Negotiation betrayed the exhaustion of Spain. The conference of the Calvinist States cemented their incipient union, and accustomed them to look up to William as their real sovereign and head.

These negotiations, in which the Grand Commander persevered, were largely due to the exhausting and humiliating repulse of Spain by the heroic city of Leyden. This memorable triumph of the Hollanders entirely changed the aspect of the war. Leyden had been closely besieged for nearly six months, when the advance of the ill-fated Louis gave it a temporary relief. Two months later a powerful Spanish army closed in upon it again. The Prince exerted all his energies to encourage the citizens, to rouse Holland to support them, and to stir up the German princes. A volume would be needed to recount in full the horrors, the marvels, the heroisms of this stupendous siege. Our simpler task is to watch the efforts of William the Silent, who never more than now deserved to be known as William the Indefatigable. He placed himself in a fortified camp between Delft and Rotterdam, and there he commanded the dykes round Leyden. Herein lay the salvation of the doomed city. It was hopeless to meet the Spanish forces on land, but they could be beaten by sea. Leyden was six miles from the sea. But the whole country round it lay below the level of high tide, and by opening the great dykes, the sea could be brought to Leyden. The genius of the Hollanders and their leader seized upon this peculiar condition, whereby an army was driven from its entrenchments by seamen, and an inland city was rescued by a fleet which sailed into its streets.

The Prince in person directed the cutting of the dykes, having persuaded the people to submit to the sacrifice. "Better ruin the land than lose the land," said they; and a fleet of two hundred vessels was collected to sail over their meadows and crops when the sea had covered them. But the sea came in somewhat slowly; and in the meantime the citizens were reduced to famine. In the midst of the crisis the Prince, worn out by his exhausting efforts in the swampy land, was prostrated with fever. Racked with anxiety and sunk in despondency, he lay at death's door, still dictating despatches, and sending messengers right and left in the intervals of his stupor. He was told that Leyden had fallen, and an envoy found him alone in bed, and in great exhaustion. Within a month his strong constitution recovered its vitality. In a letter to his brother on the 7th of September, he pours out his thanks to God, who, he trusts, will not try him beyond what the weakness of the flesh can endure; and he urgently implores John to assist him with funds, and to appeal once more to the German chiefs.

From abroad came no sign of aid. But at last Admiral Boisot came out of Zeeland with a force of wild sea-dogs, sworn neither to give nor to ask quarter, embarked in large barges charged with cannon, arms, and provisions. Again and again Boisot pressed across the flooded plain and stormed redoubts of the besiegers, whilst the famished citizens of Leyden still kept the Spaniard at bay. Orange rose from his sick bed, inspired the patriot fleet to a last effort, and ordered the cutting of the remaining dyke. By the 1st of October a gale sprung up from the west, sweeping the ocean across the drowned land, and carrying Boisot into the besiegers' entrenched camp. Terrific combats ensued night and day, till the Spanish commander, sullenly admitting that he was beaten, " but by the sea, not by the foe," took refuge in such causeways as he could find above the flood. The Zeelanders swept along the canals into the city, flinging provisions to the starving citizens as they rowed up the waterways to the great church. There Boisot and his men, the gallant Burgomaster and his famished citizens, magistrates, soldiers, sailors, women, and children offered up thanksgiving for their wellnigh miraculous deliverance. That same day, the 3rd of October, memorable in the annals of Holland— in the annals of patriotism — the great news was brought to Delft, where the Prince and the citizens were in church. It was read aloud from the pulpit, the congregation decorously waiting to hear the sermon out. The next day the Prince reached Leyden, where he did ample justice to the heroism of the citizens in their wonderful defence, gave them some honorary and pecuniary privileges, and founded that illustrious university which for three centuries has been a foremost seat of science, letters, theology, and law.

This grand feat of arms roused new life in the provinces, both Dutch and Belgian. By the end of October the Prince again sent an emissary to his brother, charged to confer with the German chiefs and

to give a report of the good promise of things in
Holland. Day after day the Grand Commander poured
out to the King his troubles and his needs, giving him
a true picture of the mutinies in the armies and the
defiance of the rebels. "They will never yield," he
tells his master, "except at the last gasp, and by
refusing supplies they mean to force his Majesty to
close the war." The next month a very important step
was taken in fixing the authority of the Prince.
Hitherto his position had been ill-defined; he could
only obtain contributions irregularly and by constant
appeals, and he was obliged to consult the States on
the conduct of the war, and involve himself in endless
disputes. He now called upon them to give him a free
hand or to take the entire control of the government
into their own hands.

So peremptorily summoned, the States conferred on
his Excellency "absolute power, authority, and sovereign command in all concerns of the common land
without exception." He required 45,000 florins a
month to prosecute the war. The States attempted to
bargain, and proposed 30,000 florins. William refused
this sum with no small warmth. He was ready to go
off and leave the country, which they could then
administer with all the economy they thought fit.
This closed the matter; the 45,000 florins were granted
without demur. Thus, within some weeks of the relief
of Leyden, the Prince was legally installed in a sovereign position over Holland, with a fixed budget that he
had estimated as necessary for the service. His effort
to bring Zeeland into the union did not fully succeed
until the following year.

In the midst of these public cares there was con-
summated in the personal life of William of Orange an
act which showed all his bold, obstinate, and masterful
nature, while strangely belying his character for prudence and exclusive devotion to the State.   It was now
seven years since his wretched wife, Anne of Saxony,
had deserted and defied him ; four years since she had
been convicted of adultery.   She was now insane, and
was practically a prisoner in Nassau.   From that time
the Prince had ceased to hold himself bound, and spoke
of her as "his former wife."   In 1575 her own family
took her back, and, at the desire of the Nassaus,
immured her in a dungeon in Dresden in the barbarous
fashion of that age.   At the same time William resolved
on contracting a third marriage ; and in the face of
violent opposition, both public and private, he carried
out his purpose with cool but desperate self-will.

Charlotte de Bourbon was a younger daughter of
Louis, Duc de Montpensier, of the royal House of
France.   As an infant she was sent from her home
and brought up in the rich Abbey of Jouarre, of which
her aunt was Abbess.   There she was forced by threats
to take the veil at the age of twelve, in spite of her
violent protests, and in violation of the canons as to
the age of profession.   And this outrage on religion
and on humanity was aggravated by the fact that this
poor child was made Abbess on the collusive resignation
of her aunt.   At the age of eighteen the young Abbess
drew up a formal document, attested by witnesses,
repudiating the outrage of which she was the victim.
Having reached the age of twenty-five, thoroughly
penetrated with the Protestant convictions of so many

of her near relations, whom she fully consulted, by the advice of the Queen of Navarre, the mother of Henri IV., Charlotte deliberately renounced her odious and forced profession, publicly abandoned the Abbey with two other nuns, and sought protection at Heidelberg with the Elector Palatine. The wrath of the Duke, her father, the indignation of her Catholic relations and of the whole Catholic world, was a natural result, which the generous support of the Puritan Elector and his wife enabled her to brave. At Heidelberg she was in the centre of the Protestant ferment during the dreadful epoch of St. Bartholomew, and there for three years she lived in continual contact with the preachers, refugees, and chiefs of the Huguenot cause. It was in the first days of her escape from the Abbey that William seems to have seen her at the Elector's Court. He cannot have seen her again. But now three years later he is seized with a resolve to make her his wife.

His lawful wife was still living. She was the heiress of one of the great princes of Germany, and he could not repudiate her without stirring them to wrath. To marry a renegade nun was to call out execrations from the whole Catholic world. To ally himself with the royal House of France was to awaken all the jealousy of rival nations and all the suspicions of his Calvinist people at home. He was immersed in debt; his life was in hourly peril; he had hardly any home that he could call his own. He was no longer young, and was older than his years. He had five living children by his two wives, and of these he had never seen much. Nevertheless he resolved to marry a woman whom he had not seen for years, and with whom he can have had nothing but a very slight acquaintance at one very short period.

William was certainly a man who craved sympathy, a man with a tender heart, and of warm temperament. For seven years, since the desertion of his wife, the break-up of his home, and the dispersion of his children, his life had been utterly lonely. All his colleagues and almost all his friends were gone. All his brothers were dead, except John, who was far away. His eldest son was a prisoner and a pervert in Spain; he had no home where he could bring his daughters or his young boy. His only intimates were a few secretaries, no one of whom was in any sense his companion. And thus, with all the deliberation and thoroughness of foresight which marked his every step, he resolved to have his existing marriage dissolved by legal forms, and to take to his home another wife.

The circumstances as well as the man forbid us to regard this as an outburst of passion. For years he had made no attempt to see the object of his choice. He addressed her as a prince desiring an alliance, not as a lover or a friend. Charlotte was extolled as a paragon of virtue and of beauty by the writers of her faith; and the venom of party and of sect has naturally denied to her both beauty and virtue. But she was certainly a woman of earnest convictions, of fine character, and of resolute temper. The preachers and refugees who had long known her were in constant relations with William; and from them he might gain a complete insight into the qualities of one who was now a mature woman, of wide experience, and of strong

nature. William then convinced himself that his life
and work would grow all the stronger if he had beside
him the grace and support of a woman worthy of him.
He believed that in Charlotte he had found her. And
a wedlock of entire happiness proved that his foresight was not a delusion. As the good John wrote in
1580—

It was a great support to his brother that God had given him
a wife so virtuous, so god-fearing, and of such high intelligence
(*solch tugentsam, gotsfürchtig, hochverstendige gemacl*), one so
entirely after his own heart and mind. He tenderly loves her.

In the spring of 1575 the Prince sent various
emissaries to propose marriage in his name to Charlotte
de Bourbon, and to the Elector Palatine, her guardian.
The Elector duly laid the offer before the King and
Queen of France as head of the lady's house, and the
Duke of Montpensier, her father. These declined to
interfere, as Charlotte herself had abandoned her family
and her religion. She declared that she regarded the
Elector as her father, and would receive his direction.
William next obtained certified copies of the legal
inquiry made by the Count of Nassau into the adultery
and desertion of Anne. The Prince then sent Hohenlohe, his brother-in-law, with instructions to propose the
marriage in form, and to arrange with his brother John
for the bride's journey through Germany to Holland.

The envoy was to give ample explanation to the
lady and to her guardian. He would first state the
facts as to the Prince's marriage with Anne; next, it
must be understood that he could give no dower out of
his estates, but he would do the best he could hereafter.
He was involved in a state of war, deeply in debt, and

forty-two years old. The good John of Nassau was greatly alarmed as well as scandalised, and wrote vehement letters of remonstrance. So too did William of Hesse, who bluntly said that William must be out of his mind (*vix compos*). The Landgrave distinguished himself by the violence of his language, which had a way of running into Ciceronian Latin. *Si pietatem respicias*, She is a renegade nun with whom scandal is rife! *Si formam*, She is simply frightful! *Si spem prolis*, Why, the Prince has too many children already! *Si amicitiam*, He will set every one against him, including his own family and hers!

Without a word in reply, William sent Ste. Aldegonde to Heidelberg to fetch his bride. She was safely escorted with a proper retinue through Germany to Embden, and thence by sea was brought to Brill, where she was honourably received with much rejoicing. Banns of marriage were published in church on three Sundays. A formal act was drawn up and signed by five eminent Protestant ministers, who, having considered the condemnation of Anne of Saxony, declared the Prince free to marry by human and divine law. The next day, 12th June 1575, William and Charlotte were married with ample ceremony and public festivities. Charlotte wrote a graceful and very dutiful letter to her new mother, the aged Countess Juliana, *ma bien aimée mère;* and soon after William wrote a characteristic letter to his brother John.

My brother—It has been my rule, ever since God vouchsafed me any understanding, to take no heed of words or of threats, in any matter which I felt able to carry through with a whole conscience, where I was doing no wrong to my neighbour, above all where I had assurance of a lawful call and the express ordinance of God. And truly, if I had chosen to take account of the talk of men, the threats of princes, and such difficulties as stood before me, I never should have plunged myself into a struggle so dangerous and so odious to the King, my former lord, and so contrary to the counsels of my friends and relations. But when I found that neither my humble prayers nor supplications and plaints availed me ought, I resolved with the grace and aid of the Lord to take up this war, whereof I do not repent, but rather render thanks to God that of His mercy He has given me the heart to bear up against all evils that beset me, however great.

I say the same of my marriage : a step I have taken with a clear conscience before God, and without cause of reproach from men. Nay, it is by the command of God that I am bound to do it. I have acted with ample deliberation and due notice. As to the objections and difficulties alleged, I have fully thought over them ; they would not be lessened by delay. On the contrary, delay would have aroused a storm of scandal and attack. All this has been avoided by the simple and rapid course of action I have taken. And when one is resolved on anything with a clear conscience void of offence towards any one, it is best to act at once, and not to go about with a trumpet as it were, and invite odious disputes, wranglings, and legal obstruction. All the difficulties as to future children have been met by a full statement of my purpose as far as this can be foreseen, and I trust that God will give me His blessing on this marriage. Why then should I consign myself to the estate of widower to which I have been so long condemned ? It is idle to tell me that by prayer and effort I could maintain yet longer the grace of continence, without resorting to marriage. I have received no such assurance, but rather am reminded of the promise which He makes to those who rightly accept His ordinance. This I am firmly convinced is the sure path to follow, not only for the sake of myself, but that of the general cause.

In the end this proved to be true. The marriage, whatever we think of its lawfulness, brought ultimate good to William, to his family, and to his cause. Much was said of its irregular form, of its extraordinary imprudence, and the high-handed way in which it was carried out. The German Protestants, since the monk

Luther had married a nun, and had authorised the bigamy of Philip of Hesse, could not say much. The opposition of the princes, Catholic and Protestant, at last died down. The Princess was warmly supported by her own Protestant relations, and ultimately reconciled to her father and to the Catholic princes of her house. Charlotte won the affection and confidence of William's children and of his family. The pecuniary difficulties were surmounted; and the Princess of Orange was soon recognised in her adopted country as the honoured wife of the Prince of Orange—in the true sense "an help meet for him." In the next year a daughter was born to them, who is the direct ancestress of the House of Hanover, and of nearly all the royal houses of Europe (see App. A).

The irregularity of form is plain. But it must not be forgotten that, within a generation of the Protestant Reformation, whilst Protestants fully recognised the principle of divorce, they had yet not instituted any regular system of matrimonial law. They had repudiated the Papal authority and the sacramental character of marriage, but had adopted no procedure for its legal dissolution. If they had done so it is not very clear what would have been the proper course. William claimed the status of a ruling prince in three countries and in three capacities, as Prince of Orange, as Count of Nassau, and as Stadtholder in Holland with sovereign power. It might be a curious puzzle to determine to what tribunal, if to any, his personal status was amenable, even by the refined and complex rules of international law as now understood.

The Princes of Nassau claimed the right to try and

put to death an adulterous wife. The trial and punishment of Anne of Saxony was informal, private, and arbitrary. It was so done to avoid scandal and to save the honour of the House of Saxony. But for this her marriage would have been dissolved in a formal way ; but this formality was never effected. Accordingly William rested satisfied with the public sentence pronounced by the five divines, based on the sentence of the Nassau private court. And this satisfied the public opinion of the people of his adoption. Those who are not satisfied are bound to regard our own Elizabeth as a bastard. For the second marriage of Henry VIII. was much more irregular and arbitrary ; and Catherine of Aragon had not deserted, defied, and dishonoured her husband, nor was she insane, an outcast, and imprisoned for life. William, indeed, did not rest this act on legal technicalities, but on substantial right and wrong. His tone was this, " My legal wife is to me dead ; the only ecclesiastical authority I recognise pronounces me free ; the attacks and threats of men do not disturb me. I am acting according to a clear conscience, and am doing hurt to no man. For my conduct I will answer to my Maker."

CHAPTER X

WE now come to the most crowded and most victorious epoch in the life of William, an epoch of such varied complications that the main results only can be stated in our space. Just before his marriage the union between Holland and Zeeland was provisionally concluded, and the Prince assumed what was practically supreme command, both military and civil. He insisted on certain modifications to give him a free hand, and he changed the suppression of "the Catholic cult," which they desired, into the suppression of any "worship contrary to the Gospel," under which vague phrase he trusted to resist the intolerance of the Calvinists.

By the middle of July 1575 all prospect of negotiation had ceased, and the Spaniards renewed the war with vigour. William was quite prepared for this. In an intimate letter to his brother John (who had begun to look for some repayment of all his advances), he gives a pathetic picture of their forlorn state and their unbroken resolution.

N

It is idle to ask for payment from us of sums advanced. This little corner of land has been crushed down by the cost of making head alone against the most mighty princes of Europe ; for it has had to fight terrible armies launched against it from all parts of the world, armies which are being daily reinforced, whilst for four or five years no prince has given us the slightest aid, for all that some of them profess a burning zeal for our religion of Christ. None have helped us save the Count Palatine, you and my three other brothers, who have freely given their substance and their lives in this just cause. Yet withal, now that peace is hopeless and the forces of the enemy daily increase, we must all strive with might and main to make face against him by every means in our power. This every man here is resolved to do as thoroughly as ever he was at any time before.

The campaign did not open well for the cause. Spain now had 50,000 foot and 5000 horse, and one after another the weak defences of the Dutch citizens were beaten down. " They stormed Oudewater," writes William to his brother, "and delivered it over to all imaginable cruelties, sparing neither sex nor age." Next Schoonhoven fell into their hands, and they laid siege to Woerden. Thence, by a magnificent stroke of energy and daring, they planted themselves in the heart of Zeeland. Starting from the island of Tholen, which had been won by Mondragon's wonderful night march through the sea, they repeated the exploit of 1572, under even greater difficulties and in face of a brave enemy. Under the eyes of Requesens a body of 3000 men forced their way in a dark and wild night through an arm of the sea, many miles wide and 5 feet deep, into the island of Duiveland, where a terrific combat ensued, in which the Dutch commander was killed and the garrison over-powered. From Duiveland these invincible veterans waded across a second arm of the sea, drove off the defenders of the island of Schouwen, captured Bom-

menede, butchered its inhabitants, and laid close siege
to the strong city of Zierickzee. Zierickzee, after a long
siege, again fell into the hands of Spain, and with it fell
the gallant Boisot. Woerden followed about the same
time. Thus in a short campaign the Royalists had
planted themselves on the sea shore, and had drawn a
belt from thence to the Rhine round Rotterdam, Delft,
and Leyden.

In this extremity William summoned the States of
Holland and Zeeland to Rotterdam, and told them that
they must now yield, unless they could find some sovereign to protect them in place of Philip. In spite of
their hesitation he forced this upon them. Though he
would prefer to look to France, the deputies decided to
apply to Elizabeth of England. As before, as afterwards, Elizabeth dallied and delayed. She wished the
struggle to go on; she wished neither King nor Estates
to be victorious; she wished both to look to her for
help. Her prudence would not allow her to accept the
protectorate : but it equally impelled her to allow none
other to accept it; she feared alike the bigotry of Philip
and the turbulence of Calvinism. All this William
perfectly understood; but he carried out the desires of
the States by again appealing to the Queen. In the
meantime he is writing to his brother imploring him to
seek for aid in Germany. It is at this time that vague
and inconsistent rumours describe the Prince as about
to withdraw across the seas, and seek a country elsewhere. His private letters and his public utterances be-
tray not a thought of the kind. They breathe nothing
but unconquered resolution. Now, indeed, his fortunes
touched their lowest ebb; and his secretary writes to

John that the Prince is "so overwhelmed with business, griefs, cares, and toils, that from morning to night he has hardly time to breathe."

From the depths of distress, they were raised up by the confusion and atrocities of the Spanish power. The Grand Commander died suddenly in the spring of 1576, leaving no successor : and government at once fell into disorder. The interim Council poured out to the King reports of their difficulties : of want of funds, of mutiny, and riot. "The license of the troops of all nations is intolerable, and is due to stoppage of their pay," wrote one report; "let the King immediately send out a Viceroy charged with a policy." Philip as usual hesitated and drifted. In the meantime, William was acting. The Union of Delft (25th April 1576) made regular and definitive the federation of the two provinces of Holland and Zeeland on the terms previously settled. This crucial act—the formal nucleus of the United Netherlands—bound the two sea-board Provinces into a permanent Union, constituted the Prince supreme authority in war and sovereign *ad interim*, and authorised him to treat with foreign princes for a protectorate. This clause he had himself forced on the unwilling deputies who had come to regard him as their real *pater patriae*, "the Father of the Land" he was now called. He was to uphold the reformed religion and put down any worship "contrary to the Gospel," whatever that might mean, "but no inquisition was to be permitted into any man's faith or conscience, nor should any man be troubled, injured, or hindered by reason thereof."

This Union, although the germ of a great power to

come, held as yet but a mere strip of reclaimed sea-swamp, barely 100 miles in length and nowhere 30 miles in breadth, containing only a few small towns, and pierced by a Spanish stronghold in its midst. No one knew its weakness better than the Prince, who, seeing the exasperation caused by the mutinous troops of the King and the confusion of his councils, strained every nerve to extend the new Union to the other Provinces. He sent forth from his post at Middelburg a torrent of appeals to the Estates of Brabant, Flanders, Artois, Hainault, and Guelderland, to governors, magistrates, corporations, and influential citizens, to rouse them to resistance, and urge them to union. For each province or person he appealed to the special motives which would most keenly be felt. These letters are masterpieces of eloquence, reason, and policy.

He told the men of Brabant how the scaffold of Egmont and Horn would be far too good for them to expect. Torture and the gallows would be their only lot if they fell into the hands of Philip. *It was not his aim to disturb religion or to introduce any novelties. To free the country from the tyranny of the foreigner, and to set up again their old constitutional rights, was their sole end and hope.* Disunion had been their ruin. Union alone could save them. Let all minor differences be referred to the States-General to settle. Let them put aside jealousies and distrust, and work with one heart and mind for the freedom of their common country and the cause to which he and his had dedicated their lives.

These appeals were greatly aided by the horrible excesses of the troops and the anarchy that was now rampant throughout the military and civil administration of Spain. The capture of Zierickzee was followed by a mutiny; and mutiny was followed by wild raids, storming of towns, and general confusion, in the midst

of which Brussels and other cities overthrew the royal
councils. A conference of the States-General was hastily
summoned. To them the Prince addressed a collective
appeal. For any success in this he saw that the question of religion must be adjourned, and he boldly
addresses them as Catholic patriots.

" Do not be beguiled," he writes, "by the superstitious idea
that loyalty involves a servile prostration to every wish of a king,
who is most ill-informed as to all that is done in his name. Our
sufferings are the result of discord. Disunion—this accursed disunion (*ceste maudite désunion*)—has ever been the direct cause of
the ruin of nations in all ages — in France, Italy, Germany,
Hungary, or in Africa and Barbary, which is given over by it to the
fury of the Turk. Your only hope is to send a joint and formal
document to the King to tell him that it is your firm resolve to
maintain the ancient rights of your country, and free it from the
insupportable tyranny of the Spaniards, but to remain subject to
the lawful sovereignty of His Majesty. Have this document signed
by all the Estates and the principal conventual orders, and by
persons of authority and credit in the land. An act such as this
will tear off all the wretched disguises and subterfuges which
paralyse action. We need a confederation which shall work
together to one end, cemented by some compact in solemn form,
as the ancients did with oaths and sacrifices, and as our ancestors
have often done now for three centuries past. Let the King see
that this is no revolt stirred up by men of influence, as he fancies,
(he said to me, *si los estados no tuviessen pilares, no hablarian tan
alto*)—but that it is the general voice of an entire people, of the
commons as well as the chiefs, of prelates, abbots, monks, lords,
gentlemen, citizens, and peasants, who, without difference of age, sex,
or condition, call aloud with one voice for justice. Let him know
that if he refuses it, you will throw yourselves into the arms of
the ancient enemy of his house. A faggot bound together cannot
be broken as easily as single sticks. You see what we of Holland
and Zeeland have been able to do in five years. We are here to
help you. But rest assured that neither the princes of Germany,
nor the gentlemen of France, nor the Queen of England, nor any
potentate of Christendom, much as they may deplore your sufferings, will ever help you, unless you help yourselves." . . .

Stirred by these appeals and by the military orgies around them, the fifteen Provinces now sent delegates to meet those of Holland, Zeeland, and the Prince at Ghent. William remained at Middelburg in practical guidance of the conference, for whose use he sent a memorandum of instructions, warnings, and politic suggestions. Within a month there was drawn up and signed (8th November 1576) the Pacification of Ghent. By this treaty the whole seventeen Provinces bound themselves in a solemn league to expel the Spaniards, and the ultimate settlement of all questions was to rest with the States-General when that was done. In the meantime the Prince was to retain supreme command in war and act as lieutenant for His Majesty. The Provinces would decide on their own religion ; but Holland and Zeeland were not to forbid Catholic rites, and private reformed rites were to be allowed in all Catholic provinces. The odious edicts against heresy were suspended. Prisoners, confiscations, and outlawries were released. Financial and administrative questions were left for the States-General to settle.

This famous "Pacification" was received on all sides, as the *Apology* declares, with shouts of joy and relief ; and for a moment it seemed as if the long work of William and his Dutch patriots was achieved. For a brief period the union seemed to be complete. A treaty called the "Perpetual Edict" was signed a few months afterwards, which ratified the "Pacification," and was based on a certain Union of Brussels, wherein Catholic and loyalist personages concurred in the national demand for withdrawal of Spanish troops and maintenance of the old charters. The "Pacification" was

undoubtedly the first effort towards a free and united
Netherlands, and was the basis of all the subsequent
federations and unions. It was a masterpiece of
diplomatic ingenuity and judicious compromise. But
nations are not made nor are they maintained by
ingenuity and compromise. It was in substance a
patriotic League between Catholic and Protestant states,
to expel the Spanish troops of the Spanish King whom
they acknowledged as their lord. But the Spanish
troops were still there, in possession of all the great
fortresses in the land. And the " Pacification " added
little to the military resources of the country. The "Pacification " had studiously avoided the problem of religion.
But the problem of religion was there in its bitterest
form. Holland and Zeeland were saturated with Calvinism, and could hardly be held back by the Prince
from exterminating the Catholic faith. The majority
in the other Provinces were Catholic, and could hardly
force themselves to act side by side with heretics.

The terrific persecution which had now persisted for
ten years had practically crushed out Protestantism in
most of the Southern Provinces. The ferocious bigotry
of the Calvinists and the atrocities committed by some
wild leaders on their side had created a deep and widespread Catholic reaction. The orgies of the mutinous
soldiers had combined Catholic and Protestant, rich and
poor, in a common loathing for the foreigner. Of this
William took advantage in his masterly scheme of a
general league. But no man could know better on how
slender a basis it rested, and how little it could promise
a permanent settlement. Yet he wrote to John full of
hope and confidence, and he never grasped fully the

depth and fierceness of the religious animosities in the midst of which he had to work.

This brief *Life* of William of Orange is not the place wherein to rehearse again the enormities of the Spanish mutinies—how troops who for ten years had been gorged with the massacre and plunder of "rebel" towns and provinces turned savagely on their own officers and rulers, and proceeded to slaughter the loyal subjects of their King, and to sack the very cities which they were stationed to guard. The "Spanish Fury," which wrecked Antwerp and butchered its inhabitants by thousands, is in many ways the most horrible frenzy in this war of horrors. The atrocities committed at Mechlin, Naarden, or Haarlem were committed in a captured city by a victorious army. The atrocities in Antwerp were the wanton outburst in cold blood of the garrison of a peaceful city—an orgy of lust, greed, and savagery. It sent through the whole Netherlands such a thrill of horror and dread as sufficed for a short space to override the innate antagonism of race, language, religion, and traditions.

The Prince had pressed on the Pacification of Ghent because he had long known of the fresh danger that threatened them in the person of the new Viceroy. Philip at last made up his mind to send out as governor his half-brother, the paladin Don John of Austria, natural son of the late Emperor, just fresh from the halo of his victory over the Turks at Lepanto. This brilliant, fascinating knight-errant of romance, now in his thirtieth year, with his chivalrous bearing and glory of crusader, was exactly the man to revive the loyal and Catholic traditions of the men of Flanders and

Brabant. But, for all his heroic and gracious airs, he was not the man to match William the Silent in policy and resolution. He arrived at Luxemburg just as the Pacification was signed; and for two years a long and subtle diplomatic duel was waged between the Prince and the Viceroy, wherein step by step the adventurous chieftain found himself paralysed by the astute and sleepless statesman.

The involutions of this negotiation are far too complex to be here set forth. The task before William was both intricate and delicate. Don John came with all the air of a royal mediator to announce the clemency of a lawful sovereign bent on closing the era of strife. To the nobles and citizens, as to William and other authorities, he showed nothing but friendship and grace. Orange could not venture to denounce such overtures in States to which he himself had just appealed as Catholic and loyal. But he well knew that to trust these overtures would be to deliver themselves bound to the incurable perfidy of Philip and the dispensing supremacy of the Pope. Whether Don John himself was sincere or not was of small importance. He was nothing but the tool of his false brother, who could thrust him aside or disown him at will. His own brain was teeming with wild ambition, desperate adventures, and personal triumphs to be won in distant lands and by the aid of royal women. All William's policy was directed to prevent the men of Flanders from yielding themselves up to the fascinations and promises of the young hero, to force on him larger and larger concessions, and, after all, to confront him with demands which the Viceroy dared neither to refuse nor to grant.

William's first efforts were to induce the States to seize the person of Don John as a hostage, and, failing in this, to regard all his overtures as false, and his real mission the same as that of Alva. To the States separately and collectively, to the leading men and councillors, he poured out a torrent of despatches in moving terms. He urges them to insist specially on two points, the entire withdrawal of the foreign troops and the ratification by the Viceroy of the Pacification. All this had to be done with extreme reserve and skill, for he could not treat Don John as an open enemy or drive the Estates into his arms. At the same time he is negotiating in France to bring in the Duke of Anjou, brother of the French king, as a counterpoise to the Imperial bastard. Don John, who meditated an attack on Elizabeth and his own marriage with Mary Queen of Scots, was quite willing to send away the foreign troops by sea; and at last he yielded point after point, and even accepted the Pacification of Ghent by a hollow truce, ill-named the Perpetual Edict.

Orange, in reply, redoubled his warnings that this paper-concession was not enough, as there were no guarantees for the withdrawal of the troops and the demolition of the citadels. Don John, on his side, was quite aware that he had gained nothing until he had gained the Prince. "He is the pilot who steers the ship ; he alone can wreck it or save it," Don John wrote to Philip. "Peace, the Catholic religion, your Majesty's rule, can only be established through him ; we must make a virtue of necessity and come to terms with him, if we are not to lose all." "I see no other way to prevent the ruin of the State but the defeat of this man,

who exerts such an influence over the nation." Don
John sent again the indefatigable Leoninus to the
Prince, who declined to be drawn from his fastness at
Middelburg. Long, subtle, politic conferences ensued.
The Prince was courteous, wary, firm, and even frank.
He could not trust the Viceroy, he said, after all that
had been done; he must take counsel with Holland and
Zeeland; he could give no hope of coming to terms.
Don John still pressed the King to give further conces-
sions. Philip even ratified (on paper) the Perpetual
Edict, and Don John withdrew the Spanish troops, and
thereupon was admitted into Brussels, where he formally
assumed the government with great pomp.

He knew how hollow was his hold on power. "The
people here," he wrote to Philip, "are bewitched by the
Prince; they love him, they fear him, they desire him
for their lord. They inform him of everything, and
take no step but by his advice." "That which the
Prince most abhors in the world," wrote Don John
bluntly, "is your Majesty." "If he could, he would
drink your Majesty's blood." Don John was in despair
as he found himself in the toils of a consummate
tactician. The Prince with his own hand replied to a
letter of Don John by a stately missive still at Simancas.
"Let his Highness rest assured that his one object was
to restore peace to the poor people of this land. For
this there was wanting only the effectual carrying out
of the Pacification of Ghent." To one of Don John's
emissaries he said, "The people form a stable force; the
will of a king is ever changing." To another he said,
"You are staking your own head by trusting the King.
Never will I so stake mine, for he has deceived me too

often.   His favourite maxim is, *haereticis non est servanda fides.*   I am now bald and Calvinist (*calbo y calbanista*— the extant Spanish despatch has it), and in that faith will I die."

Baffled, weary, despairing, Don John withdrew from Brussels after a few weeks, and returned to a policy of force.   He treacherously seized the fortress of Namur. William bruited abroad that Don John's intercepted letters told Philip that nothing now remained but fire and slaughter (*seulement avecque feu et sang* are the words as reported in the letter of the Prince's secretary). Don John learned that there were plots to seize, even to assassinate, him; and he believed that the Prince was cognisant of them.   Confusion reigned throughout the Southern Provinces; and under the incessant instigations of the Prince, the very appearance of authority was slipping away from the King's people.   The Pacification of Ghent had been followed by the second abandonment of Zierickzee by Mondragon, and the Spaniards again lost their last hold in Zeeland.   Breda was recovered to the Prince; Utrecht, Haarlem, Amsterdam, before long accepted his terms.   And Antwerp and Ghent demolished their citadels.   William was now established in full command of the northern land, from the mouth of the Scheldt to the Zuider Zee, and had predominant influence in Flanders and Brabant.

This was the apogee of William's ascendency in the whole Netherland country, and it was visibly expressed in his famous entry in state into Brussels (September 1577).   Don John had at last yielded all the demands of the States, and these, if honestly fulfilled, were ample securities of peace.   But they were only the promises of a Spanish viceroy, and Orange was resolved that they should not be taken as deeds. At last, after long preparations and with great precautions, he accepted the urgent invitations he had been receiving to enter Brussels. His progress was that of a State ceremony. Guarded by a strong force of armed citizens, he passed to Antwerp, and thence with a powerful escort by water into Brussels, where he was received with royal honours and prolonged festivities. The "rebel" chief, who for ten years had carried on unequal war with the whole might of Philip, was now welcomed with acclamations in the capital of the Netherlands, which Philip's nominal Viceroy had just abandoned in impotent despair.

Long conferences took place: should Don John's terms be accepted or not? William, using all his energy and eloquence, induced them to insist on further conditions, which Don John could not accept, and all prospect of avoiding fresh war came to an end. In his own day, and ever since, the responsibility of this act has been cast on the Prince, and undoubtedly the rupture was wholly and solely his work. The justification for it must turn on whether his conviction was sound, that no promise of Philip's ever could be trusted. As a matter of fact, Philip had already ordered his troops to return to the Netherlands; and Don John at once felt that again he was a victorious soldier, and no longer a helpless politician. In the *Apology* we read:—

The letters signed by the King's hand, sealed with his arms, and countersigned, informed us that the only difference between Don John, Alva, and Requesens was that he was younger and more foolish than they were, and was not so well skilled in concealing the poison within him, of glossing with his tongue, and restraining his hands, which tingled with desire to bathe them in our blood.

William had received in Brussels a brilliant welcome; but he well knew all the perils of the hour. His loving wife wrote letter after letter, to warn him against assassination, and to ask if he could have free exercise of his religion. Now, the Belgian Provinces in the main were Catholic, and to them William was an obstinate heretic and the chief of men sworn to uproot the Catholic faith. The great Belgian nobles were jealous of his ascendency, and for the most part hostile. The people were his ardent supporters, as against the Spanish tyranny; but the mass of them would neither tolerate Calvinism nor repudiate the Hapsburg dominion. Orange was hardly installed in Brussels when a Catholic intrigue brought upon the scene Matthias, an Austrian archduke, and brother of the new Emperor Rudolph, to be a counterpoise at once to William and to Don John. William, who neither originated nor approved this invitation, accepted it with a good grace, welcomed the feeble lad, and continued to rule under his name. As a rejoinder, the partisans of Orange succeeded in having him appointed Ruward, which was practically dictator of the interim, and they insisted on his being named Lieutenant - Governor, with the young Matthias as nominal Governor, and Don John was formally declared an enemy. Elizabeth now, in her dread of a French protector, veered round to the "rebels," guaranteed a large loan, and openly supported the Prince. A second time the Prince made a State entry into Brussels, this time as the lieutenant and minister of the Archduke. John of Nassau was named Governor of Guelderland,

and for the moment it seemed that the whole Netherlands, Catholics and Reformers at last in one, were
united to cast out the Spanish rule, with the Prince of
Orange as their virtual ruler and chief.

This fair prospect was shattered by a sudden stroke
which Philip had long. been preparing—by the arrival of
a great soldier with a new army—a mightier than Alva
with a more powerful force. By the end of January
1578, Alexander Farnese, Prince of Parma, reached Don
John with a fresh body of troops from Italy and Spain.
This other young hero of Lepanto was a son of Margaret
of Parma by her second husband, Ottavio Farnese, of the
Papal house. He was thus the nephew of Philip and of
Don John, and, more than any other captain of his age,
he combined an equal genius for intrigue and war.
With an army of 20,000 veteran troops, he swooped
down upon the ill-led army of the States at Gemblours,
near Namur, and utterly annihilated them, without loss
to himself. In an hour he had shattered the whole
military power of the Belgian States. City after city
fell into the hands of Spain and expiated their rebellion
in general massacre. Confusion and panic reigned
in Brussels and throughout Brabant. William, with
Matthias, withdrew to Antwerp; and the combination
which had cost such labours to establish was practically
dissolved.

In this extremity the Prince, with feverish activity,
carried on negotiations with three different powers at
once—Germany, England, and France. He soon found
that Matthias was a mere puppet, and that his name
would bring no real succour from the Empire. He
equally convinced himself that no more help was to be

expected from Elizabeth. And now, as always, he inclined to look towards France and was pressing on the overtures to Anjou, brother of the French king. It was an inextricable tangle, a vicious circle, in which every step involved a change of front, and each turn in the intricate game led to fresh equivocation. To make overtures to any one of the three powers was to irritate and alarm the other two. Without some help from without, William saw nothing but destruction before them. Every one of the possible friends was a master of chicanery and deceit; whilst the great enemy was the very incarnation of perfidy. The maxim of all was that which the envoy of Elizabeth so naïvely wrote to his mistress—*cretisandum semper cum Cretense*—an art of which Elizabeth herself was the greatest living adept.

At length the Prince arranged a treaty between the States and the Duke of Anjou (August 1578), which made him "defender of the liberty of the Netherlands," bound him to bring 10,000 foot and 2000 horse to the cause, the States finding an equal number. The Duke was not to take part in the civil government, but was to have the first consideration if the sovereignty were changed. And he bound himself to an alliance with the arch-heretics, Elizabeth, Henry of Navarre, and Casimir, son of the Elector Palatine. Had this treaty been honestly observed, it might have been of decisive use. But it was too much to expect that a Valois would treat it as more than a bait.

In the meantime Don John, humiliated, broken in spirit, and abandoned by all, was consumed with rage and fever. His piteous cries to Philip were unnoticed. "Our lives are at stake," he wrote, "and all we hope

now is to lose them with honour." He wasted away for
two months and died on 1st October, having just strength
enough to name Alexander of Parma as his successor.
This powerful and ruthless genius now enters on the
field, and gathering up the complex threads of that most
horrible imbroglio of force and fraud, he succeeded in
beating to pieces the larger and ephemeral fabric of the
Prince's work; and, whilst he could not beat to pieces
his stronger and permanent work in the Northern Provinces, he struck down the Prince himself by the hand
of a fanatical assassin.

CHAPTER XI

THE last years of William's life were years of almost
hopeless struggle to keep united the frail fabric of the
seventeen Provinces of the Netherlands in presence of
a mighty and relentless foe. Vast labour and address
had brought them together in a time of outrageous
oppression ; but they were perpetually torn asunder by
religious hatreds, difference of race, of language, and
tradition, by personal jealousies and party cabals.
Modern history presents no story more pathetic than
the energy, sagacity, ingenuity, and resolution with
which the Prince faced the crisis. If it were ever
given to political genius to ride the storm and to weld
the incompatible, it might have succeeded even now.
As it was, the larger scheme failed, but had an indirect
result : the smaller had a permanent and glorious
success.

The elements of confusion were these. The Protestants of the Northern Provinces, in Ghent and some
other Belgian cities, were seething with fanatical intolerance, and prone to rush into persecution them-

selves. The Catholic Provinces of the South, and especially the official and noble class, however hostile they might be to Spanish oppression, clung to the ascendency of their ancient Church. The Belgian nobles, with the Duke of Aerschot at their head, were secretly jealous of the Prince's authority; they hated his Calvinism; they feared his alliance with the people. The people were the only element where he could find support, or which he could rouse to enthusiasm. And the people of the cities, both North and South, Protestant or Catholic, were constantly a prey to unscrupulous demagogues or foreign adventurers. The Catholic nobles by a secret intrigue brought in the young Archduke Matthias, brother of the Emperor, as a rival at once of Don John and the Prince. The Southern Catholic cities again brought in the Duke of Anjou, brother of the French King, for the same purpose. And the Calvinists on their side brought in John Casimir, son of the Puritan Elector Palatine. They were all mischievous and selfish schemers, without capacity or influence—the Archduke and Anjou without courage or character of any kind. Each of these rivals in turn was courteously welcomed by the Prince, who made them his puppets, checkmated their schemes, used them for his own ends, and politely induced them to withdraw.

Down to the successes of the terrible Prince of Parma, the popularity of Orange with the burghers amounted to extravagance. "They love him, they fear him, they want to make him their master," wrote Don John to Philip. "The people believe in no god but in him," wrote Renon de France. "They welcome him as

the Jews would their Messiah," wrote another Royalist.
The public entries of the Prince into Brussels, Antwerp,
and Ghent were triumphal processions, wherein men
and women flung themselves on their knees before him,
and the citizens formed voluntary guards of honour
around him, and stood sentinel day and night at the
door of his abode.

This popular effervescence was only a part of the
general excitement. The violence of the reformers
was answered by reaction amongst the Catholics. In
Holland the Calvinists instituted persecution of priests
and papists. In each city the local bodies, swayed
from side to side by demagogues and partisans, acted
independently and fell into arbitrary disorder. "There
was nothing," writes the Dutch historian, "but dissen-
sions, jealousies, heart - burnings, hatred; every one
claimed to rule, no one would obey." Dutch, German,
Walloon, and Fleming were in fierce antagonism. The
Northern Provinces tended to a republic. Burgher
juntos gave orders on military affairs to their own
captains, or sullenly refused to admit garrisons to
defend them from Spain. From Brussels Ste. Aldegonde writes that the cause of true religion is strangely
hated and suspected everywhere, and "it seems that
they would rather be ruined without us than saved
with us " (*qu'ils ayment mieulx se perdre sans nous, que
de se sauver avecque nous*). Again he writes to the
Prince—"The malady is deeper than I had supposed "—
"I find here dire confusion in everything"—"On our
side there is neither order, nor money, nor content"—
"Unless your Excellency comes, we are certainly lost."

Well might honest John write to the Landgrave:

"There is gross negligence, rivalry, avarice, and stupidity (*grosze negligentia, aemulatio, geitz, und unverstand*), and great hatred of our evangelical religion"; "Civil war is inevitable : I find few patriots but many priests, raw young gentlemen, and paid officials, greedy of money and advancement, and not a few of them cowardly and spiritless as well." The Landgrave, with his biting way and Ciceronian tags, might well write to John complaining of *privata odia et simultates.* All that had been done by Alva was but *praeludia* to the horrors that were to follow—*omne regnum inter se divisum desolabitur.* "It was all a queer *olla podrida* [*ein seltzamb ollo putrido*"]; "it was a mere *confusum chaos.*" And the French Protestant historian writes : "*Res Belgicae in immensum chaos abire videntur.*"

It was but too true. And around this whirlpool stood hostile and self-interested powers. The German princes hated Catholics and Calvinists alike. The Landgrave was caustic and suspicious; the Elector of Saxony was angry and contemptuous; John of Nassau was honest but wooden. Germany, France, and England would take no part themselves, but they jealously counter-intrigued against each other. Elizabeth changed her tactics from hour to hour ; Anjou and the Valois dreamed of a dominion for themselves. And in front of them all stood the Prince of Parma, with his fierce veterans, his wiles, and his gold, the incarnation of Spanish chivalry and Machiavellian craft.

The revolutionary outbreak of Ghent (October 1577) was most disastrous in its results, and one of those acts of the Prince which it is most difficult to justify. Two nobles of Flanders, demagogues of unscrupulous ambition and bad character, de Ryhove and de Hembyze, at the head of their reforming partisans, seized and imprisoned the Duke of Aerschot, the Governor of Flanders, and several other men of rank and authority. The Duke was undoubtedly the leader of a cabal formed to overthrow the Prince and to suppress the democratic and Protestant movement in Flanders. There can be no doubt that the agitators had the secret sanction of the Prince, who disavowed their action at Brussels, but sent troops to their aid. He induced them to release the Duke after a few weeks' imprisonment, as being a mere weak fool; and then he went himself to Ghent and established some order, practically placing de Hembyze and de Ryhove in power, but making no real effort to have the other reactionaries released. The democratic dictators soon established in Ghent a "calvinist tyranny." They sacked churches and monasteries, suppressed religious orders, and actually burnt alive several monks in the market-place by a Calvinist *auto-da-fé*. They then proceeded to extend this reign of the Saints throughout Flanders. The efforts of the Prince to moderate their violence only succeeded in turning the demagogues into his own worst enemies.

For a time the energetic appeals and action of the Prince effected a temporary lull, but in the following year fresh disorders broke out. De Ryhove murdered two of the prisoners in cold blood; and, under the incitement of de Hembyze and the unfrocked monk Peter Dathenus, the Protestant mobs sacked churches, expelled Catholics, and committed excesses, "as if the whole city had gone mad." Again the Prince came to Ghent, and succeeded in establishing peace, and restoring the

Catholics. A third outbreak in the next year recalled him again to Ghent, where de Hembyze and Dathenus were denouncing him as a papist, a traitor, and an atheist. In a grand message he justified himself to the citizens, and appealed to their patriotism and good sense. A third time he came to Ghent; de Hembyze and Peter, the incendiary monk, hid at his approach. Both were seized and dragged before him. He sternly rebuked them and sent them away unharmed. They fled to John Casimir; and years afterwards de Ryhove caught de Hembyze in manifest treachery, and had him executed. Such were the elements of discord with which the Prince had to deal, and such were the men with whom he was forced to work.

In the clash of these competing bigotries William of Orange strove to enforce mutual toleration by stirring appeals, by indignant rebuke, and by vigorous action. Time after time he drew up and obtained assent to a scheme of religious compromise or peace, on the basis of each party being free to exercise their own worship, subject to conditions to secure public order, and to avoid offence to their opponents. Both Catholic and Reformed communions were to have equal liberty, where either were in sufficient numbers to form a congregation, and were to have separate churches assigned to them. The rites, ornaments, and property of all religious bodies were to be held free from interference, attack, or insult by word or deed. Open-air and tumultuous preaching was forbidden, and everything which could invite strife or wound the conscience of believers in any creed. William now extended this toleration even to Anabaptists, by which his own chief agent was much

scandalised. He obtained assent to a new "Union of
Brussels," destined to prove so evanescent that it has
almost escaped notice. By it Catholics and "Dis-
sentients" bound themselves to protect and help each
other on equal terms against the national foe. His pro-
ject of *A Religious Peace* was formally accepted by many
of the principal cities, but it soon appeared to give a new
ground for discord.

In his zeal for real and complete toleration of creed
William of Orange was in advance of his age by many
centuries. And in this he stood absolutely alone. Some
Catholics could be brought to abstain from persecuting
heretics ; but none could be brought to surrender the
exclusive prerogatives of their own Church. Calvinists
clamoured for protection and freedom, but they all used
both as an engine to suppress Catholicism. Catholics
could only endure Protestant worship in private, and
provided it did not menace the Church ; and in like
manner Protestants, where they were in a clear majority,
strove to get rid of the Church altogether. Not one of
the best and ablest of the Prince's supporters had risen
to his conception of mutual tolerance and respect for
differing faiths. The good John of Nassau would not
endure papistical rites in a Protestant province. Ste.
Aldegonde himself protested against the breadth of the
Prince's charity. The zealots of all creeds held him to
be a Gallio, if not a godless man at heart. To all, his
suffering false belief to exist betrayed a secret proneness
to it in himself. Nay, more ; the formal proclaiming of
full religious freedom roused alarm in all : the Catholic
saw in it the eventful triumph of heresy ; the Protestant
saw in it the prelude to a new persecution.

Thus the codification of a real "Religious Peace," coming on the top of the outrages at Ghent, actually conduced to fresh religious divergence. In the Walloon Provinces abutting on France, there arose a new party of "Malcontents"—a Catholic revolt against the religious compromise or "Pacification of Ghent." By the *Treaty of Arras* (January 1579) the Southern Provinces bound themselves "to maintain the Roman Catholic religion," and practically to submit to Philip. And in the same month the Northern Provinces—Guelderland, Holland, Zeeland, Utrecht, and its districts—formed the *Union of Utrecht*, which bound them to promote the Protestant creed, and practically to abjure allegiance to the King. Here were shattered the Pacification of Ghent, the Perpetual Edict, and the Union of Brussels, and all the other laborious efforts to unite Catholic and Protestant in a national league. The Catholics of the South pledged themselves to the old Church; the Reformers of the North pledged themselves to the Protestant cause; and both to the exclusion of the other. Yet here too, in the dissolution of the larger confederation, lay the germs of the future history of the Netherlands, that contrast of race, religion, language, and institutions which to-day we see in Belgium and Holland.

The Union of Utrecht was essentially the work of John of Nassau, now Governor of Guelderland, and was cast in the mould of his dogged Protestantism and anti-French prejudices. In one sense it was a blow to the Prince's policy, for, professing Calvinist as he was, he never encouraged any attempt to establish a Calvinist ascendency, and for a whole year he had abstained from joining in any public worship, in order to prove his neutral position as a Moderator. He was now sincerely anxious to make use of Anjou, who for the moment had the favour of Elizabeth. For some five months he declined to assent to this new Union, which had taken a form so contrary to his own ideas; and it is difficult to accept the claim of the *Apology* that it was his work, except in a highly indirect and general sense. But, eager for union as he always was, and seeing how hopeless each day was becoming the broader union of all, William, with his invincible genius towards compromise and "opportunism," frankly accepted the narrower Union of Utrecht; he made it his own; and, surrendering his ideal of a great nation to be built up by North and South, by Catholic and Protestant, so as to stretch from the French frontier to the Zuider Zee, he loyally adopted the smaller Union which proved to be the germ of the State of Holland.

He still did not abandon effort to obtain a general settlement; and in this spirit he allowed himself to be informally represented in the negotiations that took place at Cologne in April 1579. The Emperor, Rudolph II., had long desired to act as mediator; Philip and the States, both now exhausted in the long struggle, were equally willing to find a tolerable issue. Accordingly, on the Emperor's invitation, high and mighty commissioners were sent to represent the Empire and the Electors, Philip, the Pope, the States, and indirectly Orange and the Duke of Parma. The Conference lasted for several months and ended in nothing. As was his practice in all such affairs, the Prince began by full and courteous attention to all the propositions made; step by step he drew the envoys on to disclose the utmost limits of concession; he gradually elicited what to them was secondary, what was *sine qua non*. He then, very positively and almost bluntly, laid down his own *ultimatum*—and it was always the same thing, just as he had told Bonte, Leoninus, Requesens, Don John, and Parma. His terms were, identification of his own interest with that of the States, withdrawal of the Spanish soldiery, freedom of worship for all, and solid guarantees. These granted, he was willing himself to quit the Netherlands for ever, and live at peace in Nassau. His policy was subtle, hardly straightforward (if such a word exists in the lexicon of diplomacy), and it was the cause of prodigious waste of patience, paper, and oratory. But to William it was a means of exhausting every conceivable chance; it gained him time and opened to him secrets; and in final result it manifested his own indomitable consistency and constancy.

It is the more instructive and interesting because it is only in recent years that research has discovered at Simancas, in Spanish despatches and translations, the secret negotiations which the Duke of Terranova held with the Prince on behalf of the King. The Duke was quite as much convinced as were Requesens, Granvelle, or Don John, that everything depended on the Prince. He was authorised to offer Orange the release of his eldest son, de Buren, from Spain, the restoration to him of all the honours and estates of his house, and 400,000 ducats to discharge debts—the sole condition was that the Prince should quit the Netherlands.

William allowed these terms to be discussed, and sent Brunynck, his secretary, to Cologne as his plenipotentiary. The commissioners, ducal and episcopal, were fluttered with hope ; Swartzenberg, the Imperial envoy, was offered 20,000 ducats and a command worth 5000 more, if he won over the great rebel.   And after months of negotiation, the Prince calmly sent a despatch (which exists only in a Spanish copy) wherein, after truly Castilian compliments, he declares that he and the States are absolutely at one ; he cannot treat separately; he asks nothing for himself—nothing but to free the land from foreign tyranny ; and he accepts whatever the States accept.   As to the splendid offers of Philip, well, if his son were released from his prison, and he himself were restored to all his offices and estates, if he were reimbursed his outlay in Germany (calculated at 2,000,000 florins), and, all his losses and damages were made good,—and, besides this, *if free worship according to the Protestant ritual were guaranteed in all places where it had been introduced*,—then the Prince would withdraw. The mitred, imperial, and royal deputies broke off in wrath—which is not unnatural.   Terranova abetted a plot to poison the Prince, and the Count Schwartzen-berg, the main agent of the secret overtures, became his enemy for life.   Such is the portion of those who trifle with their friends, even for a great patriotic end.

In the meantime the sleepless Alexander of Parma was winning his way by intrigue and by arms.   The leaders of the Southern Provinces were gained by pro-mises and gold, the masses by fear of his army and sincere devotion to their ancient Church.   Soon the Walloon Provinces were almost entirely reconciled to Spain.   Then swooping down the Meuse, Parma laid siege to Maestricht, below Liège, the gate into Germany. It was a strong and rich town of some 34,000 inhabit-

ants, hardly recovered from the massacre it had suffered
three years before.   It was defended by about one
thousand soldiers, by bodies of trained burghers, and
some thousands of peasants who had taken refuge there.
Parma invested it with a veteran army of 20,000 men,
to which he received reinforcements of about 10,000
more.   He built bridges across the Meuse, above and
below the doomed city, and fortified a complete line of
circumvallation with ramparts and towers.   All that
was heroic and horrible in the sieges and defence of
Haarlem and of Leyden was repeated at Maestricht.
Alexander led his men to the storm again and again,
and left them repulsed and crushed under the walls.
Mines, explosions, cannonades, hand-to-hand conflicts
went on night and day—men, women, and children
joining in the fight.   For four months the townsmen
held out, and slew a large part of Parma's force.   At
last, the weak garrison, worn out by toil, hunger,
wounds, and slaughter, were overpowered in a furious
night assault, and the city was given over to indiscriminate massacre.   Butchery, pillage, and outrage
lasted for three days ; the population was exterminated ;
and Maestricht was reduced to a deserted ruin.

The fall of Maestricht inflicted an almost irreparable
blow on the patriot cause and on the influence of the
Prince.   He had laboured throughout the siege to rouse
the States to the defence; and for the most part he
laboured in vain, for the incurable divisions of party and
of provinces made them slow to succour a town in
Limburg, far to the east.   By desperate efforts he had
raised 7000 men, whom he sent under John and Count
Hohenlohe to raise the siege ; but, when they reached

it, they found Parma entrenched in an impregnable camp
with an overwhelming force, and they were forced to
retire.   In the last extremity, William sent in a message
promising succour, a promise which it was impossible for
him to keep.   Loud outcries were raised about treason,
apathy, blundering, and the Landgrave's agent wrote
home that " people everywhere ceased to trust him, and
thought that the Prince must regret that he had ever
left Holland at all.   He had lost all authority in the
Netherlands, after allowing so many thousands to be
butchered.   He cannot even withdraw with honour ; he
is not safe even in Antwerp, where his popularity is
gone."

One after another, cities, provinces, and chiefs fell
away.   John wrote to Dillenburg that nearly every one
but Lalain had deserted the Prince.   But Lalain, Count
of Rennenburg, one of his stoutest supporters, now made
private terms, and was bought by Spain for money and
a title.   An anonymous letter was sent to the States-
General accusing the Prince of treachery and personal
aims.   William took the letter from the hand of the
clerk, who hesitated to read the libel, calmly read it
aloud to them himself, as if it were an ordinary trifle,
and then he proudly told them that he was ready to
depart from them, if they desired it, and could believe
the calumnies of which he was the butt.   This was one
of the darkest hours of his long agony ; but he still
toiled on, and henceforth he toiled on alone.

And now, the Spanish Cabinet, having finally realised
that the Netherlands could not be crushed whilst Orange
lived, and that no arts and no offers could bend or break
his will, resorted to more systematic ways of compassing

his death.   Years before, Antonio Perez had written to
Don John that he must " finish Orange," if he desired to
satisfy the King.   And now Cardinal Granvelle, whilom
the Prince's mentor, friend, colleague, and rival, kept
urging Philip to offer a reward of 30,000 or 40,000
crowns to deliver the Prince dead or alive.   " The very
fear of it," wrote the deadly prelate, "will paralyse or
kill him."   The King listened to his counsel, wrote to
Parma, by Granvelle's hand, to offer the sum for the
death of *l'homme si pernitieux*, and issued his famous *Ban*,
dated Maestricht, 15th March 1580, which may be thus
condensed.

Philip, by the grace of God, King of Castile, and so forth, etc.,
etc., to all to whom these presents shall come.   Whereas, William
of Nassau, *a foreigner* in our realms, once honoured and promoted
by the late Emperor and by ourselves, has by sinister practices and
arts gained over malcontents, lawless men, insolvents, innovators,
and especially *those who were suspected of religion;* and has instigated these heretics to rebel, to destroy sacred images and churches
and profane the sacraments of God ; and has promoted revolt by a
long series of offences, encouraging the public preaching of heresy,
and persecuting priests, monks, and nuns with a view to exterminate
by impieties our Holy Catholic faith ; whereas he has taken a consecrated nun and abbess in the lifetime of his own lawful wife, and
still lives with her in infamy ; whereas he has been the head of the
rebellion against our sister, the Duchess of Parma, against the
Duke of Alva, and our brother Don John, and still persists in this
treason, refusing all our offers of clemency and peace, and support-
ing the "damnable League of Utrecht"; whereas the country can
have no peace whilst "this wretched hypocrite" troubles it with
his insinuations (as do those whose conscience is ulcered like Cain
or Judas), and, foreigner as he is, puts his whole happiness in ruining our people :
        Now we hereby declare this head and chief author of all the
troubles to be a traitor and miscreant, an enemy of ourselves and
our country.   We interdict all our subjects from holding converse
with him, from supplying him with lodging, food, water, or fire

under pain of our royal indignation. And, in execution of this Declaration, *we empower all and every to seize the person and the goods of this William of Nassau, as enemy of the human race ; and hereby, on the word of a king and as minister of God, we promise to any one who has the heart to free us of this pest, and who will deliver him dead or alive, or take his life, the sum of 25,000 crowns in gold or in estates for himself and his heirs ; we will pardon him any crime if he has been guilty, and give him a patent of nobility, if he be not noble, and we will do the same for all accomplices and agents.* And we shall hold all who shall disobey this order as rebels, and will visit them with pains and penalties. And, lastly, we give command to all our governors to have this Declaration published in all parts of our said Provinces.

In due course the Prince caused to be drawn up and published his reply, the famous *Apology,* his official defence of his whole life and career. The document covers more than one hundred pages of close print. It is rhetorical and diffuse, and apparently modelled on the orations of Cicero by a learned and eloquent scholar. The hand of an ecclesiastical scribe is as evident in it as in the *Ban* itself. It was said to be drawn by de Villiers, an eminent Protestant divine and once an advocate, now William's chaplain. The Prince himself composed the argument throughout, and certainly is responsible for it as a whole.

The Prince of Orange, Count of Nassau and so forth, etc., etc., Lieutenant-General in the Low Countries and Governor of Brabant, Holland, Zeeland, Utrecht, and Friesland, and Admiral thereof, to the States-General Greeting :—

I take it as a signal honour that I am the mark of the cruel and barbarous proscription hurled at me by the Spaniard for undertaking your cause and that of freedom and independence ; and for this I am called traitor, heretic, hypocrite, foreigner, rebel, enemy of the human race, and I am to be killed like a wild beast, with a price offered to my assassins. I am no foreigner here, no rebel, no traitor. My princedom, which I hold in absolute sovereignty, and all my baronies, fiefs, and inheritances in Burgundy, and in

P

the Netherlands, are mine by ancient and indisputable right, and have the sanction of my good friend the late Emperor and the public law of Europe. My ancestors were powerful Lords in the Low Countries, long before the House of Austria set foot therein, and, if need be, I will rehearse the ancient history of the House of Nassau to whom Dukes of Burgundy and the Emperors have owed so much for generations past. So far back as the year 1039 my ancestors were reigning Counts and Dukes in Guelderland for centuries, whilst the ancestors of the King were mere Counts of Hapsburg in Switzerland. King he may be in Spain or Naples, or of the Indies, but we know no King here : we know only Duke or Count—and even our Duke is limited by our ancient privileges, to maintain which Philip has pledged his oath on his accession, though he professes to have been absolved from it by the Pope.

Traitor, he calls me, against my lawful sovereign—he himself deriving his crown through Henry, the bastard, that traitor and rebel against Pedro, his liege lord, his own father's son, whom he killed with his own hand. If Don Pedro were a tyrant, what is Philip ? What was Philip's own ancestor, then a Count of Hapsburg, when he turned his sword against my ancestor, his liege lord Adolphus, the Emperor ? Adulterer, he calls me, who am united in holy matrimony by the ordinances of God's Church to my lawful wife—Philip who married his own niece, who murdered his wife, murdered his own son, and many more, who is notorious for his mistresses and amours, if he did not instigate Cardinal Granvelle to poison the late Emperor Maximilian !

The mischief has all arisen from the cruelty and arrogance of the Spaniard, who thinks he can make slaves of us, as if we were Indians or Italians ; of us who have never been a conquered people, but have accepted a ruler under definite conditions. This is the cancer that we have sought to cauterise. I was bred up a Catholic and a worldling, but the horrible persecution that I witnessed by fire, sword, and water, and the plot to introduce a worse than Spanish Inquisition which I learned from the King of France, made me resolve in my soul to rest not till I had chased from the land these locusts of Spain. I confess that I sought to ally my friends and nobles of the land to resist these horrors, and I glory in that deed. And of the resistance to the tyranny of Spain in all its stages I take the responsibility, for I view with indignation the bloodthirsty cruelties, worse than those of any tyrant of antiquity, which they have inflicted upon the poor people of this land. Has not the King seized my son, a lad at college, and immured him in a cruel prison. Does he not delight in *autos-da-fé?* Did he not order me to kill worthy persons suspected of religion? Never! I say. By fire and sword no cause can be gained (*par les feus et les glaives on n'advance rien*). Did he not send here the monster Alva, who swore eternal hatred to this people, and boasted that he had put to death 18,000 persons innocent of everything but differing from him in religion, a man whose tyranny and cruelty surpass anything recorded in ancient or modern history?

He accuses me of being a demagogue, a flatterer of the people. I confess that I am, and whilst life remains, shall ever be on the popular side (*je suis et serai toute ma vie populaire*), in the sense that I shall maintain your freedom and your privileges. And all the offers that have been made to me, the release of my poor son, the restoration of all my estates and honours, and the discharge of all my debts—I have treated these with scorn, for I will never separate my cause from yours. And equally I spurn his setting a price on my head. Does he think he will frighten me by this, when I know how for years I have been surrounded by his hired assassins and poisoners? Does he think he can ennoble my assassin ; when, if this be the road to nobility in Castile, there is no gentleman in the world, amongst nations who know what is true nobility, who would hold converse with so cowardly a miscreant?

As for myself—would to God that my exile or death could deliver you from the oppression of the Spaniard! How eagerly would I welcome either! For what think you have I sacrificed my whole property, my brothers who were dearer to me than life, my son who was kidnapped from his father; for what do I hold my life in my hand day and night, if it be not that I may buy your freedom with my blood? If you think that my absence or my death can serve you, I am willing. Here is my head, of which no prince or monarch can dispose, but which is yours to devote to the safety of your Republic. If you think that my poor experience and such industry as I have can serve you yet, let us all go forward with one heart and will to complete the defence of this poor people, with the grace of God, which has upheld me so often in dire perplexity and straits, and let us save your wives and your children, and all that you hold dear and sacred.

JE LE MAINTIENDRAI.

CHAPTER XII

AFTER the mortal defiance exchanged between King and Prince by the *Ban* and *Apology*, nothing remained but war to the knife. William formally submitted his defence to the States with an earnest appeal to them offering them his devotion through life. It was adopted with enthusiasm. He thereupon printed the *Apology* in French, Dutch, and Latin, and sent it forth with a really passionate circular letter from himself to the leading princes of Europe (4th February 1581). He evidently desired to show the whole world that he had burnt his ships and meant to fight Spain to the death; for William always had his eloquence under the control of his judgment. But the violence of the *Apology* alarmed some and disgusted others. "Now the Prince is indeed a dead man!" said the cautious Ste. Alde-gonde. Honest John of Nassau shook his head, and the German chiefs grumbled. John at length withdrew from Holland altogether; he married a second wife; and settled down as a patriarch in Nassau. From the Lutherans nothing more could be hoped; they had ceased to take any further part. And this fierce war of words led up to its inevitable result (as William designed it should) — the abjuration of Philip as sovereign of the Netherlands.   Before men's minds could be ready for a step of such unparalleled audacity, they needed a rude awakening out of inveterate tradition.

It is the testimony of Catholic historians, of that age and of ours, that the *Ban* and *Apology* injured the credit of Philip with the Netherlanders and raised that of the Prince.   The sagacity of Parma anticipated this result; Renon de France complains "that the people always side with the oppressed."   And William took advantage of the thrill of indignation caused by these tremendous "Philippics" — (it is his own word) — to press on the abjuration of the King.   Within a few months it was voted by the States of Holland.   And after long debates and urgent appeals from the Prince, the States - General declared their independence, and renounced their allegiance in a memorable Act (26th July 1581).

It was indeed no slight or simple change.   To the traders, it meant confiscation and outlawry in Spanish ports; to the Catholics, it meant Protestant ascendency; to the ordinary citizen, it was a formidable defiance of all the traditions of loyalty and civil society.   It was the first great example of a whole people officially renouncing allegiance to their hereditary and consecrated monarch; and it was by two generations in advance of the English Commonwealth, by two centuries in advance of the American and French Republics.   It was destined to have a crucial influence over the course of modern civilisation.

A prince (they said), is appointed by God to be the shepherd of His people. When he fails in this duty, when he oppresses them, violates their rights, and tramples on their liberties, as if they were slaves, then he is not a prince but a tyrant. And the Estates of the land are then justified in deposing him and placing another on his throne. They rehearsed in formal and moderate language the story of the persecutions and tyrannies they had endured from Philip during twenty years, dwelling mainly on acts of oppression rather than on religious persecution. They then declared the King of Spain deposed from sovereignty over them, and refused to recognise his authority or his officials. And this was clenched by a new Oath, whereby Philip was renounced and *allegiance was transferred to the United Netherlands.*

" *Facinus,*" writes the Jesuit Strada in horror, "*quasi abhorrente animo hactenus supersedi.*" It was, as he truly felt, the knell of absolute, indefeasible monarchy "by the grace of God." And the wrath of Heaven, he adds, was signified by a terrific earthquake (*ingens insolitusque terrae-motus*).

No one knew so well as the Prince that to abjure allegiance to Philip was not enough—that without some protector they were lost. In his own age and in ours he has been reproached for not frankly accepting the sovereignty himself. The States of Holland, a year before, had offered him the Countship of Holland, which he steadily refused. And now he risked his reputation and influence by almost forcing on the United States the sovereignty of a French prince. William refused sovereignty himself for the same reasons and in the same way as Cromwell. He felt that acceptance by him would hopelessly alienate the Catholic and Belgian elements. He did not see the possibility of a Republic. Like Cromwell, he was willing to take on himself the whole responsibility of power; he would not accept the formal titles of sovereignty; yet he felt that a titular sovereign of royal rank was inevitable. He sought for a titular sovereign in the royal House of France; and, in spite of all the follies and falsehood of the Valois, he stuck to the Duke of Anjou with an obstinacy which is part of his character, but is not very easy to explain.

Ample materials exist to show us all that was passing in William's mind in this intricate and tangled problem. He addressed a set of powerfully-reasoned messages to the States-General; he wrote a set of long and intimate letters to his brother John and to others. His reasons are the same in substance throughout. They may be thus condensed.

The condition of the Provinces, after a fierce struggle during twelve years, is almost desperate. A great soldier, with an army of veterans, never yet defeated in the field, is winning back town after town. The Provinces, and even the great cities, act separately, and can scarcely be brought to act as one, even in extreme crises. They have neither generals of experience nor trained soldiers of their own. They can hardly raise money to pay the foreign men-at-arms they need as garrison; and these are continually turning against them, betraying, or plundering them. Religious differences are a constant source of division, suspicion, and intrigue. Philip has at last been abjured; but his place can only be taken by a prince of some great royal house. The Empire, the Dukes of the Rhinelands, England, and France have all been tried and besought in vain. As to the German chiefs, they are all now hopelessly alienated, and are oppressing the Calvinists at home. England might help them now and then as it served her turn. But she has refused to take them under her protection. Without the protection of some great Power, there is nothing before them but anarchy within, and crushing defeat from the sword of Alexander.

There are but three courses to take: (1) submission to Spain, tyranny, and the Inquisition; (2) to fight it out alone; (3) to call in the brother of the King of France. The first they must all reject with indignation to the last gasp of breath. The second is beyond comparison the best, if it were not impossible. Without

men, generals, money, or arsenals, how were the remnant of the
Provinces to contend against the most powerful King in the world,
when, even united, they had been crushed in a series of cruel
defeats? If we had the support of a great Power we could hold
our own till we wore down even Philip of Spain. Thus nothing
remains but the third course, alliance with a French prince.

It is true that Anjou is a Catholic, a foreign adventurer, and
deeply distrusted by our best friends. The House of Valois has a
black record, and the Duke may be as bad as any of his House.
But he is the heir to the throne of France. Henry III. must be
forced to support a cause to which his brother and heir is committed. He, and he alone, could form an effective counterpoise to
Philip. Bad as is the conduct of the French Court, Protestants
have from time to time been protected by Anjou, and still more by
the King of Navarre, the next heir to the Crown. In any case,
France is no such enemy of the Reformation as Spain is and must
ever be. Anjou can bring us a powerful French force, and France
blocks the passage against Philip. To defy France and Spain at
the same time is certain ruin. Anjou may at any moment succeed
to the Crown of France ; he is the accepted suitor of the Queen of
England ; he has supporters in the Empire. His rank and connections might bring us invaluable aid ; and if he seeks to become
a tyrant, we can easily master him. In any case we must muzzle
him, and make him our instrument ; we will never suffer him to
become our master. His exalted rank will attract the waverers,
and will unite the factions and provinces, if any name can do so.
The fact that he is a Catholic is so far a gain that he may win
over our Southern brethren to join us. To forbid Protestants in
the hour of need to seek help from Catholics is rank fanaticism,
repudiated often by most truly religious men. The man who,
on his way to Jericho, fell among robbers and was left for dead,
was succoured by the Samaritan when the priest and Levite passed
by on the other side.

William was under no illusions as to the character of
Anjou. This meanest of his vile race was hideous in
person, depraved in nature, fickle, treacherous, and
grasping. He had abilities and power of fascination.
In spite of his vices, cowardice, and falsehood, the accident of birth had made him a centre of great importance ;

and, in that age of intrigue, change, and counterpoise, men of sense and virtue believed that they could use him to a good end. Henry of Navarre, a keen judge of men and Anjou's deadly enemy, said he was *malin, volage, cauteleux, et déloyal,* no unfair estimate of his whole career. "*Il me trompera bien,*" said the stout Gascon, "*s'il ne trompe tous ceux qui se fieront en luy.*" Orange did not trust him; he was not deceived; in his extremity he clutched at Anjou's name, and believed that he could use him. Her *grenouille,* as Elizabeth called him, was now playing Bottom to the Queen's Titania. And so, like the sagacious Queen, like Ste. Aldegonde, like Burleigh and many more, William of Orange persuaded himself that it was worth while to make a friend even of "false, fleeting, perjured" Francis of Valois, Duke of Anjou and of Alençon.

Overtures had been begun long ago. In 1573, at Blamont, Louis of Nassau reports to the Prince their whispered conference. In 1576, soon after the Union of Delft, William persuaded the States of Holland and Zeeland to offer their sovereignty to Anjou. With the "Peace of Monsieur," their hopes from France rose high. For years negotiations were suspended, renewed, or dropped, as the Emperor, Elizabeth, the German chiefs, or the enthusiasm of the States themselves, alternately grew hot or cold. When Matthias, Casimir, and Don John were all pressing forward after the massacre at Gembloux, in 1578, Anjou came in on the invitation of the Catholics as a counterpoise to the Calvinists. William had not invited him, and did not want him, but he obtained for him the title of "Defender of the Netherlands," used him, checkmated him, and induced him to withdraw. But, after the fall of Maestricht, the Prince took up Anjou in earnest, and pressed on the alliance with singular force and pertinacity, in spite of the warnings of his brother and the German chiefs, and the dogged aversion of Hollanders and Calvinists to a Frenchman and a Valois. As John put it, *non sunt facienda mala, ut eveniant bona.*

Beating down all opposition, the Prince effected the Treaty of Plessis-les-Tours, ratified at Bordeaux (December 1580), whereby Anjou, effectively "muzzled," was to receive the sovereignty of the Netherlands in return for military aid. In the following year he brought an army from France and had some success. Returning from his grotesque suit to Elizabeth, who thrust him on the States with cynical recommendation as *ung aultre soy mesmes*, Anjou was solemnly installed at Antwerp as Duke of Brabant (February 1582). The Prince, however, remained the real sovereign. By a private arrangement, Anjou understood that Holland and Zeeland would accord him nothing but a nominal acceptance. And now again they formally offered the Prince the titular Countship of Holland, which at last William accepted (August 1582). To this act he attached no great importance. It pacified the irritation of the Calvinists, but it was a fresh bar to any hopes of a United Netherlands. He little saw that it was destined to be the root of a dynasty which has grown and flourished for three centuries.

The restless, greedy, insolent Valois now complained bitterly of his treatment. He demanded a civil list of 350,000 florins and the authority of a king. Elizabeth by her own hand warned William not "to torment a prince of such quality and merit." And now the Duke contrived an outrage worthy of a Borgia or a Visconti. He had been installed with gorgeous ceremonies as Count, Duke, and Lord of various Provinces when suddenly he ordered a *coup-de-main* on Antwerp in the midst of entire peace. His French men-at-arms dashed into the city, killed the guard, and charged through the streets, shouting, "Anjou! the Mass! Kill! kill!" The citizens rallied at their own doors, drove out the soldiers, slaying them in heaps. Anjou and his brigands were repulsed. And the "French Fury" remains a monument of treachery and ferocity, surpassing even the "Spanish Fury" in villainy, though not in bloodshed. Part of the plot had been to inveigle and seize the Prince. He escaped this peril, and rushed in to stop the fighting, shouting out that it was a misunderstanding.

Even now the Prince would not give up Anjou, who wrote shameless appeals to William, as did the Queenmother in France, and Elizabeth from England. On a balance of dilemmas, the Prince still held to the last of his three courses, and, in spite of all, thought that France was their best hope. He refused for himself the Dukedom of Brabant, and with incessant labour, and in the teeth of hot remonstrances, he effected a hollow reconciliation with the Duke. "Better have Philip than Anjou!" they cried. "Then kill me at once," replied William. At last the irritation at Antwerp was so fierce that William was personally threatened and insulted as a traitor. He left Antwerp for ever and established himself at Delft. But he succeeded in obtaining the formal acceptance of Anjou, which remained a mere form, as perhaps the Prince had expected. The false Valois, who had more than once plotted against the life of Orange, was now secretly intriguing with Parma. After a few months of futile conspiracy, he retired into France, a physical and moral wreck under mortification and disease. He expired in torment, pouring out blood, and so passes out of history, leaving nothing good but the fact that he thus opened France to the Bourbon.

The obstinacy with which Orange clung to the French alliance, after all the perfidies of Anjou, carried to the utmost limit his maxim of "using what you can get, not what you would like," of keeping all passion out of policy—his habit of inexhaustible patience, compromise, forgiveness, suppressing of resentment, and resorting to the most dangerous instruments in pursuit of a great end and with infinite precaution. He was a man using dynamite in a desperate strait. He felt himself to be treating not so much with the wretched Anjou as with the French Crown. And, before we can condemn his policy, we must thoroughly study his elaborate despatches, both public and private, wherein he justified his course. It served at least to show his sincerity and absence of personal ambition. At any time for years he might have placed on his own brow the coronets which he forced the Provinces to confer upon Anjou— advice which they resented with insult and outrage.

It is not so clear why he did not make more of Henry of Navarre, his wife's cousin-in-blood, unless it be that the Hollanders still looked on Henry as a *frondeur* and a madcap; and during the life of William, the gallant

Gascon was little more than a powerless pretender. Henry himself spoke of William and his cause with lively sympathy, and signed himself to the Prince *vostre plus affectionné Cousin et plus parfaict amys.* It was not until after the death of Orange that Henry became heir to the throne and a great power. Speculation may revel in the thought of a close alliance between William of Orange and Henry of Navarre. Henry might have become perhaps Stadtholder of the Netherlands; but if so, he would never have been King of France.

During all these years it is amazing to contemplate the industry of the Prince and the whirlpool of business in which his life was passed, as we review the documents preserved in the archives of Holland and Belgium, Paris and London. They combine all conceivable details of diplomacy, administration, and war. Negotiations, both public and secret, are carried on simultaneously with various courts, statesmen, and agents. Incessant appeals to the States for unity, energy, moderation, and courage are mingled with minute and intricate directions to local officials, and these with orders to officers on land and sea. On a casual scrap we may see memoranda for dealing with twenty questions of urgency awaiting decision. What about those ships in Zeeland? —about the artillery from Brussels?—what instructions for Ste. Aldegonde? What as to the fortifications at Muide? Is papistry to be tolerated in Zierikzee? For years the Prince remains the sole arbiter of all things ecclesiastical and civil, military and diplomatic, financial and judicial. He was like a man, he said, sitting on a stool with one leg broken off; if he inclined to one side

or other, he must fall down. And all this mass of business had to be settled in the midst of a ferocious and
invincible foe, discord in each province, the outrages of
Catholic zealots in one town and of Protestant fanatics
in another town, demagogic faction, foreign intrigue,
local animosities, the desertion of friends and hired
assassins. When William, Count de Berghes, another
brother-in-law, turned traitor, and with his sons enlisted
under Parma, the Prince drank to the dregs the cup of
bitterness. He might well take as his device—*saevis
tranquillus in undis.*

And now the *Ban* began to work in earnest. From
the Rhine to the Tagus, avarice, fanaticism, and ambition were stirring the secret thoughts of wild men.
Gold, heaven, and nobility were all to be won by a bold
stroke. From kings, generals, and prelates came words
of encouragement; and priests blessed the weapon
suggested by the deadly Cardinal. For ten years
William had been dogged by assassins—French, Scotch,
Spanish, German, Flemish had all tried at the instiga-
tion first of Alva, then of Requesens, of Parma, Mendoza,
Terranova, and other grandees of Spain—and all
attempts had failed. The dagger, the pistol, poison,
explosion—none hit the mark. At length an elaborate
conspiracy almost succeeded. A Spanish official at
Lisbon obtained from Philip a promise of 80,000 ducats
for the Prince's death; he entered into correspondence
with one Añastro, a bankrupt Spanish merchant at
Antwerp. The merchant induced his clerks, Jaureguy
and Venero, both young Biscayans, to undertake the
murder. Timmermann, a Dominican monk, gave
Jaureguy absolution, the sacrament, and a blessing.

The lad, armed with a pistol, and protected by an *Agnus Dei*, a Jesuit catechism, a holy taper, and a charmed toad-skin, heard mass devoutly, and then forced himself into the hall at Antwerp, where the Prince was dining in public according to custom.   He was thrust out, but hung about the door, pretending to be a suppliant.   As William passed forth, Jaureguy presented a petition, and placing his pistol close to the Prince's face, shot him through the neck, the palate, and the cheek.   The assassin was instantly pierced with scores of swords and halberds.   The Prince fell, calling out, "Do not kill him !—I forgive him my death."

The plot was thought to come from Anjou and the French ; but young Maurice, then barely fifteen, closed the house doors, searched the dead assassin, found the conspiracy to be Spanish, and arrested Venero and Timmermann the priest.   Añastro escaped and ran off to claim the reward.   Anjou burst into tears and sobbed for half an hour, swearing that he had lost a father. The Prince was carried to bed, the blood was stanched, and he prepared for his end.   To the burgomaster he said, " If it please God, in whose hand I am, to take me, I submit with patience to His will.   I commend to your care my wife and children."   To his chaplain, de Villiers, he said, " Will God pardon all the blood spilled in these years ?   I put my trust in His mercy.   In His mercy alone can be my salvation ! "

His fine constitution and serenity of nature saved his life, which hung upon a thread for weeks.   They could not stop the bleeding, as pressure choked the breathing; and when the wound was healing, a fresh hemorrhage broke out, which was at length stopped by

the continuous pressure of attendants' thumbs on the
vein, maintained by relays night and day. He lost
forty ounces of blood; but in six weeks he was well.
He had lain motionless and speechless, calm and thoughtful, writing his last instructions on tablets. His great
anxiety was to clear the French Prince and his people,
to appease the excitement in the city, and to confirm
them in the alliance with Anjou. When Venero and
Timmermann were condemned to death, the Prince wrote
from his bed to spare them torture—

I have heard that to-morrow they are to execute the two
prisoners, the accomplices of him who shot me. For my part, I
most willingly pardon them. If they are thought deserving of
a signal and severe penalty, I beg the magistrates not to put
them to torture, but to give them a speedy death, if they have
merited this. Good-night!

William survived: the shock killed his wife.
Charlotte de Bourbon, rushing forward at the sound
of the shot, swooned and fell from one fit of fainting
into another, until she calmed herself sufficiently to
tend her wounded husband. The second hemorrhage,
with its agony of suspense, brought on fresh convulsions,
which exhausted the remaining strength of a mother
with a baby of three months. She wrote to her brother a
last letter full of affection and meek devotion. Three days
after her husband had attended a solemn thanksgiving
on his recovery, Charlotte expired at the age of thirty-
five (5th May 1582). Her end was soothed with
evangelical piety and Christian resignation. Just before
the birth of her last child she had made a careful will, full
of devout expressions, with gifts of personal ornaments,
and mementoes to all her children, relations, and house-

hold.   And she left to all who had known her the memory of a fine and loving nature endowed with conspicuous dignity and charm.

The married life of Charlotte de Bourbon, of less than seven years, had been one of complete happiness and of noble example.   William had given her his whole confidence, and trusted her with most important duties. Her letters to him, to her father and her brother, to her mother-in-law, and to her step-children, are beautiful models of thoughtfulness, good sense, and affection. With loving persistence she at last overcame the anger of her father ; and before her death she was reconciled to him, and to all who had so bitterly resented the marriage.   She 'left William six daughters, all of whom had an eventful history, which is fully stated in Appendix A.

Louisa Juliana, named after Charlotte's father and William's mother, married Frederick IV., Elector Palatine, and became the grandmother of Prince Rupert and the Electress Sophia, and thus the ancestress of the reigning houses of England, Prussia, Austria, Russia, Italy, and Spain, and also of many men and women famous in history.   Elizabeth, god - daughter of our virgin Queen, married the Duc de Bouillon, and became ancestress of that famous House, and mother of Marshal Turenne.   Catherine Belgia, born at the height of the Prince's fortunes, had for sponsors William's sister and the States-General.   She married the Count of Hanau-Münzenberg.   Charlotte Flandrina, the god-daughter of the States of Flanders, was sent as an infant to her cousin, the Abbess of Paraclete. She was brought up, on her mother's death, by her

Catholic relations, and died Abbess of Poitiers. Another Charlotte, named Brabantina by her sponsors, the States of Brabant, married the Duc de Tremoïlle, and became ancestress of that illustrious race; she was mother of the heroic Countess of Derby, who, fighting with her cousin Prince Rupert, defended Lathom House in our Civil Wars. Lastly, Emilia, called Antwerpiana, from her sponsors, the magistrates of Antwerp, married Frederick Casimir, Count Palatine of Zweibrücken. Amidst the profound sorrow of her husband and splendid honours from his people, Charlotte de Bourbon, after her romantic and crowded life, was laid to rest; and for centuries her descendants filled many a stirring page in the annals of Europe.

The marriage with Charlotte, for which William had fought so obstinately against a torrent of opposition, brought him a domestic life of perfect love and singular charm. It is rare that a statesman, whose life was a series of desperate struggles, has left behind him such touching memorials of domestic virtue. He was a man of keen sympathies and thirst for sympathy, of steadfast fidelity and expansive heart. In his noble letters to his saintly mother, to his brothers Louis and John, to Charlotte, he pours out his inmost thoughts, his hopes, anxieties, and prayers. They breathe a deep personal communion with his God, without a trace of preference for any creed, doctrine, or Church. His letters to all his relatives and friends, his dealings with his family and dependants, are stamped with affection, forethought, judgment, and indulgence. He was the father, master, and judge not only of his own children, but of his family and relations for many degrees. And his children were worthy of their father. The young Maurice had already begun to show his mastery and his genius (*divinum ingenium*, said his tutor). Marie, the eldest daughter, now twenty-six, became a second mother to her motherless sisters. Even the captive Philip of Buren had the grace to kill in a fit of passion a villain who traduced his father. Few great rulers of men have ever known more profoundly than William the Silent how the love of wife, mother, brother, sister, daughter, son, and friends can sustain in peace a life that to the world without was one long crisis of battle, agony, and toil.

CHAPTER XIII

WILLIAM, who had been a widower nearly a year, now contracted a fourth marriage; and again he chose an illustrious French Protestant, with whose family he had long had intimate relations, both public and private. Louise de Coligny was the eldest daughter of the famous admiral, and had been married in extreme youth to his beloved comrade, the gallant Charles de Téligny. In the awful night of St. Bartholomew she witnessed the massacre of her father and her husband; the bride, but just seventeen, escaped imminent death, fled to Savoy, where she was cruelly treated, and at length returned to France. For eleven years she lived a widow in mourning and close retirement. She then accepted the Prince of Orange as her second husband, and they were quietly married at Antwerp on 12th April 1583: she being twenty-eight, and he just fifty years old. They had not met since her widowhood. Thus a second time William married a lady of eminent character and mature age, whom he had not seen for many years.

Louise de Coligny was one of the noblest women of

her time, worthy of her father and her noble race, worthy of her husband, the devoted helpmeet of William, the able counsellor and guide of her stepson and of her own son, successive Princes of Orange. Contemporary portraits preserve for us the refined and beautiful face, so full of intellect, energy, and courage. Documents, letters, anecdotes in abundance, testify to the graces and force of her character; nor did these fail her in all the crises of her tragic and illustrious life. She was destined to a great part in the long struggle for independence which she witnessed for nearly forty years, and she became the ancestress of a long line of Princes of Orange and of the reigning families of Holland, of Prussia, and of Russia.

The grace, tenderness, and wisdom of Louise soon won the affection of her numerous step-children by three mothers, of John her brother-in-law and his children, and indeed of all around her. In January 1584 her only son was born, and was christened Frederick Henry after his godfathers, the King of Denmark and the King of Navarre. He was destined to succeed his two half-brothers as Prince of Orange; on the death of Maurice in 1625 he was for twenty-two years also Stadtholder of the United Provinces; and after a long and glorious career he practically established the freedom and power of the United Provinces. As neither Philip-William, nor Maurice, the only other sons of William, left any descendants, it is through this child of Louise de Coligny, the late-born son of his old age, that William the Silent transmitted his name and title to our own William III., and to the line of the House of Orange.

Absorbed in unending labours, bowed down by disasters, but happy in the midst of his family, William was living in the old convent which had been given him as a residence in Delft. The priory of St. Agatha stands on the long canal and shady quay called the *Oude Delft*, just opposite the Old Church. It is a modest brick edifice built in a quadrangle round a courtyard, with a large inner dining-hall, reached by a dark winding staircase. Since he had made it his home, it had been called, and is still known as the *Prinsenhof*. It has recently been made a national memorial, and there are collected portraits, engravings, arms, and relics of the Founder of Dutch Independence. The old town of Delft, with its picturesque walls, its spires, turrets, its gateways and towers, with its sluggish canals winding along beneath avenues of trees, with its churches and mansions in the quaint fashions of the fifteenth and sixteenth century, still remains little altered by time, and is the very ideal of the quiet, industrious, and thriving Dutch town.

In habits, in outward form, and in heart, William was deeply changed from the magnificent grandee on whose youth the Emperor had lavished his favour. In the modest and somewhat makeshift residence of a provincial Governor the Prince lived a simple and domestic life, open to all, and too deeply absorbed in work to give any thought to the outward man. His shabby dress, said an English courtier, with a loose old gown and a woollen vest showing through an un- buttoned doublet, was that of a poor student or a water- man, and he freely consorted with the burgesses of that beer-brewing town. Yet, in conversing with him, our fine gentleman admits *there was an outward passage of inward greatness.* Now, at the age of fifty-one he was bald, worn with wrinkles, and furrowed with ague and with sorrows; the mouth seems locked with iron, the deep-set watchful eyes, the look of strain and anxiety, give the air of a man at bay, who has staked his life and his life's-work (see App. B).

He was overwhelmed with debt, and often in actual need of necessaries. Ten years afterwards, his liabilities to his brother John were stated at 1,400,000 florins. On his death he had not a hundred guilders in cash; and his plate, clothes, and effects were sold to satisfy his creditors. His wife, for whom on her bridal entrance into Delft nothing better could be found than a rude country cart, wrote piteously on his death to John describing her forlorn and destitute state. Yet no man could bear reverse of fortune and incessant anxieties with an air more cheerful and calm. In spite of his most paradoxical surname, William was all his life, and never more so than at its closing hours, one of the most affable and gracious of men, brilliant in speech, and famous for his charm of manner. It was said of him "that every time he put off his hat, he won a subject from the King of Spain." He enjoyed the frugal meal with his family around him, whom he cheered with a flow of lively conversation. The history of those times has no more fascinating picture than that of the weary politician seeking rest from a thousand complications of state, in a family circle of his wife, sister, sons and daughters, nephews and nieces—the young people of various ages, from Marie, now twenty-eight, and seven other daughters from fifteen to three years old, down to the boy baby of just five months. There the Prince seemed to find repose and safety. No man could pass the gates of the town unchallenged, nor could he enter the door of the Prinsenhof unnoticed by the guards and sentries.

It was now two years since the failure of Jaureguy's attempted assassination and the execution of his confederates, and during that time incessant plots were being made with the knowledge of Parma and other agents of Philip to carry off his arch-enemy. The dagger, the pistol, and poison were all proposed. The assassins as yet had all failed. Either their courage gave way, or they were betrayed, or were caught and executed, or else they turned traitors and revealed the plot. The Prince received constant warnings, nor did he at all neglect them. But now appeared an assassin of a different type. Balthazar Gérard was a young Burgundian, small, mean, and feeble, sinister in aspect, a fervent Catholic, and a devoted servant of the Spanish Crown. From boyhood he had nourished a fanatical desire to be the instrument of freeing the world of the arch-heretic and master-rebel. When the royal *Ban* was issued against the Prince, Balthazar went to Luxemburg to carry out his design. There he heard that "a gentle Biscayan," as he called Jaureguy, had already murdered William; he thanked God, and entered the service of Marshal Mansfeldt.

On learning that the Prince had recovered from his desperate wound, Balthazar resumed his design. He communicated it to the Prince of Parma, who wrote to Philip that he did not think him a man who promised well for an enterprise of such importance,—*toutes fois je le laissay aller.* The assassin was then encouraged by Councillor Assonleville, and by his own confessor, who promised to remember him in his prayers. He reached Delft; and taking the name of François Guion, he succeeded in winning the confidence of the Prince's people by means of some seals which he had purloined from Count Mansfeldt, and by a story of persecution for the reformed religion of which he declared he was the victim. Finally, as bearer of a despatch to the Prince announcing the death of the Duc d'Anjou, he was introduced alone into the room where the Prince was in bed. Having no weapon, he could no' nothing. He still hung about the Prinsenhof, professing fervent devotion to the Calvinist faith, borrowed a Bible, and begged for help by way of charity. Thereupon the Prince ordered twelve crowns to be given him. With these he bought pistols from one of the men on guard. This poor fellow who sold them hanged himself when the deed was done.

On 10th July 1584 the Prince dined with his family in the hall which is now hung with his portraits and various relics. His wife, his sister, and three of his daughters were there, and one or two persons were admitted on business. William left the room and had just reached the circular staircase when Balthazar, who had posted himself in a dark corner, drew his pistol and fired three balls right into the Prince's breast. It is related that he just murmured the words : "My God, have pity on my soul! My God, have pity on this poor people !" He was caught as he fell by an attendant, laid on a couch, commended his soul unto Jesus Christ in a word whispered to his sister, and breathed his last.

The assassin was pursued and caught. The soul of fire, in the mean and ill-favoured frame of the fanatic, blazed out with a superhuman courage and self-sacrifice, which made him a hero and a martyr in the whole Catholic world. He gloried in the deed, and made a full confession. For four days he endured the most revolting torments which the ingenuity of demons could devise, and he was put to death with a horrible barbarity which disgraced his executioners and not a little sullied the cause of his victim. All this Balthazar bore without a murmur, and with a stoical endurance which his tormentors held to be witchcraft, and his patrons held to be the inspiration of Heaven. The history of William the Silent need not be defaced by rehearsing the atrocities with which his murder was avenged—atrocities against which his whole life was an enduring protest. Cardinal Granvelle and the Prince of Parma expressed delight in the murder, and begged that the murderer should be rewarded. Philip grumbled that it had not been done before; but "better late than never," he wrote; and he publicly declared that "by an act of great valour Gérard had performed an exploit of supreme value to all Christendom." Philip, however, was not the man to pay the 25,000 crowns he had formally promised; but in lieu of money he issued a patent of nobility to the family, exempted them from taxes, and settled on them *certain estates that belonged to the Prince. And when these estates were at last restored to his son, they were charged with annuities to the murderer's family.*

William was buried with great pomp in the town of Delft, his son Maurice being chief mourner, and a magnificent mausoleum was raised in the New Church in the Great Market. There lie also Louise de Coligny, Maurice, and the princes of the House of Orange, to whom has been added in our own day the remains of the last Prince of Orange-Châlons. The effigy of William in marble lies surrounded by a canopy, beneath which are the four emblematical figures of Freedom, Justice, Prudence, and Religion, with the mottoes, *je maintiendrai piété et justice—saevis tranquillus in undis*. And in this case, neither emblems nor mottoes are conventional untruths.

William died in one of the darkest hours of the long struggle that for twenty years he had waged against the power of Spain. The consummate genius of Parma, both in policy and war, handling his splendid veterans, and making lavish use of promises and gold, was steadily winning back the Catholic and Southern Provinces. Before the Prince's murder, nearly all of them were lost to the Union; and Flanders and Brabant were on the verge of surrender. Bruges and Ghent soon gave way; Brussels and Antwerp and the other cities of Brabant followed in the next year. With the loss of Antwerp, the key of the Scheldt, the fate of the Catholic and Flemish Provinces was finally determined. Nor is there any reason to think that the genius and tenacity of William could have changed the issue. The whole of their subsequent history for three centuries down to our own day remains to prove that permanent union between the Dutch and Belgian races cannot be maintained,—that Flanders, Brabant, Hainault, and Namur will neither ally with, nor submit to, a Calvinist, bourgeois, maritime

Republic. To-day these Gallicised Provinces are the strongholds in Northern Europe of ultramontane Catholicism and conservative zeal. Nor could all the resource of William and the heroism of Holland have long preserved them from submitting in the end to their historic Church and their ancestral lords.

Then, was the whole of William's policy since the Union of Delft, the last eight years of his career, but labour in vain, a struggle after the impracticable, an attempt to construct an imposing edifice on sand? Not so. The toils, the agonies, the triumphs, of the effort to save Belgium from Spain during the Prince's lifetime, and all those which followed for long years after his death, served a real end, though that end was not the permanent union of the seventeen Provinces. It gave strength, self-confidence, and time to the seven Protestant Provinces of the North to consolidate their union; and it ultimately enabled the ten Catholic Provinces of the South to obtain such a modified scheme of rule as that which the tyrant conceded at last. The long struggle, whilst it created the Dutch nation, saved the Catholic Netherlands from being crushed into a mere outlying fragment of Spain.

Could William by any ingenuity of compromise have effected a permanent union of the two creeds, as Elizabeth of England secured a settlement which was neither Catholic nor Calvinist, as Henry of Navarre ultimately closed civil war by a free-and-easy conversion to a faith which was neither that of Philip nor that of the Colignys? He could not. His difficulties ran deeper than those of Elizabeth or those of Navarre. The indelible features of race, language, religion, and temperament which divided the seven United Provinces from the Southern Netherlands were far too clearly cut to make any compromise conceivable. William, a man far more deeply religious in heart than Elizabeth or Henry, was incapable of the cynical imperiousness of the Tudor Queen, or of the cynical humour of the jolly Béarnais. He was forced to make a choice between the Vatican and Geneva. He chose Geneva as the creed of the toughest, truest-hearted, more defensible section of the Netherland peoples, albeit far the smaller, poorer, and more modest section. He chose them, and he stuck to them; and his choice has been ratified by their history from his day to the day of Wilhelmina, the girl-queen.

It was in vain for him in writing, in speech, in act, to labour for mutual toleration, Christian fellowship, and national union,—things of which he alone in that age had conceived the beauty and the force. "The difference," he kept on repeating in his large way, perhaps his somewhat too philosophic way, " *the difference is not enough to keep you apart!* " It was enough, and more than enough. And in this matter his error, his noble error, was this, that his serene vision of spiritual fellowship in humanity—a vision which was opened to him alone amongst the men of thought and the men of action in his age—blinded him, more than a statesman should be blinded, to the madness and theological bigotries in the midst of which his work was cast. With all his profound insight, he did not quite understand that the Netherlands formed not one nation, one religion, one race, but two, and even more; and that differences in these things go deeper down than the most obvious claims of safety, prosperity, and peace. But, battling in vain to make these nations one, he and his in the end did make Holland indestructible and great, and did enable Belgium to become at last both prosperous and contented.

The greater union of seventeen provinces for which he struggled for twenty years against hope, against fate, which he had seen, for a short space, as a real and promising fact, this greater union died with him, and it was dying of itself in the last year of his life. But the lesser and more vigorous union of the seven Provinces of the North grew and flourished beyond his utmost dreams, till for a time it rose to be an Empire. The murder of their chief filled the Dutch people with rage and desire of revenge, but not with dismay. Elizabeth's English agents wrote home "that the wickedness of the deed hath hardened their stomachs to hold out as long as they have any means of defence"; "it had animated them with a great resolution of courage and hatred engraved in them, . . . to defend their liberties to the uttermost portion of their substance, and the last drop of their blood." And on the very day of the murder, the Estates of Holland resolved "to maintain the good cause, with God's help, to the uttermost, without sparing gold or blood." They kept their word, and under the sons of William, successive Princes of Orange, and Stadtholders of Holland, they carried on a successful struggle for some sixty-four years more. Heroism might make possible the final triumph of Holland, but genius itself could as little foresee it in the hour of Parma's victory, as it could fathom the approaching decadence of Spain.

This decisive battle for national independence was not only the earliest, but it was the most prolonged, and the most desperate of all the revolutions of which it was the prelude. It was the first example on a great scale of a people defying an alien oppressor, and founding a free commonwealth in the teeth of a mighty despotism. It directly inspired the Revolution in England of the seventeenth century, as also that in America of the eighteenth century; and, by its intellectual influences, it indirectly contributed to the Revolution in France. In the lifetime of "Father William's" youngest son and successor, Holland became the home of spiritual and political freedom—an asylum wherein were nurtured seeds of priceless value to the civilisation, policy, and thought of Europe. And this may solve the apparent paradox that a statesman whose whole career was an almost unbroken chain of humiliation, failure, and defeat conferred immortal services on after ages of mankind. The blood of the martyrs is the seed, not only of the Church, but of the State.

The malignity of sect has even ventured to accuse the great Stadtholder of personal ambition, and the echoes of this scurrility linger in some who in our own day call themselves historians of truth. Unscrupulous ambition did indeed stain the career of William's descendants and successors. But as to William the Silent, it is a more difficult task to defend his memory from the charge of being backward to assume the manifest headship into which he was forced by events and by his people. Should he not have urged from the first the repudiation of the Spanish Crown? Was he right to have toiled for twelve years, by a thousand schemes, and in spite of rebuffs, failure, and treachery, to find a protector for his country in some foreign prince

—German, Austrian, French, or English? Was he not infatuated in clinging to the last to the fickle and treacherous Anjou? Should he not early have accepted the sovereignty in name as well as in fact? Should he not have recognised at once how hopeless was the effort to drive out of Belgium the House of Hapsburg and the creed of Rome? Should he not, quite early in the struggle, and at least at the Union of Delft, have concentrated the defence upon Holland, and had himself boldly proclaimed its Sovereign Lord and Count? These are all questions most complex and obscure, which from the vantage-ground of three centuries of subsequent history we may now attempt to solve.

William was himself a sovereign Prince, the heir of two ancient ruling houses, and had been brought up from boyhood in the Cabinet of Charles V., where he had seen how traditions of loyalty and king-craft sufficed to hold nations together in that age of confusion, re-settlement, and new birth, in the throes of civil and religious wars. By temperament, conviction, and training, William was saturated with the ideas of the ruling caste, and with respect for hereditary rights and duties as the foundation of social order. There had been no large or recent example in Europe of a nation defying their lawful sovereign, much less of their founding anew a free independent commonwealth. All this coloured the early career of the Prince; but at last, having exhausted every possible scheme to avoid this issue, he resolutely accepted it as final.

A royal personage, as foreign protector, always meant the open or secret assistance of some foreign power, whether German, or Imperial, or French, or English.

As a fact, the various protectorates towards which the Prince laboured—even the offer of them—did bring help to the cause in some form, direct or indirect, material or moral. He was no doubt right in believing that the open or veiled assistance of one of the great powers, when the German Lutherans so cruelly abandoned the Calvinists of Holland, was absolutely indispensable to successful defence. He was certainly right in looking to France as his best friend, and in parading his hopes from France as a means of procuring help from the rest. In the issue the United Provinces gained more from France than from Germany, Austria, or England. And had the knife of Jacques Clément struck earlier home, had the bullet of Balthazar Gérard failed to strike at all, had William of Orange and Henry of Navarre lived to act together as allied sovereigns, great things might have been seen in the Netherlands and in Europe. William stuck to the wretched Anjou with perhaps culpable tenacity. As they died within a few weeks of each other we have no means of knowing what William's course would have been with Henry of Navarre, heir to the French throne. He could not be expected to look forward for a hundred years when, in a transformed Europe and with a decadent Spain, Holland would be engaged in a death-grapple with Louis XIV.

As to the sovereign title, had it been claimed by the Calvinist William, and he but one of the vassal counts of the Netherlands, it would have involved the instant defection of the whole Belgic Provinces—now predominantly Catholic and full of chiefs who regarded themselves as his peer, and his ascendency with jealousy and scorn. He who was Count of Nassau on the Lahn, and titular

R

Prince of Orange on the Rhone, was in Brabant a mere Baron of Breda; and for such an one to claim the splendid succession of the great House of Burgundy in the Netherlands was simply to abandon all prospect of union between the seventeen Provinces at all. William therefore abstained, and wisely abstained, from any suggestion that he looked to be titular Prince of the entire Netherlands, though he fully and frankly accepted the real and paramount authority.

Long before his death he saw that even this was not possible or lasting. And slowly, reluctantly, and with reserve he accepted the simple Countship of Holland, which in effect was to fall back on the seven Northern Provinces, and to take up for himself and his successors the sovereign rule. At last—almost, as it were, with his dying breath—he recognised the logic of events, founded the smaller nation which for three centuries has had so glorious a history, and transmitted to his descendants under various titles, and with some rude intervals of break, the throne of Holland, which the young Queen now fills amidst the devotion of her own people, and the cordial friendship of the Powers of Europe.

Gloomy as were the prospects of William's family as they followed his body to the tomb in the great church of Delft, the future had in store for them much that was beyond all hope in the dark hour of their bereavement. The forlorn widow, left destitute in a strange land with her infant of hardly six months and ten young step-children, the only son a lad at college, bravely set herself to her overwhelming task. For thirty-six years more she lived, toiled, protected, and guided that large household, a pattern of all wisdom, goodness, and grace.

She lived to see and to be the help of her stepson
Maurice, and of her own son Frederick Henry, as they
carried on heroically to triumphant issue the work of
their slaughtered father—both amongst the foremost
soldiers and statesmen of their time. She married eight
out of the nine daughters of the Prince into the most
illustrious houses of Europe, Charlotte Brabantina alone
remaining unmarried as the Catholic Abbess of Poitiers.
Philip William, the kidnapped and perverted son of the
Prince, ultimately returned to his native land, and was
partly reconciled to the family from which he had
been alienated so long. And to-day the nation which
William founded by his sweat and blood three centuries
ago is flourishing and honoured; his granddaughter in
the eleventh degree sits on the throne of Holland; the
blood of the greatest of the Nassaus runs in the veins of
almost every royal house in Europe; and amongst his
descendants may be counted for three centuries some of
the most valiant soldiers and some of the ablest chiefs
whose deeds adorn the history of Europe (see App. A).

APPENDIX A

The Family of William the Silent

William I., *b.* 25th April 1533, eldest of twelve children of William the Rich, Count of Nassau-Dillenburg, and Juliana von Stolberg-Wernigerode. Prince of Orange by devise, 1544. Killed, 10th July 1584. He married four wives—

1. Anne of Egmont, daughter of Maximilian, Count of Buren, etc.; *m.* 6th July 1551 ; *d.* 24th March 1558.
   She left one son and one daughter.
2. Anne of Saxony, daughter of Maurice, Duke and Elector of Saxony ; *b.* 23rd April 1544 ; *m.* 2nd June 1561 ; repudiated, 1571 ; *d.* 18th December 1577.
   She left one son and two daughters surviving.
3. Charlotte de Bourbon, daughter of Louis, Duc de Montpensier ; *b.* 1547 ; *m.* 12th June 1575 ; *d.* 5th May 1582.
   She left six daughters.
4. Louise de Coligny, daughter of Gaspard de Coligny, Admiral of France ; *b.* 28th September 1555 ; widow of Charles de Téligny, August 1572; *m.* Prince of Orange, 12th April 1583 ; *d.* October 1620.
   She left one son.

William the Silent, at his death in 1584, left twelve children by his four marriages, of ages from thirty to five months—three sons, who all became in succession Princes of Orange, and nine daughters—three other children having died in infancy.

Sons of William the Silent

I. Philip William (by Anne of Egmont), *b.* 1554, Count of Buren ; *m.* Eleanor, daughter of Henri, Prince of Condé, of the royal House of Bourbon. This Henri was cousin and comrade of Henri IV., King of Navarre and France, and was grandfather of the great Condé. Eleanor was a distant cousin of Charlotte de Bourbon, the Prince's third wife. Philip William became Prince of Orange in 1584.
d. 1618 without leaving issue.

II. MAURICE (by Anne of Saxony), *b.* 14th November 1567, Count of Nassau. Prince of Orange, 1618, on death of his half-brother, Philip William.

    d. 23rd April 1625, unmarried and without legitimate issue.

III. FREDERICK HENRY (by Louise de Coligny), *b.* 29th January 1584, Count of Nassau ; became Prince of Orange, 1625, on death of his half-brother, Maurice.   .

    m. Emilia of Solms-Braunsfeld, 1625 ; he *d.* 1647.

Frederick Henry (sometimes called Henry Frederick), by his wife Emilia, had nine children, of whom one son and four daughters married and left descendants.

  1. William II., Prince of Orange, and Stadtholder of Holland ; *b.* 1626 ; *d. (œtat.* 24) 1650.

He married Mary, daughter of Charles I., King of England. Their son, William III., *b.* 1650, Prince of Orange and Stadtholder of Holland, *m.* his first cousin Mary, daughter of James II., and was King of England, 1689-1702.

They had no issue, and the male line of descent from William the Silent then came to an end.   .

Thereupon the headship of the House of Orange-Nassau was settled on John William Friso, whose grandfather, William Frederick of Nassau, a grandson of John of Nassau, had married Albertina Agnes, granddaughter of William the Silent. From them descends the royal family of the Netherlands.

DAUGHTERS OF FREDERICK HENRY

1. Louisa Henrietta, *m.* Elector of Brandenburg.
2. Albertina Agnes, *m.* William Frederick, Count of Nassau-Dietz.
3. Henrietta Catherine, *m.* John George II., Prince of Anhalt-Dessau.
4. Marie, *m.* Louis Henry, Count Palatine of Zimmern.

DESCENDANTS OF DAUGHTERS OF FREDERICK HENRY, PRINCE OF ORANGE

I. LOUISA HENRIETTA, *b.* 1627 ; *d.* 1667.

    "Excellent Louisa ; Princess full of beautiful piety, good sense, and affection ; a touch of the Nassau-heroic in her" (Carlyle, *Friedrich II.* vol. i. 364-367).

She married 1646, Frederick William of Brandenburg, the Great Elector, who *d.* 1688.

This Great Elector was the son of Elizabeth Charlotte, daughter of Frederick IV., Elector Palatine, by Louisa Juliana, eldest daughter of William the Silent and Charlotte de Bourbon.

Thus the Great Elector, a great-grandson of William the Silent through his daughter Louisa, married Louisa Henrietta, a granddaughter of William the Silent through his son, Frederick Henry.

From them the royal House of Hohenzollern of Brandenburg combines these two lines of descent from the Prince.

> Frederick I., the first King of Prussia (1701, *d.* 1713), married his second cousin, Sophia Charlotte, sister of George I. of England, and daughter of the Electress Sophia of Hanover, who was a granddaughter of Louisa Juliana, eldest daughter of William the Silent by Charlotte de Bourbon.
>
> > The son of Frederick I., King of Prussia, was Frederick William I., King of Prussia (1713-40). He married Sophia Dorothea, daughter of George I. of England, and granddaughter of the Electress Sophia. By her he was the father of Frederick II., called the Great.
> >
> > Frederick the Great thus combined descent from William the Silent in four lines, one being through Louisa Henrietta, daughter of Frederick Henry, William's third son, by Louise de Coligny, and three lines being through Louisa, eldest daughter of Charlotte de Bourbon.

Being in the direct line from Frederick I., William II., present German Emperor, thus unites descent from William the Silent in many different lines—first from Louisa Henrietta, eldest daughter of Frederick Henry, Prince of Orange, and also from Louisa Juliana, eldest daughter of Charlotte de Bourbon, through many lines. The Empress Frederick, mother of the German Emperor, is also in direct line of descent from the Electress Sophia of Hanover.

Charlotte, sister of William I., first German Emperor, who died 1888, married Nicolas, Tzar of Russia, from whom are descended the last three Tzars, who thus, with their descendants, trace their descent from William the Silent, through the same lines as the Kings of Prussia.

II. ALBERTINA AGNES, *b.* 1634, *d.* 1697, was the second surviving daughter of Frederick Henry, Prince of Orange; she possessed all the virtues of her grandmother and her sister.

She married William Frederick of Nassau-Dietz, grandson of John of Nassau-Dillenburg, the only one of the brothers of William the Silent who left children.

> Their grandson in the male line was John William Friso, Stadtholder of Friesland, recognised as his heir by King William III., and by the testament named Prince of Orange, in 1702.
>
> From him descends the royal family of Holland.

William IV., Prince of Orange, and Stadtholder of Holland (1748-1751), the son of John William Friso, married Anne, daughter of George II. of England, who, like the rest of

the House of Hanover, was descended from Louisa Juliana,
eldest daughter of Charlotte de Bourbon.
> Their son, William V. (1751-1802), *d.* 1806, *m.* Wil-
> helmina, daughter of Augustus of Prussia, brother of
> Frederick the Great.
> She, like her husband, was fifth in descent from
> Frederick Henry, Prince of Orange.
>> Their son William I., King of the Netherlands,
>> 1815, and King of Holland, 1830-43, *m.* his
>> cousin Frederica, daughter of Frederick William
>> II., King of Prussia, both of them being sixth in
>> descent from Frederick Henry, Prince of Orange.
>>> The son of William I. was William II., *d.*
>>> 1849, whose son was William III., King of
>>> Holland, *d.* 1890.

Thereupon the male line of Orange-Nassau became extinct.

William III., King of Holland, *m.*, 1879, Emma, Princess of
Waldeck-Pyrmont, *b.* 1858, daughter of George Victor,
Prince of Waldeck, and of Helena Wilhelmina Henrietta
Paulina, of Nassau, daughter of William George Augustus,
Duke of Nassau, whose grandfather Karl Christian *m.*
Carolina of Nassau, a granddaughter of John William Friso,
Prince of Orange.
> Queen Emma is thus tenth in descent from William the Silent,
> through Frederick Henry and Albertina Agnes. Her
> husband, King William III., was ninth in descent from the
> same stock.
>> Their daughter, Wilhelmina, the present Queen, *b.* August
>> 1880, combines all these lines of descent from William
>> the Silent, and also the lines from his brother, John of
>> Nassau.
> On the death of King William III., in 1890, and the previous
> death of his sons, Wilhelmina succeeded as Queen, her
> mother Queen Emma being Regent during the minority.

III. HENRIETTA CATHERINE, *b.* 1637, *d.* 1708, was the third surviving daughter of Frederick Henry, Prince of Orange.
> She *m.* John George II., Prince of Anhalt-Dessau.
>> Their son was Leopold, "the old Dessauer" of Frederick
>> the Great's wars ; see Carlyle, *Friedrich II. passim.*
>>> "The biggest mass of inarticulate human vitality"
>>> (*Friedrich II.* vol. i. p. 401).
>>> The sons of Leopold were Leopold, "the young Des-
>>> sauer," and Maurice, famous in Frederick's cam-
>>> paigns ; see *Friedrich II. passim.*
> The family has long flourished with the same name.

IV. MARIE, *b.* 1642, *d.* 1688.
> She *m.* the Count Palatine, Lewis Henry Maurice, Duke of
> Zimmern.

Daughters of William the Silent

1. Marie [by first wife], *m.* Philip, Count of Hohenlohe.
2. Anna [by second wife], *m.* William Lewis, Count of Nassau.
3. Emilia [by second wife], *m.* Emmanuel, Prince of Portugal.
4. Louisa Juliana [by third wife], *m.* Frederick IV., Elector Palatine.
5. Elizabeth [by third wife], *m.* Henry, Duke of Bouillon.
6. Catherine Belgia [by third wife], *m.* Lewis, Count of Hanau.
7. Charlotte Flandrina [by third wife], Abbess of Poitiers.
8. Charlotte Brabantina [by third wife], *m.* Claudius, Duke of Trémoïlle.
9. Emilia Antwerpiana [by third wife], *m.* Frederick Casimir, Count Palatine of Zweibrucken.

Descendants of Daughters of William the Silent

1. Marie (only daughter of Anne of Egmont), *b.* 1556, *d.* 1616, god-child of Queen of Hungary, Countess of Nassau and Buren.
   She *m.* (1595) Philip, Count of Hohenlohe-Langenburg, a valiant soldier and officer of the Prince. He was younger brother of Wolfgang, Count of Hohenlohe, commander in the war against Spain, and ancestor of the princely House of Hohenlohe.
2. Anna (daughter of Anne of Saxony), *b.* 1563, *d.* 1588.
   She *m.* (1587) her first cousin, William Lewis, Count of Nassau, eldest son of John of Dillenburg. He *d.* (1620) without issue, and the succession to the House of Nassau-Dillenburg ultimately passed to the descendants of the younger son, Ernest Casimir.
3. Emilia (daughter of Anne of Saxony), *b.* 1569, *d.* 1629.
   She *m.* (in 1597) Emanuel, Prince of Portugal. He was the son of Don Antonio, pretender to the throne of Portugal, whose adventures fill many pages in the history of these times. Emilia inherited the self-will of her mother, and her passion for Prince Emanuel and her quarrel with her brother Maurice form one chapter in the romantic annals of the House of Nassau.
4. Louisa Juliana (eldest daughter of Charlotte de Bourbon), *b.* 1576, *d.* 1644.
   She inherited the virtues of her mother and her grandmother, after whom she was named, and she became, after the death of Louise de Coligny, the ruling spirit of the family.
   She *m.* (in 1593) Frederick IV., Elector Palatine (1583-1610), the grandson of Frederick III., Elector Palatine and guardian of Charlotte de Bourbon.
   The son of Frederick IV. and Louisa Juliana was Frederick V., Elector Palatine, 1610-32, who *m.* Elizabeth, daughter of James I. of England, the famous "Queen of Hearts."

Frederick V. and Elizabeth were the King and Queen of
Bohemia, whose misfortunes fill so many pages of
history, till they found a refuge with the Nassaus in
Holland.

The children of the King and Queen of Bohemia (amongst others)
were :—

(1.) Charles Lewis, Elector, 1649-80.
(2.) Prince Rupert ⎱ nephews of Charles I. and his officers in the
(3.) Prince Maurice ⎰ Civil Wars.
(4.) Sophia, *m.* Ernest Augustus, Elector of Hanover.

(1) Charles Lewis, the Elector, had a daughter, Charlotte
Elizabeth, who *m.* Philip, Duke of Orleans, only brother of
Louis XIV. of France.

From them descended Philip, the Regent, Philippe Égalité,
Louis Philippe, and the whole House of Orleans.

The present Duc d'Orleans is descended in the twelfth degree from William the Silent.

Elizabeth Charlotte of Orleans, daughter of Philip, first
Duke of Orleans and Charlotte Elizabeth of Bavaria,
m. Leopold Joseph of Lorraine.

Their son was Francis Stephen I. (1745-65), who
m. Maria Theresa of Hapsburg, daughter of the
Emperor Charles VI.

Their descendants were the Emperors from 1765 down to
Francis Joseph, the reigning Emperor of Austria, who is
descended in the eleventh degree from William the Silent.

Theresa of Tuscany, wife of Charles Albert, King of Sardinia,
was a great-granddaughter of Maria Theresa.

Adelaide, the wife of Victor Emmanuel, King of Italy, was
also a great-granddaughter of Maria Theresa.

Humbert, King of Italy, is descended in the eleventh degree
from William the Silent.

From Francis I. and Maria Theresa were descended Marie
Antoinette and her children, Maria Louisa, wife of
Napoleon I., her son the King of the Romans, and also the
so-called princes of the family of Jerome Napoleon.

Similar descents might be shown for the deposed royal
Houses of Naples, Parma, Modena, and Tuscany.

Alfonso XIII., reigning King of Spain, is descended in the
eleventh degree from William the Silent, as is also the
King of Portugal.

(2, 3) Princes Rupert and Maurice left no legitimate descendants.

(4) Sophia, the youngest but one of the children of Frederick
V. and Elizabeth, King and Queen of Bohemia, *b.* 1630, *m.*
(1658) Ernest Augustus, Elector of Hanover. She was
the niece of Charles I. of England, and cousin of William
III., Mary, and Anne.

By the Act of Settlement (12 & 13 Will. III. c. 2, 1701) the

succession to the Crown of England, on failure of descendants of Mary and Anne, was settled on Sophia and the heirs
of her body, being Protestants.

The Electress Sophia, great-granddaughter of William the
Silent, is thus not only ancestress of the House of Hanover,
but is the root from which the succession is to be traced
under the Parliamentary constitution of the United Kingdom.

> *Queen Victoria is ninth in descent from William the Silent,
> and thus is nearer to him than any other royal personage
> in Europe.*

The Electress Sophia left numerous descendants. Amongst
them are the following :—

Her great-granddaughter Anne, a daughter of George
II. of England, *m.* William IV. of Orange, *d.* 1751,
and is the ancestress of the reigning family of the
Netherlands, who thus combine descents from Frederick
Henry, John of Nassau, and Charlotte de Bourbon.

From the Electress Sophia also were descended the four Kings
of Denmark, from 1766 to 1863, down to the accession of
the House of Glucksburg. And the reigning House of Denmark has made many alliances with royal houses continuing
the blood of William the Silent.

Sophia Dorothea, granddaughter of the Electress Sophia,
m. Frederick William I. of Prussia, and is ancestress
of the reigning family of Hohenzollern.

Similar descents could easily be shown for the extinct royal
Houses of Brunswick, Hanover, and Westphalia, and for the
royal families of Sweden, Belgium, and Roumania.

5. Elizabeth (2nd daughter of Charlotte de Bourbon), *b.* 1567, *d.*
1642. She was god-child of Queen Elizabeth, and was born
at the time of William's highest success.

She *m.* (1595) her first cousin Henri, Duc de Bouillon, Prince of
Sedan, etc., son of her mother's sister, Françoise de Bourbon.
Henri and Elizabeth were the parents of—

(1) Frederic Maurice, Duc de Bouillon, and of
(2) Marshal Turenne—both famous in the wars of the
seventeenth century ; and also of
(3) Marie ; *m.* her cousin, Henri de la Trémoïlle, Duc
de Thouars, etc.

From Elizabeth descended the famous House of La Tour
d'Auvergne ; see Baluze, *Histoire Généalogique de la
maison d'Auvergne,* folio 1708, vols. i., ii.

6. Catherine Belgia (3rd daughter of Charlotte de Bourbon), *b.*
1578, *d.* 1648.

She was adopted by the United Provinces.

m. (1596) Philip Lewis II., Count of Hanau-Münzenberg ; and
from her descended Philip Maurice and Philip Louis III., in
succession Counts of Hanau-Münzenberg.

7. Charlotte Flandrina (4th daughter of Charlotte de Bourbon), *b.* 1579, *d.* 1640.

    She was adopted by the States of Flanders, and in infancy was entrusted to her mother's cousin, Abbess of Paraclete. She was only three years old at her mother's death, was brought up by her Catholic cousins, and ultimately became Abbess of Poitiers.

8. Charlotte Brabantina (5th daughter of Charlotte de Bourbon), *b.* 1580, *d.* 1631.

    She was adopted by the States of Brabant, and was born in the year of the *Ban* of Philip.

    She *m.* (1598) Claude de la Trémoïlle, Duc de Thouars, and from them descended the Dukes of Trémoïlle.

    > Their son Henri, Duc de la Trémoïlle, *m.* his cousin, Marie de la Tour, daughter of the Duc de Bouillon and Elizabeth before mentioned.
    >
    > Their daughter Charlotte de la Trémoïlle, *m.* James Stanley, seventh Earl of Derby, 1642, and was famous in the Civil Wars of England as the defender of Lathom House with her cousin Prince Rupert.
    >
    > From her descended the Earls of Derby down to 1736, and the present Dukes of Atholl, etc., in England.

9. Emilia (second) Antwerpiana (6th daughter of Charlotte de Bourbon), *b.* 1581, *d.* 1657.

    She was born at Antwerp a few months before the crime of Jaureguy and the death of her mother.

    She *m.* Frederick Casimir, Count Palatine of Zweibrücken, 1604-45.

    > Their son was Frederick Lewis, Count Palatine (1643-81), *ob. s.p.*
    >
    > John, a brother of Frederick Casimir, *m.* Louisa, daughter of Louisa Juliana, the Electress Palatine.

The family history of the Nassaus is one of the most copious and interesting of modern times. It is remarkable for the tenacity and valour of the men and the energy and goodness of the women. The blood of Nassau ran in the veins of an immense number of the illustrious men and women of the seventeenth and eighteenth centuries, and it runs still in very many of the royal and noble houses of Europe. It was a family remarkable for its incessant intermarriage, its general fertility, and the predominance of female progeny. The parents of William the Silent had nineteen children by their own double marriages. William had born to him fifteen children by four wives. John of Nassau had twenty-four children by three wives. Charlotte de Bourbon had six daughters and no son, Frederick Henry four daughters and one son, William II. had only one son, and William III. had no children. The House of Orange-Nassau is now represented by one young girl.

The public and private life of this extraordinary family may be studied in the following works :—

GROEN VAN PRINSTERER. *Archives ou Correspondance de la maison d'Orange-Nassau.* 1re série, Leiden, 1841-47 ; 2me série, Utrecht, 1857-61.

GACHARD. *Correspondance de Guillaume le Taciturne.* Brussels, 1847-57.

COUNT J. DELABORDE. *Charlotte de Bourbon.* Paris, 1888.

—— *Louise de Coligny.* Paris, 1890.

VORSTERMAN VAN OYEN. *Het Vorstenhuis Oranje-Nassau.* Folio. Leiden en Utrecht, 1882.

LORENZ (OTTAKAR). *Genealogisches Handbuch der Europäischen Staatengeschichte.* Berlin, 1895.

DR. K. VON BEHR. *Genealogie der in Europa regierenden Fürstenhäuser.*

ORLERS (JAN). *Genealogia Comitum Nassoviae.* Leiden, 1616.

HOPF (KARL). *Historisch-Genealogischer Atlas.* Folio. Gotha, 1858.

THE portraits of the Prince, both paintings and engravings, are very numerous ; but, with few exceptions, they are copies not taken from life ; indeed, many of them are copies taken from copies of a single original which has disappeared. The earliest in date is the fine picture in the gallery at Cassel, representing the Prince at the age of twenty-five in a suit of rich armour, his hand on his helmet. From the inscription giving his titles it is believed that this portrait was painted about the year 1558, and probably by William Key. An early copy of this was made in 1581 for the Landgrave of Hesse, and perhaps the original was burnt at Dillenburg in 1760. A copy of the Cassel portrait was recently presented by the Emperor William II. to the Queen of the Netherlands, and is now in the palace at the Hague. This most interesting portrait is the only authentic record of the early manhood of William. It is nobly impressive and convincing, and bears every mark of profound intellect and indomitable character.

The portrait at the Hague with the inscription—Antonio Moro, 1561—is doubtful, and it is disputed if it represents the Prince at all ; but eminent critics (perhaps rightly) believe it to be an authentic portrait, but with the features somewhat altered by an injudicious restoration. Another portrait, now in the Prinsenhof at Delft, is perhaps a copy of Pourbus, and may date about five years later. The Prince is then becoming bald, and the look of stern resolution and intense anxiety is deepening upon his whole aspect.

In his later life, almost all the extant paintings are by Miereveld, or are copies and duplicates of Miereveld's portraits. Miereveld was only seventeen years old when William was assassinated, and the fine paintings by his hand could not have been taken from life. In one of the best, that in the Royal Museum at Amsterdam, Miereveld's inscription states that the face is copied from Cornelis de Visscher. We know *aliunde* that Visscher of Gouda did paint the Prince's portrait *ad vivum ;* but it is not known what is become of it. The grand head in armour with a ruff, in an oval form, now at the Mauritshuis at the Hague, also by Miereveld, seems also to have been taken from Visscher's original. Miereveld, who lived to a great age and had a large school of disciples, painted or fathered a series of portraits of the Prince—the features and expression apparently all being taken from the lost original portrait by Visscher. And these have been scattered over Europe in copies, imitations, engravings, busts, and medallions.

After a careful study of the extant portraits and engravings of the Prince, it is impossible to doubt that, although we depend for his look in mature life almost entirely upon copies made after his death, we have an almost unerring record of his outward man. The best portraits, especially those at Cassel, the Hague, and Amsterdam, are in wonderful harmony with the inward character and qualities of which we have so perfect a record. The authentic paintings by Miereveld's hand are not only noble works of art, but they reveal a nature which no thoughtful beholder can misunderstand. We see before us a powerful spirit in a frame worn down to premature old age, a brow alert with observation and furrowed with care and thought, an eye of keen penetration, a jaw of iron grip, a look of indomitable tenacity and patience—the entire aspect that of a fencer on guard, or a watchman awaiting an assault. We may rest assured that, after three completed centuries, we know to-day the real aspect of the man as completely as we know that of Henri IV. or Oliver Cromwell.

[The history of the portraits has been thoroughly examined by E. W. Moes of Amsterdam, *Oud Holland*, 1889. It is fully treated by Miss Putnam in vol. ii. App. H, and also by Mrs. Lecky in a most interesting paper, with four engravings, in *Good Words*, March 1897.]

NOTE

This *Life* has been compiled from the contemporary authorities, and *in all cases the passages cited have been quoted and translated afresh from the original texts.* The archives of Holland, Belgium, Spain, and Germany contain an immense series of documents, which, supplemented by those of Paris and of London, picture for us every phase of an age remarkable for the extraordinary volume and importance of its written records. The principal statesmen of the age carefully committed to paper their most secret thoughts and instructions in voluminous papers intended solely for their own agents and intimates. And an immense body of these papers have been preserved at Brussels, the Hague, Simancas, Paris, and London. This vast store, in six European languages, has to a great extent now been published, edited, and calendared by the labours of generations of experts. But for this, a long lifetime would not suffice to master ·the original sources in MSS. for the reign of Philip II.ˑ and contemporary rulers. There have been few epochs when the chanceries of Europe have been supplied with so complete a mass of original documents, composed with inexhaustible industry, and often with profound sagacity.

The great storehouse of the documents relating to

the life of William the Silent is to be found in the voluminous collections of the Dutch and Belgian archivists,—notably Groen van Prinsterer, Gachard, and Kervyn de Lettenhove. The magnificent works of van Prinsterer and of Gachard supply a mass of contemporary material for the entire life of William, largely in his own words. Altogether we have 1770 documents, more than 1000 of which were signed by the Prince himself. And many less important letters and memoranda are scattered in other works. Besides these, the *Justification* and the *Apology* published by the Prince make a small volume in themselves. Many of these papers are long and elaborate despatches to confidential agents, or else intimate letters to his brothers and colleagues. The present volume is the result of a complete study of all these documents. The following authorities have been consulted :—

CONTEMPORARY AUTHORITIES

Groen van Prinsterer. *Archives ou Correspondance Inédite de la maison d'Orange - Nassau.* 2nd ed. Vols. i.-ix. 8vo. Leiden, 1841-47.
—— *Archives ou Correspondance Inédite de la maison d'Orange-Nassau.* 2de série. Vols. i.-v. and Supplement. 8vo. Utrecht, 1857-61.
Gachard. *Correspondance de Guillaume le Taciturne.* Vols. i.-vi. 8vo. Brussels, 1847-57.
—— *Correspondance de Philippe II. sur les Affaires des Pays-Bas.* Vols. i.-v. 4to. Brussels, 1848-79.
—— *Correspondance de Marguérite d'Autriche,* etc. 4to. Brussels, 1867.
—— *Actes des États-Généraux des Pays-Bas.* 8vo. Brussels, 1861.
Cardinal Granvelle. *Papiers d'État* (ed. C. Weiss). Vols. i.-ix. 4to. 1841-52.
—— *Correspondance.* 4to. Brussels, 1877.
Bor. *Oorsprongk der Nederlandsche Oorlogen.* Vols. i.-iv. Folio. Amsterdam, 1679.
Hoynck van Papendrecht. *Analecta Belgica.* 6 parts. 4to. The Hague, 1743.

Hoynck van Papendrecht. *Epistolae Vigli ab Aytta*. 4to. Liege, 1671.
Hopperus. *Vita Vigli* (in Hoynck, 1743).
—— *Recueil et Mémorial*, etc. (in Hoynck, 1743).
Pontus Payen. *Mémoires*. Vols. i. ii. 8vo. Brussels, 1861.
Renon de France. *Histoire des Troubles des Pays-Bas*. Vols. i.-iii. 4to. Brussels, 1886-91.
La Huguerye (Michel de). *Mémoires Inédits*. Vols. i.-iii. 8vo. Paris, 1877.
Kervyn de Volkaerbeke. *Documents historiques Inédits* (1577-84). 2 vols. 8vo. Ghent, 1847.
Strada (Famianus). *De Bello Belgico*. 4to. Frankfurt, 1651.
—— Continued by Foppens. *Supplément à l'histoire de Strada*. Vols. i. ii. 12mo. Amsterdam, 1729.
Van Meteren. *Histoire des Pays-Bas (traduite)*. Folio. The Hague, 1618.
Meursius. *Gulielmus Auriacus*. 4to. Leyden, 1621.
Aubéry du Maurier. *Mémoires*, etc., 1740. 12mo.
Brandt. *History of the Reformation*, etc. (translated) Folio. London, 1720.
Digges. *Compleat Ambassador*. Folio. London, 1655.
Ellis (Sir H). *Original Letters*. 11 vols. 8vo. 1825-46.
T. Wright. *Queen Elizabeth and her Times*. 8vo. 1838.
The Calendars of State Papers (Foreign), 1566-77, and 1558-86.
La Pise. *Tableau d'Orange*, etc. Folio. 1639.
Orlers. *La Généalogie des Nassau*. Folio. Leyden, 1615.
Lacroix. *Apologie*, etc. 8vo. Brussels, 1858.

NON-CONTEMPORARY AUTHORITIES

Blok (Prof. Pieter J.) *Geschiedenis van het Nederlandsche Volk*. Vols. i.-iii. 8vo. Groningen, 1896.
Kervyn de Lettenhove. *Les Huguenots et les Gueux* (1560-85). Vols. i.-vi. 8vo. Bruges, 1883-85.
—— *La Flandre pendant les trois derniers siècles*. 8vo. Bruges, 1875.
—— *Relations politiques des Pays Bas et de l'Angleterre*. 4to. Brussels, 1882-91.
—— *Chroniques Belges Inédites*. 4to. Brussels, v.d.
Delaborde (Count Jules). *Charlotte de Bourbon*. 8vo. Paris, 1888.
—— *Louise de Coligny*. 8vo. Vols. i. ii. Paris. 1890.
Juste (Théodore). *Guillaume le Taciturne*. 8vo. Brussels, 1873.
Arnoldi. *Geschichte der Oranien-Nassauischer*. 8vo. Hadamar, 1799.
Motley. *Rise of the Dutch Republic*. 3 vols.
—— *United Netherlands*. 4 vols.
Prescott. *Philip II*.
Stirling-Maxwell (Sir W.) *Don John of Austria*. Vols. i. ii. 8vo. 1883.
Martin (H.) *Histoire de France*. Vols. ix. x.
Michelet (J.) *Histoire de France*. Vols. iii. iv.

Froude. *History of England.* Vols. viii.-xi. incl.

Beesly (Prof. E. S.) *Queen Elizabeth.* 8vo. London, 1892.

Burgon. *Life of Sir T. Gresham.* Vols. i. ii. 8vo. London, 1839.

Arnaud (Eugène). *Histoire des Protestants en Provence.* Vols. i. ii. 8vo. Paris, 1884.

Hopf (Karl). *Historisch-Genealogischer Atlas.* Vols. i. ii. Folio. Gotha, 1858.

Vorsterman van Oyen. *Het Vorstenhuis Oranje-Nassau.* Folio. Leyden, 1882.

Hymans (Louis). *Bruxelles à travers les Ages.* Brussels, 1882-89.

Special mention should be made of the most recent, most elaborate, and most scholarly work on this period, *William the Silent*, by Ruth Putnam : New York and London.—Putnam's Sons, 1895. 2 vols. 8vo., with numerous illustrations, tables, etc. At every step a subsequent writer has to admire Miss Putnam's immense industry and accurate learning.

THE END

Printed by R. & R. CLARK, LIMITED, *Edinburgh*.